I0692749

NO MORE TEARS TO SHED

'Dipo Toby Alakija

© Copyright 2012 by 'Dipo Toby Alakija

All rights reserved by Calvary Rock Resources. No part of this book may be reproduced or transmitted in any form or by any means without written permission of the publisher through any of the addresses below, apart from the use of short quotations or occasional page copying for personal or group study.

ISBN: 978 - 978- 49874-3-1
978-49874-3-0

Printed in United States

First published in 2012 and republished in 2016 by the publishing house of

CALVARY ROCK RESOURCES

19, Ajina Street, Ikenne Remo,
Ogun State,
Nigeria.

36, Thomson road
Gorton
Manchester
M18 7QQ
United Kingdom

270 Madison Avenue
Suite 1500, New York, NY 10016
United States

www.calvaryrock.org

CHAPTER ONE

The class was full of life as Mary Toba was introduced to other students who were getting prepared to go on recess.

A non-teaching staff of the high school who came to introduce her was a tall blond lady of about twenty-five while Mary was a tall, slim and light complexioned girl of sixteen.

Mary just came from Nigeria with all the attractive features and virtues anyone would expect from a simple African teenager. She was dressed in the typical African made attire that was common in the 1980s. The dress made her so outstandingly beautiful that most of the male students in the class could not keep their eyes off her, making her very uncomfortable and bashful. Her appearances were enough to indicate that she was an international student. Although the school was so full of students from various parts of the world that it was not strange to see her yet, for quite a while, she held everybody's attention. What made her exceptional was her peculiar dressing and simple though beautiful looks. She wore no make-up except that her hair, which must have taken hours to braid, still looked freshly touched.

In spite of her seemingly naïve looks and shy expressions, she was a real beauty queen, who most boys would be proud to go out with.

'Hello, everybody,' the staff said, looking round at the students that were made up of teenage boys and girls. 'We've got another student joining us this session. As you can see, she is new in this country and she's new in this school. She came from Nigeria last Friday. She needs friends and you are going to be her good friends.' She looked at Mary. 'Tell them your name, my dear.'

Feeling more uncomfortable, Mary said, 'I'm Mary Toba.'

The teacher smiled at the students. 'She told me she has heard a lot of good things about America. So you must not give her any reason to think otherwise. I want you to show her how friendly we are, especially in this school.'

She later ushered her to her seat before she left the class. Mary walked to the seat, holding her school bag and looking bashfully on the ground. Soon most of the students crowded round her, shaking hands

1

with her.

'Hi, I'm Linda.'

'Hello, Mary. I'm Victoria. I'm from South Africa. So we are sisters.'

Mary smiled at her, shaking her hand.

'Hi, Mary. My name is Thomas. I have a friend who is also a Nigerian. Would you like to meet him?'

Trying to be modest, Mary replied, 'perhaps later.'

Before long, Mary had gotten more than enough friends that were ready to give her their attentions.

Mary lived with her uncle called Leke Toba in one of the less busy areas in Brooklyn in New York. The place was not far from St. James College, her new school. Leke, a busy businessman who dealt with exportation of fairly used cars to Africa among so many other things tried as much as he could to make her adjust to her new environment. Although Mary had never left the shore of Nigeria since she was born, she has a way of adapting to every environment she found herself. Her parents, uncles and aunties and friends thought she would miss Nigeria terribly much but the people she met in the country; especially those in her school made things different from what everybody expected. Even Leke thought she was going to find it a little tough to adjust. So he toyed with the idea of taking her to his wife in Chicago where she would be surrounded with her cousins. He had asked her before putting her in St. James College if she would prefer Chicago instead of staying with him in New York where his exporting business was located. Mary did not hesitate to choose New York. She knew she would have more freedom if she stayed with him. She did not quite appreciate being ordered around by his wife whom she knew to be a disciplinarian. Besides, the few days she had spent with him, doing nothing except to cook what she would eat; clean the house; read her books; watch the television and sleep for as long as she wanted proved to her that she wouldn't get any better treatment anywhere in the world not even in Nigeria. She was not ready to sacrifice the luxuries and the freedom in New York for anything, not even for her cousins in Chicago.

As she expected, Leke was not at home when she returned from school. She went to her bedroom straight to change, had a shower and went to get herself something to eat in the kitchen. She was already eating when the telephone began to ring. At first she ignored it because she did not feel the call was meant for her. If the call was meant for her uncle, the caller ought to know better than to call around this time.

2

After ringing for a while, it suddenly occurred to her that it was probably one of her new friends in the school calling. She remembered she gave a few of them her telephone number. She rushed to pick it.

'Hello,' she said.

'Hello,' a male voice said. 'Is that Mary Toba?'

'Yes,' Mary said. 'Who's calling?'

'I'm Charles.'

The voice and the name did not sound very familiar though he was able to pronounce her last name very well. She thought of the faces of the people she had met in the school but none of them went with that name. The proper way he pronounced the name showed that the caller was probably a Nigerian. No one in school was able to pronounce the name like that.

'Thomas gave me your telephone number,' the caller explained after a brief pause. 'He told me to call you. He said you might need my company.'

'I'm not sure I do,' she said almost impolitely. She was already familiar with the naughty games which most of the boys loved to play. Down in Nigeria, many boys normally offered their unsolicited friendship with the intention to date her. She always found a way of frustrating their efforts to come closer to her. Only one boy called Sesan was able to walk into her life but the rest had failed - woefully. Even then, she had to call it a quit with Sesan when he got involved with another girl.

'If at all I need someone to keep my company, it is definitely not a stranger or a guy I need. I really don't appreciate anyone giving my number to strangers,' she added.

'I'm a Nigerian too,' Charles said.

'So what?'

'I'm sorry,' he said quietly. 'Thomas thought I might be able to help you get familiar with your new environment.'

'That won't be necessary,' Mary said. She was anxious to get rid of him. She wanted to get back to the dinning table and finish her meal.

'You don't sound so friendly, do you? No one means any harm. We just want to be your friends. That's all.' He paused for a while before he added. 'I'm sorry to bother you. I thought I could be your friend.'

'I wonder why you want to be my friend.'

'We are from the same country. Isn't that enough for me to offer you my friendship? I thought I could take you to many places around the city on week-ends.'

She thought he sounded nice. She decided to be friendlier even though he was still a stranger to her. Being a Nigerian made little or no difference to her. She said, 'I'll give it a thought.'

'When can I call you again?' he asked almost eagerly.

'I'll send Thomas to you.'

'Alright,' he said. 'Good day, sister.'

'Thanks for calling, Charles.' She dropped the telephone and went back to take her meal.

When she finished eating, she packed the plates to the kitchen and went to sit down in the sitting room to think about the life in America as opposed to Nigeria. Unlike in Nigeria where the military ruled with brutality, America was a free country. Although there was no way she could have known so much about the United States within the period she arrived in the country but the little she had experienced and read revealed a lot to her. There were lots of differences. Americans would have considered Nigeria a strange country if they knew what exactly was going on there. The country was characterized with extreme poverty and sufferings even though she had more than enough resources to meet all the needs of all her citizens, including unborn children. She produced oil in so large quantity that it was exported to other countries yet she could not take care of the local consumption. The leaders were more interested in what to make out of the oil than meeting the needs of the people. The country had other natural and human resources that were enough to make her one of the richest nations, if not the richest in the world yet her economy was a disaster. The military government has so much destabilized the economy and the political set-up that even the unborn generations would spend all their lives, trying to rebuild them. Most advanced countries like America had predicted war in Nigeria when everything seemed to be going from bad to disaster but Nigerians would rather die, struggling to survive in the midst of them all than to go into war. Consequently, a lot of things that were frowned at by other countries formed part of the norms of the society. Fraud, swindling that was popularly coded as 419, bribery and other serious malpractice were what many Nigerians engaged in. The malpractice which extended abroad gave the people bad names and terrible images. Many Nigerians who could not distinguish themselves as good citizens were regarded with disrespects. The people found it very hard to trust Nigerians. To obtain a visa in any foreign embassy, the applicant would have to prove that he was not a criminal. She would not forget the first time she appeared at the American embassy with her uncle and how one of the officers had told one of the visa applicants point-blank that he didn't trust Nigerian police reports. It was as bad as that. If anyone attempted to put things right in the country, he or she would end up in jail or most likely in the grave as in the case of many prominent Nigerians who lost their lives while trying to put things right. Even then, many people outside Nigeria wondered why the people could not strike the government in the place that would hurt but, as her father normally argued, they failed to realize that many who struck weak blows never lived to strike another one. The outsiders felt that the people could make the country ungovernable but again they failed to realize that millions of lives were at stake in the society where the government ruled by the force of the artillery. The military government did not know the difference between the civilians that opposed them and the soldiers that planned coup d'etat. If any civilian tried to stop the military from ruling the people through any way or by any means, it was going to be war between the civilians and the military. Since the civilians were defenseless, especially when they knew that the military would stop at nothing but to wipe out their families, all they could do was to call on God to save them.

And then there was this difference in the American and Nigerian mentalities. Americans were brave. They were always too willing to die for their freedom. They were always ready to sacrifice anything for their country. That was their mentality from the beginning. She read little about the history of the United States in a book for young ones. She read about the battle of Bunker Hill, which proved that Americans would die for freedom. Their question about life had always been: 'what is the use of the life of a captive?' To them, the life of the captive must be used to get freedom for others. In a way, this was opposed to Nigerian ways of thinking. Typical Nigerians always referred to a proverb that said, 'anybody that offers his head to be used to break coconut would not live to eat out of it.' Very few people in Nigeria felt the need to die for the benefits of others. That was why only few saw reasons to fight the military government even when there was every reason to fight it. Up till the time she left the country, Nigeria was still going through what Americans would call hell...

The telephone rang again, jerking Mary out of her chains of thoughts. Guessing that the call must be hers, she went to pick it. The call was from one of her few closest friends in Nigeria, who knew she was coming to the United States.

'Hello. This is Bola, calling from Nigeria.'

'Bola?' Mary found it hard to believe. 'Hay, Bola!'

5

'Yeah,' the caller replied. 'Is that you Mary?'

'Yes! I can't believe this!'

'I just thought I should give you a surprise by calling you.'

'How did you get this number?'

'Your mum gave it to me,' Bola replied. 'I was in Ibadan with some of my friends two days ago. I went to confirm from her if you've left the country. She told me you've gone. She gave me your postal address, including the telephone number.'

'It's so nice to hear from you,' Mary said. 'I have so many things to tell you.'

'Hay, Mary, if I spend so much time on international call, my father would beat the shit out of me when the bill comes.'

Mary laughed.

'Did I sound like American?'

'Yeah. But I don't want you to speak to me like American. I am not an American, remember? I am Naija. I dey kampe!' she said,

Bola laughed at other end. That was one of the things she loved about Bola. She was always full of fun and laughter. She was also kind, cool headed and brilliant. 'Are you in your father's house right now?'

'Yeah,' Bola replied.

'I'll call you now,' Mary said and cut the line. A moment later, she called Bola who quickly picked the phone again. 'My uncle is footing the bill now.'

'You sound so American now. Oh, girlie, let's talk Naija,' Bola said.

Mary laughed. After a while, she began the long discussion. She told her about her first experience in America. She told her how she landed in the country with her uncle, how she was registered in the school and all he planned to do for her, including training her to become an accountant. 'Bola,' she went on, 'I really like it up here. It's so pleasant that it didn't take me time to adapt to the environment. You know, it's easy for you to get used to any environment if you're just coming from Nigeria. It's easy to enjoy luxuries than to endure hardship even if you're in the midst of your people.'

Bola laughed whole-heartedly. 'I wonder what you mean by that.'

'With those military boys in government, Nigeria is such a terrible place to live, you know. As soon as you get to America, you just feel you're a prisoner who is newly released from cell.'

'You are lucky you got out of here,' Bola said. 'But what would you say of the people who are not fortunate to leave the country like you?'

'You know, I just pity everybody under the government of the

6

military. Sometimes I wonder how the people would survive in that country.'

'You sound as if you're not going to come back. Are you sure you're coming back to Nigeria?'

'I'll come back, of course. Nigeria is still my country, no matter how terrible the place is right now. I believe Nigeria is going to be great again. If this present generation can tolerate the military government, there's going to be a generation that will not take it lightly with the dictators.'

'Mary,' Bola said with a chuckle, 'you're in a free country now. So you're free to say whatever you like and go away with it. Nobody will come and pick you up with Black Maria. You know what will happen to anyone that tries to oppose or criticize the government.'

'Yeah, yeah,' Mary said, giving a smile. 'The State Security Service men are always around the corner to make sure that everybody keeps his mouth shut even though they are suffering. They are always watching and listening to whatever you say. If you say anything against the military, you'll be dragged to the prison without trial just like one of my father's friends.'

'What happened to him?'

'Well, he was having some drinks at a beer parlor with few other men. Unknown to him, one of the men drinking with him was a SSS man. He said some things against the government. He said, "the military is terrible! We don't want the military. They belong to the barracks. Let them go to the barracks. We don't want them as rulers!" That's all the man said. You wouldn't believe it. He landed in jail. He was still in prison up to the time I left the country. The last time my father saw his family, they were living in extreme poverty. He had to do all he could to make sure that the family had enough to eat.'

Their chat was endless. They spent almost an hour chatting before she eventually put down the telephone.

Finding nothing to do at the moment, she decided to go to the kitchen to clean the place before her uncle returned.

Leke returned home late in the night, long after Mary had gone to bed. He gained access into the house with the use of the extra key he always carried with him.

He went straight to his bedroom after locking the door back, put the briefcase he was carrying on the table and began to get undress. He was just too tired to think of anything except to get a shower and go to sleep.

He went to the bathroom in the master's bedroom which he

occupied and had a snappy shower. He put on his pyjamas and went to lie in the bed, switching off all the lights. He soon surprised himself when he found himself in chains of thoughts instead of dozing off.

He was a forty-two year old man who was quite successful in exporting and importing business in America. Although he had suffered a lot of racial discrimination yet the country had offered so many opportunities in his business career that it didn't take him time to become successful. He knew if he had been in Nigeria where he was so much respected, he would never have been so successful. Although Nigeria has her own advantages but the business climate was just too bad - so bad that many businesses crumbled like a pack of cards, making businessmen to look for better places to establish their businesses. The military government had been the most frightening spectre that was destroying everything that constituted the republic of Nigeria including the people.

He had left the country for America when he studied the trend of things. It appeared the military enjoyed power and they were not ready to let it go. In fact, some military men joined the army with the determination to rule the nation by force. When he discovered that he was not likely to achieve much if he stayed in Nigeria, he contacted one of his friends who was an American citizen. He told him that he needed his help to get out of Nigeria to the country. His friend had helped him to secure a visa and within a short time of his stay in the country, he had become financially comfortable. With the understanding that he came from the country that offered little or no chance to become financially successful, he utilized all the opportunities America offered him as best as he could. He had to play the fool and the role of a helpless person several times just to get the co-operation of many arrogant Americans he came in contact with. He had admitted inferiority complex for the sake of getting what he needed whenever he found himself in the midst of haughty looking businessmen who have the money, the connection and the names to get him through tight protocol to get goods in or out of the country. Within the few years of getting himself established, he had gone far ahead of many other foreigners who had been in the country long before him. Sometimes he wondered why success was so cheap to get in the United States. Many argued with him that he was just lucky although he could not quite see the role of luck in all his activities. He knew what he wanted in the country and he knew exactly how to get it. Those who claimed that he was just lucky needed to listen to his side of the success story. He had faced a lot of challenges that were

8

enough to make him give up but he simply pressed on, knowing fully well that if he did not get through, his whole life would be filled with defeats. Feeling of defeats, of course, was the main cause of real failures in life. He knew that if he was not defeated in the inside of him, there was no way he could be defeated from the outside. As he always told people, it was what they determined to get from life that they received. If they did not have enough determination to get what they wanted, they would get far below what they bargained for. What actually made him so determined to make so much money was because of his background. He had seen the ugly faces of poverty and sufferings back in Nigeria and he was simply determined never to see them again. Poverty and sufferings destroyed potentials of people and made them to compromise. It caused them to do things against their wills. People in other parts of the world loved to point accusing fingers at Nigerians when they behave in a particular way but none of them could go through what they have gone through over the years without going crazy. Even though he never justified any of the fraudulent practices of some Nigerians, he did not feel anyone who had never been through what they have experienced has the right to label his country as a criminally disastrous area. After all, every normal person was expected to compromise with some moral principles in the bid to survive in critical situations. Nigerians were in critical condition much more critical than anyone who was not inside could imagine. Most of the malpractice of some Nigerians were traceable to the havoc, which the military had wrecked on the economic, social and political structures of the country. For anyone to have the right to condemn Nigerians, he must first imagine what he would have done in the situation that threatened his life, health, family and future. Crisis, as he learned later, was usually the period of test of the strength of character. It was usually a period people compromised with what they stood for. Because it was a very difficult test, most people failed it. So compromise that constituted anti-social behaviours and even crimes in the past became the order of the day in the bid to survive. Nigerians were going through the period of this difficult test and so many of them were failing. It was a pity that those who have never been through the period of the test were the ones assessing the performance of his people. Many prosperous nations were yet to grasp the understanding that it was a lot easier to criticize and assess the weakness of characters of those going through crisis than for them to go through it. If they found themselves in similar situations, they might misbehave as well.

Even though the crisis has made a lot of Nigerians to develop so much negative attitudes that they were unwilling to change when they found themselves in a better place, there were still many of them like his brother (Mary's father) who still stood firm in the storm. They refused to compromise with their principles. They refused to leave the country even when they have the chance. They would rather stay in the country and do all they could to either fight back or help those who were too weak to survive the crises. He was not bold or strong enough to stay behind and fight the military but he managed to help some of those who were there. There were a good number of families that were counting on the money he normally send to them for survival. He was always celebrated each time he visited the country but the real heroes were those who had the courage to stay and fight the evils of the military government. A lot of these heroes were killed while fighting for the masses. Some were rotting away in the prison. It was very hard to still find people standing in the situation that was either threatening their lives or driving them into insanity. Many communities have gone back to the Stone Age when conventional farming was the major source of income. So many marriages have crumbled just because the husbands could not provide for their families. Many house wives and mothers who were once responsible have turned into prostitutes just to make ends meet. A lot of children have dropped out of schools to become either area boys or pickpockets or sex hawkers. Brilliant girls who were supposed to start building their careers in colleges were outside, hawking goods and exposing themselves to rowdy men that were ready to take them as bed partners in exchange with peanuts that looked so much; making them mothers whose children would later constitute nuisances in the society. The moral values that were once cherished by the people had become things of the past. And so a lot of Nigerians became what they were, not by choice but by compulsion.

He was attracted to a lot of people both in the United States and Nigeria because somehow success has a way of attracting attentions. In fact people did not like to be identified with failures but many would go extra mile to be identified with successful people. Thus it was a lot easy to get involved with series of ladies until he eventually settled down with Christie, a charming lady from South Africa who promised to make his home a haven and his family saints.

Christie just arrived from South Africa when he met her. He would never forget how he met her. They were traveling together in a train, sitting beside each other. They were engaged in a pleasant conversation that lasted through out the journey. They had exchanged telephone numbers. Strange enough he started thinking about her when he got home. He could not understand how he felt so much for a lady he met in a day. He had called and asked her if she did not mind him spending the weekend with her. She did not object. He traveled from New York to Chicago where she worked as a nurse. They had spent a very romantic weekend together. The weekend was to remain one of the most memorable days of their lives. He was helplessly in love with her and she was crazy about him since they met in the train. Before they could think properly about it, they were in the Church before a priest to get married.

His family in Nigeria, especially Mary's father who was the first-born of his late parents and now the leader in the family reacted negatively to the marriage. He had hoped he would come to Nigeria to pick a wife so that, at least, there would be no room for divorce; which everybody knew was common in America. Africans have a way of tightening marriage knots, making it difficult if not impossible for the couple to untie without the co-operation of either the family of the wife or husband. The families could take a decision on behalf of a couple and enforce it if they were Nigerians. They normally did all they could to maintain stability and unity in the family. Unlike in many other places, the people in Africa knew the way to call members of their families to order, no matter how unruly he or she might seem to be. Africans were ready to disown any member of their families that tried to break the norms and orders. Any member that was rebellious to the prevailing customs and order was usually regarded as a bastard. For someone to be regarded as a bastard in Africa was a terrible shame to him and his mother. The case was different in America. In sharp contrast, Americans were paying too much to have freedom in every area of their lives. There was a limit parents could go to discipline their children in America. It was different from African ways of doing things. Parents could do anything to discipline their children. There were lots of differences in the way parents disciplined and related with their children in the two continents.

He had to take Christie to Nigeria to assure his family that he had not married an American who could harm him or his family in the name of freedom. Although few members of the family observed that Christie was a little stern in her dealings, especially with young ones; most members of the family including Mary's father soon approved of her. They were really impressed by the way she participated in the cultural activities. Although she had not yet learned the ethnic

11

language, she easily fit into the system because some of the ceremonies performed for the newest wife in the family were similar to the ones performed in South Africa. As an indication that she has become part of the families in the town, she was asked to carry basket of brooms and dance round the town. She was immediately spotted as a foreigner in the way she danced and that really impressed the people....

At last, after what seemed like hours of thinking of what was happening in his country and what has happened some years ago, Leke slept.

CHAPTER TWO

Thomas went to Mary just before they started the class work and said, 'my friend; Charles said he called you yesterday. He said you're suspicious of him.'

'Did he say I said that?'

'No, but you gave him that impression.'

'I don't know why you have to give him my phone number in the first place.'

'You needed a friend - a brother. I thought, as a Nigerian like you, you could at least trust him. You don't seem to appreciate him even as Nigerian.'

'Thomas, I don't trust boys. They are too naughty for my liking.'

'You need to give someone a chance to be your friend.'

'I've got enough friends. I don't need a date.'

'He's not a date for goodness' sake.'

'That's what it looks to me.'

'He wants to be your friend or brother. He is a nice guy. You are going to like him if you meet him. Don't put him off with your attitude.'

'Okay. I'm sorry. Okay?'

"He said you told him you would think about going places with him.'

'Yeah.'

'When can he….'

'I'm Mama's girl,' she interrupted. 'So I need to get to know him first before I can go out with… Are you sure this is not dating?'

'Whatever it looks like, it's not dating. I want you to meet him, at least.'

Mary smiled. 'It really matters to you I meet him, isn't it?'

He returned the smile, nodding.

'Is he a student too?'

'Yeah.'

Their discussion ended immediately the teacher entered the classroom. It continued during the recess.

'He's in the college. He studies civil engineering,' Thomas later explained to her.

'I see,' Mary said. She had the feeling that he hoped something would come out of the friendship he wanted her to develop with his friend. Whatever might be their plans; she wondered how they hoped to succeed without her co-operation. With the way her parents have brought her up in Nigeria and with the counsel her mother had given her before coming to America, which she was determined to follow strictly, they stood no chance to cajole her into any relationship.

'He'll call you later.'

'Okay.'

Mary was attracted to many students who wanted to know about Africa, especially Nigeria. They have heard so many frightening stories about the place. They wanted to know if truly Africans lived on the trees. They wanted to know if there were certain Africans that have tails. They wanted to know what made them different from animals, going by what they have seen on the television about their ways of life.

Mary spent enough time to explain that Africans were human beings like them though some may live a primitive life. They might not be as developed like some countries but they were definitely not animals as they were portrayed in some films. The more she told them about Africa, the more they wanted to know. She was amused by many of their questions. She was delighted to answer them. Her intelligence and understanding about the issue and other things endeared her to many students. They were really enchanted be her attributes.

About two days after the discussion she had with Thomas about Charles, he called her. She just returned home from school then, going through the routine she normally went through. She had a shower, took her meal and cleaned the kitchen. She lay on the couch to read one of the magazines her uncle had brought for her. She just finished reading an article about lifestyles of some black Americans when the telephone rang. She went to pick it. It was Thomas' friend.

'Hello.'

'Hi, Mary,' the caller said. 'It's me, Charles. Thomas told me to call you again.'

'How are you today?'

He hesitated for a while before he said, 'I'm fine. What are about you?'

'I'm getting used to the life in America.'

'How do you find it?'

'Well, it's fine except that I miss my parents back in Nigeria.'

'You'll get used to that too. I missed my mother when I first got here.'

'Your mother is in Nigeria?'

'Yeah.'

'How are about your father?'

'He's here.'

'Why are they apart?'

'They are not together. My father has another family here. I'm the only one among my mother's children that managed to get here.'

'I see. It must be hard for you to cope.'

'Not really. I can easily adapt to any environment. I want you to adapt too.'

'I think I'm doing fine here.'

'That's good - very good,' he said. 'Mary, you sounded so unfriendly the last time I called. I was reluctant when Thomas urged me to call you again. You see, I don't mean any harm. I just want to treat you like my sister since we are from the same country.'

Mary suddenly felt guilty. All the while, she had mistaken his call as a way to start a mischievous game, which most boys were fond of playing. 'I'm very sorry, Charles. I didn't mean to be unfriendly really.'

'Well, then,' Charles said. 'How do I get to know you better?'

'I don't know,' Mary said reluctantly. 'If Thomas can bring you to our school after closing, that'll be okay.'

'Alright,' Charles said. 'I'll inform him about it.'

'Thanks for calling, Charles,' Mary said. 'I'll be expecting you in the school.'

'Okay. Bye.'

'Bye,' Mary said and dropped the telephone.

* * * *

The school just closed for the day and everybody was getting prepared to go home when Thomas went to inform Mary that Charles was waiting to take her home. At first, she was reluctant. She did not quite like the idea of a stranger taking her home but she didn't want to make Thomas feel offended again.

'Alright,' she said.

'Then let's go and meet him right away.'

Charles turned out to be a slim and tall young man around twenty. He was quite handsome with dark smooth skin. He has naturally curly hair with bright and lovely eyes. His slightly bushy eyebrows

15

complemented his good looks. He was dressed in jeans and fine looking short sleeve shirt.

Contrary to what Mary expected, she liked him at once. She liked his looks. He looked handsome and trustworthy. Charles on the other hand was somewhat overwhelmed by her outstanding beauty. Thomas did not really give him the full description of her by saying she was a beauty from his country. She was in fact a paragon of African beauty. He had assured him that he would like her and he surely did. What he was not sure of was whether she would appreciate him or not.

He was relieved a little, however, when she smiled at him. Charles quickly offered his hand in handshakes although Thomas thought that was a little stupid of him. It easily indicated that she thrilled him.

'I'm glad to meet you, Mary,' Charles said. 'I didn't know you're such a beautiful lady.'

'Thank you,' Mary said although she felt strange to be regarded as a lady. Charles must be a real gentle guy to accord her with that kind of respect.

'I have to meet someone now,' Thomas said. 'I'm sure you guys don't mind if I get missing.'

'If you get missing,' Charles said; smiling at him, 'you're going to be difficult to find. But you are free to go without getting missing.'

Thomas was amused. He waved at them. 'See you, guys, later.'

Mary smiled at him and waved back.

'He's a nice guy,' Charles said, turning to look at Mary.

'Funny,' she said. 'He said the same thing about you when he was trying to persuade me to meet you.'

'Really?'

She shrugged.

He smiled at her, taking a moment to study her face. She looked so innocent that he wondered if she had any boy friend and he wondered if he could find a way to befriend her. Actually, he only longed to make friends with people from his country but he definitely did not plan to meet someone that would captivate him to the extent of thinking of something deeper than mere friendship. Thomas had predicted that he was likely going to develop a relationship with Mary if he met her but he had argued with him that there would be nothing but friendship. He could now see why he made that prediction.

'Do you live nearby?' Charles asked after a while.

'It's not quite near but it's a walking distance.'

'Can we take a stroll to the place together?'

She looked reluctant.

16

'It's okay if you don't want me to walk with you. I guess I'm still a stranger.'

She looked at him. She could not help playing into his hands. She knew her uncle would frown at the idea of a man walking her home. But then, she could not resist a charming guy like him.

'You know I live with my uncle?' she asked.

'I know you have a guardian,' Charles replied. 'I suppose your parents are in Nigeria.'

'That's right.'

'Well, I promise you I won't do anything against your interest.'

Mary tried to interpret what he meant. When she could not, she looked at him expressionlessly and said, 'I wonder what you mean by that.'

'Oww,' Charles said quickly. 'I mean if you don't want me to walk home with you because of your uncle, I won't. I know I'm still a stranger.'

'Charles,' she said, looking deep into his eyes, 'tell me the truth. Why do you want to meet me? Are you looking for a girlfriend?'

He looked at her briefly and smiled. 'Mary, I'm not looking for a girlfriend. If I'm looking for one, there are plenty of girls I can fool around with. Like I said, I simply want to help you adjust to American ways of life and be your friend. That's all.'

'No foul play?'

'Not at all,' Charles said. 'Please, believe me.'

She shrugged. 'I believe you, Charles,' she said.

They walked for sometime before he asked, 'what do you like to do? I mean your hobby.'

'I like reading novels, listen to good music and I like watching films.'

'We have a lot in common then,' he said. 'How about going to the cinema on weekend together?'

'Charles,' she said softly. 'You must realize I'm Mama's girl who just came to the States. How do you expect me to go to a cinema, not even alone but with you? You don't seem to know what that means in Nigeria, do you?'

'Oh, I'm sorry. I guess I've lost touch with the way we think in Nigeria. You see, it's not a big deal to go to the cinemas here. I'm indeed sorry.'

'There's nothing to feel so sorry about,' she said quickly. 'There's still plenty of time to go places together. And remember we are just friends, not dates. You have to understand this from the beginning.'

Charles knew he was pushing his luck too far or rather attempting

17

to do what he did not plan to do. Somehow, he was acting out of impulse and he knew he was probably going to end up falling in love with her, if at all he had not fallen in love with her already.

They talked about her school and his. It was a good discussion. It at least covered up the few lapses which she must have observed so far. When they got to where she lived, she stopped; indicating that she was not inviting him inside. He looked deep inside her eyes and smiled. 'Well,' he said after a brief silence, 'I guess we have to call it a day here.'

'I guess so,' she sighed

He smiled, nodding. 'It's lovely talking with you, Mary,' he said. 'I hope to see you again.'

She returned the smile. It was a very sincere smile that jolted him out of his senses. 'Thanks for your friendship. I hope to keep it if it doesn't go beyond that level.'

'You're still suspicious of me, aren't you?' he asked with somewhat rueful looks.

'You wouldn't blame me for that if I am. Why would a nice looking gentleman like you go this far to offer his friendship to someone who does not really deserve it?'

He smiled. 'The problem with witty girls is that they are always too suspicious.'

'Witty girls? You must be dealing with a lot of them.'

'Oh, no.'

'Then how come you know so much about them?'

'Oh my God! I really need someone to rescue me from you.' He laughed.

She loved the way he laughed. She smiled pleasantly at him.

'There are girls in my school. At least, I relate with them as friends. Is there anything wrong with that? Mary, I just want you to remember that I didn't see you before I offered the friendship. What made me interested in you is simply because you are a Nigerian a Yoruba person like me.'

She went to hold his hand for a brief moment, smiling. 'I think I feel better, brother.' Then she went towards the house, waving at him.

He waved back before he went away, feeling fulfilled for that day.

* * * *

Mary lied on the bed, feeling restless. She had no idea how long she had lied on the bed, thinking of the beginning and the trend of her life including the feelings she had developed towards Charles. Bola was right to think she was very fortunate to leave Nigeria to the place she could build a very good career. She was thinking of becoming an accountant. She could work with her uncle who was obviously very fond of her. She remembered the time she was a kid, the time she was old enough to understand that family ties in Africa went beyond father, mother, brothers and sisters. It extended to uncles, aunties, grand and great grand parents. When her uncle, Leke and other relations were gathered in the family house to celebrate the Christmas together in Sagamu, she had wondered whom most of them were until her uncle Leke exclaimed when she saw her. 'Is this the little Mary I left behind years ago?' He carried her and turned to her father, 'Egbon mi o.' "Egbon mi" literarily means an elder brother or sister, especially of the same nucleus family. 'Mary has grown into a big girl now! She was so small like a kitten when I saw her last. I will take her from you sooner or later.' He always sent things to her when he went back to New York, making other children in the family to be envious. Her parents felt so secured in her uncle's love for her that it was a lot easy for them to release her to him. Being their only child, there was no way they would have let him have her if they were not sure he would take good care of her. In fact, her father feared that because he loved her so much, he would find it difficult to discipline her when she did something wrong. She would never forget what he told him. 'I'm giving you a child I've disciplined so far. Don't pamper her for whatever reason. If you do, I'll take her back from you.' Her uncle had promised to do his best to train her to become not just a responsible lady but also a seasoned accountant. 'If there is any reason to change that plan, I'll let you know.' And so she could not even complete her secondary school before her uncle told her it was time to come to America. She had gotten a letter of transfer from her school to St. James College before she could think of reading accountancy in the university. She dreamt of going to study in one of the most prestigious universities in America. She wanted to be the kind of lady her family and even her country would be proud of.

As she thought of her life and dreams, the thought of Charles invaded her mind. She was involuntarily carried away by his good looks and attributes. Charles was a charming guy who could easily captivate any girl. Although to think of him as her boyfriend was not an acceptable idea, she could not help toying with the idea. It was repugnant to the prevailing norms in the ethnic group she belonged to back in Nigeria. Besides it was grievously against her father's policy.

She could imagine how he would bellow at the idea if he managed to read her thoughts about keeping a boyfriend. 'What! You must be insane to think of having a boyfriend at this stage of your life. You're not even sixteen yet. You have not even completed your secondary school.' As principled as he was, her mother once told her that he proposed to marry her when she was a teenager. That was to prove that love was that powerful. If there was real love, age did not really matter but the problem was how to recognize true love in this morally decadent generation. The moral values of the people, especially among the youths were at a very low level. There were high moral and family values during the time of older generation. That of the people in the present days was deteriorating seriously. She had witnessed the cases of her friends dropping out of school after getting pregnant. She did not think the situation in the United States was better. The moral decadence in the country was about the same if not worse. The little interaction she had with many of the students in her new school indicated that it was no big deal for a teenager to have a boyfriend. In fact, the moral values in the country had degenerated to the extent that condoms were distributed in the schools. It was not unusual for a girl to give a condom to her boyfriend, an indication that she wanted him to make love to her. A lot of American ladies were always on pills, which prevented them from getting pregnant. If by mistake or sheer negligence, a lady got pregnant, she would simply go for an abortion. The case was different in Nigeria. If a lady got pregnant, nobody would openly encourage her to go for an abortion because the act was illegal. Besides, the norms regarded it as a murder. Many Americans did not believe that abortion of pregnancy was a murder. She remembered the argument she read between a pro-life and pro-abortion in a magazine. The pro-abortion was saying in one of the busy streets in Atlanta, 'if abortion is made illegal, the blacks tend to loose. The white will always get a way out…' Mary wondered why no one asked her how. 'We must retain the law that supports getting rid of unwanted pregnancies.' A pro-life had challenged her sincerity. She wanted to know why she was asking the people to kill their babies. 'Did I tell the people to kill their babies?' the pro-abortion asked. 'Pregnancy is different from a baby. I suppose every idiot knows that.' The pro-life claimed that she not know the difference. So she explained, 'the difference is: babies are already born while pregnancies are still in formation stages.' Before the audience got carried away by her explanation and argument, the pro-life who was obviously a Christian had shot the question at her, 'formation of what?

Animals? Virus?' The debate was over before anyone knew it.

Mary wondered how many unwanted babies had been rid of in America. According to the argument of the pro-life, many people who could have been great leaders and inventors like Thomas Edison, Abraham Lincoln, Albert Einstein and a host of others had been murdered in the womb before they were born. How incredibly insane it was for a woman to kill her baby before he was born. As great as America was, she needed a lot of orientation in some areas. In fact, her observation in the country proved to her that no country was an island of knowledge. Just as every country must learn from Americans, they also need to learn from other people all over the world.

She rolled to another side on the bed, still wrapped in thoughts. She thought of what America has got to offer in building her career and family. There were vast golden opportunities in America although many did not seem to notice them. Everyone who has ever lived in Nigeria would not fail to see them. Everything, which people in Nigeria have to struggle to get was almost free in America. Air, water, train and some times land transportations were for the privileged; the kinds of food that posed threats to people's health in America were the kinds that many Nigerians struggled to get for survival. Expired and substandard drugs that were hazardous to the body system were always exhibited for sales in the buses and streets of Nigeria. Even though the country was referred to as the giant of Africa, being the most populous nation in the continent, she has more problems than most other countries in the entire world. Though, on a whole, the country was not completely bad but she has far too many political, social and economic problems that could be attributed to the military regime. The country was going through a trauma under the dictators who had murdered so many promising political leaders. Because of the political problems, so many ugly things were coming from the country. The military have virtually destroyed every aspect of life in Nigeria including the moral values. The economy was in shambles, resulting into greed, lack of considerations for others, fraudulent practices and so many other crimes. If the country was going to remain like that, it would be stupid of her to think of settling down there; no matter how much she loved the country. Even then, she would need to consider the person she would marry before she could think of where to live.

Then the thought of marriage began to occur to her. She wondered how the person she would marry would look like. Would he look like

21

Sesan, the boy that once won her heart in Nigeria? No, she told herself aloud. They didn't fall into the same class any longer. How about Charles? She asked herself. He seemed so nice and gentle but that sounded like a stupid question. How could she consider someone like Charles who she knew barely two weeks ago for marriage? Besides, she has a long way to go before she thought of marriage. Before she knew it, she was thinking of the things she loved about him. He might be pretending but he seemed like a cool guy to her. He looked like a serious minded and virtuous person. He has impressive features with sharp mind. He was the kind of guy she could introduce to anyone as her boyfriend. But then, was she not being totally stupid to have that kind of thought, knowing fully well that she has a long way to go before she could think of submitting herself to any man? Definitely, she argued with herself, she would marry one day. The earlier she knew whom she was going to marry, the better for her. She could plan her life with his right from the onset. The combination of their efforts and determinations could make them very focused and successful. After all, her new teachers used to say success was a process. Success did not just come by chance. It was always planned for and worked out. Her favourite teacher who was more or less a motivational speaker that read a lot of books on motivation once said while answering a student's question on general issues, nobody is born to fail or succeed in life. People failed because they choose to fail and people succeeded because they choose not to be a failure. She once heard her uncle telling someone, "success was very cheap to get if people were not cheap enough to give in to failure and if they did not go about success in a cheap way." The bottom line was that they should be ready to give what it took to be successful.

The few weeks she has spent in the school so really affected the way she viewed things. Most American schools always challenged their students to be successful in whatever they chose to become. They gave them support and provided the right text and supplementary books that would encourage the students to be successful. Nearly all the schools were conscious of the fact that anyone could become anything by reading. Hence, their libraries were always treasures of knowledge. Unlike in Nigeria where most workers, including the teachers were not motivated, America believed so much in their citizens that she invested a lot in them by providing quality education, reliable means of communications and means of developing the brain of individuals including the handicaps. There was far too much brain drain in Nigeria. The youths were not empowered with necessary infrastructures that would help them make best use of their potentials. They were usually at the mercy of polluted environment that made criminals out of them. As intelligent as many Nigerians were, most of them engaged in malpractice like corruption, nepotism, abuse of power, tribalism and even religious riots. It was difficult to talk about Nigeria without mentioning these unpleasant characteristics that could be attributed to the inhuman leadership. A lot of lives were always wasted if anyone tried to say the right things or put things right. Nigerians were one of the easiest sets of people to govern despite so many differences in each tribe and ethnic group. They would readily adapt to the unpleasant government policies. They were always willing to co-operate with the government in everything by giving all they have, including their freedom and start all over again rather than to fight back. That was why and how they continued to survive in the ocean of insanity. Many political experts around the globe once predicted another civil war in the country but Nigerians stunned them by making themselves comfortable in the midst of conditions that were enough to drive people in other part of the world into insanity. They would rather look for other options to survive than to go to war. From history, Nigerians were not cowards as many people assumed. Apart from being peace-loving, the people knew that the price of civil war far outweighed price of peace. So it was not a surprise that the country managed to help other African countries to stop wars. The military government knew that Nigerians did not like to see blood, especially the blood of their fellow citizens. So the government captivated on the people's weak spots to rule them anyhow. The consequence of not going into war made many Nigerians fraudulent, which unknown to them, outweighed the price of war. There was nothing as dangerous as making the people to develop negative attitudes. It has a lot of chain reactions. If bad leaders was wiped out, the people would keep their positive attitudes. It would be easy to boost the people's moral values then. Since the bad leaders were not rid off, the drive to survive would influence the people to accept and get involved in anti-social and criminal acts. The consequence of criminal acts like armed-robberies was to see more blood in the streets than that of the price to be paid to remove the bad leaders. In fact, it was more difficult to build a country that was made up of people with negative attitudes than the one that was ravaged by war. There was far more hope to build the nation that was a heap of ruins if the citizens possessed patriotic spirits than the one whose citizens were full of negative attitudes. No matter how rich a nation may be, if the people were not patriotic, they would constantly work against the progress of the country and no matter how well the political system was built, it would be destabilized. So, like her father used to argue, if anyone wanted to build his nation, he must start with the people. People were much more valuable than wealth because it was the people that created wealth. The people were the greatest wealth or problem of any given nation. Wealth could never create the people but people could create wealth. The people could also destroy wealth if it was not invested to build and empower them. America would continue to grow strong because the people were not only empowered but were also characterized with positive attitudes. Unlike in the attitudes of many Nigerians, many Americans would rather opt for presidential handshakes that would go into the record than to make millions of dollars in a crooked manner. Even if a Nigerian opted for a good name that would go into the record, other people; including his family would consider him insane. Some might even ask him if he could eat good name. They would get a proverb to buttress this which said, 'you see a mad man's leg; you don't cut it off for rituals. Where on earth do you expect a sane man to you offer his?' The military government had made the people so greedy that many of them looked for money with the passions, not caring how they got it. To many Nigerians, money was the ultimate. A child who was supposed to be in school was looking for money, his parents were looking for money and so was everyone. Mary would never forget an incident that occurred in the school she attended in Nigeria.

There were three girls in the final year in secondary school. They were good friends. They were so close that they studied together and stayed together at times when they were preparing for examinations. Two of the girls conspired to sell the third girl to a witch doctor who would use the parts of her body for rituals. Rituals were so common in Nigeria that many people were found missing on a daily basis. The witch doctors normally use parts of human body to bring about mysterious wealth. So it was not headline news when people were found missing.

The two girls told their friend to follow them to see a man in another town. Unknown to her, they have made arrangement with the witch doctor that they were bringing someone to him for sale. They hired a taxicab that would take them to and from the town where they were to carry out the evil deal. The taxi driver was instructed to wait in the car while they went to a nearby bush where the witch doctor was waiting to receive them. After selling their friend, the girls collected their money and went back to the taxi driver who asked them of their friend. One of the girls told him that she would meet them later. The driver became suspicious as they left the place. To add to his suspicion that something mischievous was going on, the girls started counting huge amount of money in the cab. Instead of driving them to the place they were going, he drove them straight to the police station and informed the police officers on duty what was happening; adding that there was something fishy about the two girls. The police questioned the girls about the other girl. They gave flimsy excuses that they left her with her family. The policemen told the taxi driver to take them and the girls to the place. Before they got to the place, the body of the poor girl had been dismantled for rituals. The entire nation was full of shock when the story came out as news item in media houses. If secondary school girls could go as far as selling their friend for rituals, what was the hope of the people that the country would be better? What was the future of the nation if young ones like that could be so heartless enough to sell their friend to evil men?

Every sane person in Nigeria knew what the military had turned the country that was once peaceful and wealthy into hell. Mary wondered how things were going to come back to normal. A friend of her father called Mr Lekan Jagun once said that the national progress was the sum of individual industry, energy and uprightness as national decay was of individual idleness, selfishness and vice. In other words, the change in any nation began with a change in the individual. As another of her father's friend pointed out while having discussion about the condition of the nation, 'if all Nigerians are taken to Britain, they would turn the country into another Nigeria and vice visa.' This, according to him, was due to the attitudes of the people. It was the attitudes of the collective people that changed the environment and not the environment that changed the collective people. The environment that was created by the collective people could only influence an individual and not vice visa.

Now that she was in America, far away from the polluted environment like the one in Nigeria, she would make best use of the opportunity and see what she could do for her family and relations just as her uncle was trying to help those that were in need. There was little or nothing she could do for her country at the moment except to educate people who did not understand the situation back there. No matter how terrible the situation might be, she would never deny her identity as a Nigerian. Nigeria was her root. She would be proud of it, no mater how. In fact, she desired to marry a Nigerian. Yes, she would marry a Nigerian. Did she mean she would go to Nigeria and get married? She asked herself with a frown. There were many Nigerians in America. Charles was one of them. Charles? Why did the thought of Charles constantly invade her mind? Was she in love with that guy or something? She could not say. She was sincere enough to tell herself that she liked him but she was no sure if it has anything to do with love. How could she possibly fall in love with a guy she met not quite long? Besides that, she was just sixteen years old. If at all there was anything like love, it was not for her - not for someone of her age.

After a long chain of thoughts, she heard the door to the sitting room opened. She knew it was her uncle. She thought of going to welcome him even though he expected her to have slept. He barely has much time for her. He was always working even on weekends. Although he had promised her that he would take her to Chicago on one of the weekends to see her cousins and their mother but he had not been able to spare the time. Perhaps she should get out of the bed to welcome him home and use the opportunity to remind him of his promise to take her to Chicago. If she continued waiting for him to spare the time, she might wait a long time.

She got out of the bed. She was wearing her nightdress. She went to the sitting while Leke was going to go to his room.

'Mary,' Leke said with a frown, 'what are you doing by this time of the day?'

'I couldn't catch some sleep.'

'I see,' he said. 'I hope there is no problem.'

'Not at all.'

'Are you sure?' he asked.

'There's no problem, Uncle.'

'You're sure you're not feeling bored.'

'No,' she replied. 'This place is hardly boring but I just wonder when you're taking me to Chicago.'

'I don't have the time,' he said. 'I'm sure you know that. You can go by yourself, can't you?'

Mary looked excited. 'Can I really go by myself?'

'Why not? Even if you are baby, I can easily hand you over to the air hostess to deliver you like a parcel to your aunty who will be waiting to receive you in Chicago.'

'Is it that easy?'

'It's much easier than that. This is America. Nobody would steal you from me.'

She laughed. 'But I used to hear cases of kidnaping and things like that.'

'Oh, that happens when the kidnappers want to take something big from a Mr Big Shot. You know what I mean?'

'Yeah. You are Mr Big Shot, aren't you, uncle?'

'I'm not, my dear. At least, not yet.' He paused for a while, looking thoughtful. 'I'll arrange for the time you'll go by air and call Christie to pick you up at the airport.'

'That'll be lovely,' she said, looking excited. 'Thanks, sir.'

'Would you be able to catch some sleep now?' he asked, smiling.

'Oh, sure.'

'Alright,' he said, switching off the light. 'I'll see if I can arrange the journey for this weekend. Good night.' He headed for his room.

'Thank you, sir,' she repeated, going to her room.

When she went back to bed, she thought of her cousins and their mother for a while before she slept.

CHAPTER THREE

Mary was so excited to meet her cousins and their mother, Aunty Christie that she did not observe the differences between the environments in Chicago and New York. To her, America was beautiful. Even the areas that were considered slums in the country were better than so many areas in Africa.

She did not have to struggle to see her relations whom she had come to visit in Chicago when she got down from the plane before Christie came with her three cousins Linda, Koya and Lola. Linda who was just fifteen years was already in the college, studying chemical engineering. Koya who was a thirteen-year-old boy was in the senior high school while Lola, an eleven-year-old girl was still in the junior high school.

They were all excited to see Mary. It was the first time they were going to meet her since she came to America. The last time they met was about five years before. That was the time they have gone to their hometown, Sagamu in Nigeria to celebrate the Christmas and the New Year. Although they were all still very young then, they would never forget the exciting time they had together. Mary and one other relative who was very familiar with the town had taken them round the place. Everything they found in the town was new - completely different from America. Nearly through out the time they stayed in Nigeria, the natives celebrated one thing or the other; making the town very lively with merriments. Instead of the gunshots which they were used to in the environment in America or films, it was merriment galore; making their entire stay in the country very exciting. Apart from being friendly, the natives were happy and accommodating people. They were treated with special care.

Christie grabbed Mary from the waist as if she was one of her babies and decorated her with kisses. She was always fond of Mary. In fact she was her favourite among all her husband's nephews and nieces.

She was not only hardworking and beautiful but also very intelligent. She normally dazzled her with her views about many things each time they interacted. Although she needed not be surprised at

28

her display of intelligence for she only exhibited the trait of her father yet she wondered a girl of her age could be so knowledgeable. Again, when she got to know her father more closely, she came to the conclusions that she did not only took after her father but also learned so many things through him; making her to think like an adult at her tender age. She always had the opportunity to hear her father's views. She sometimes listened to intellectual debate between him and his friends. It was a great advantage to have her kind of father. Besides, as her mother once told her, her father made her read newspapers and a lot of books.

Through what Christie observed in Mary, she could see that she has a great deal of potentials. She knew she could become great in future. So she encouraged Leke to get her to study in America when he informed her about his intention to invest in her. She had hoped she would live with her in Chicago but Leke would rather have her with him in New York.

Her three cousins hugged and kissed her cheek each. Christie soon bundled everybody with Mary's bag into the car and drove them away.

For the first time, Mary noted that Chicago was also full of many tall buildings like the ones in New York. She was impressed by everything she saw in the area.

They chatted all the way. They talked about beautiful and ugly things in America. Mary told them that Nigeria was becoming more uncomfortable to live under the military dictators.

'Can't the people do something?' Linda asked, irritated.

'What do you expect the people to do?' Mary asked.

Christie fell into deliberate silence, pretending to be more engrossed in the driving. She knew the teenagers were about to go into a serious debate. She wanted to know how reasonable the girls would sound in their argument.

'They could make the country ungovernable,' Linda said. She was truly angry with the military government in her country.

'You'll be asking for another civil war.'

'Does that matter when the freedom of the people is at state? I mean it's like everybody in the country is in bondage. No one is free. You can't find something good to eat, no good transportation, no - medical facilities, no good education - nothing good. Tell me what good thing you can find in the country where you can't even express yourself without landing in jail. For how long will the people continue to live like that? We hear all sorts of stories about the place. I don't like it.

The situation in the place does not make me feel proud of the country. I don't like people to tell me there is nothing they can do.'

'You talk and think like Americans,' Mary said. 'I know an average American would say, "give me freedom or kill me." But what would you say if the war is between the inhumane military and the helpless civilians?'

'The civilians can become militant if they really want freedom,' Linda argued. 'There's nowhere in the world that freedom is obtained on the platter of gold. You must struggle to get it. Blood must be shed to get it, no matter how. If the people don't die for freedom from the military now, they would die of something else later. What's the point of keeping your life when millions of lives, including that of the unborn generations are at stake? In my mother's country, the people are ready to die for their freedom. They have been fighting apartheid system for hundreds of years. I'm sure they'll not stop shedding blood until they get their freedom. So it's not only in America that people will die for their freedom. If the people in Nigeria do not fight for their freedom from the military now, when their children grow up to see all the mess their parents have allowed, they would feel betrayed. Do you know what kept on the struggle for freedom in South Africa for so long?'

Mary shook her head, completely carried away by her points.

'It's the number of people that have died for freedom. The death of one person who stands for freedom will always nurture other people to be ready to die for the same course. When the people think of their relations or friends or even mentors that have died in the course of fighting the apartheid system, they are provoked the more. I use to think that if I can get the chance to talk with the freedom fighters, I will not only encourage them but also teach them how to manufacture cheap and easy explosive that can be used to destroy those bloody racists!'

It was when Christie laughed that the girls realized that she had been listening to them.

Linda looked at her mother laughing. Before anyone knew it, everybody was roaring with laughter.

'I must admit that you really have a point,' Mary said, 'but there are a lot of differences in the mentality of Nigerians and other people. You see, Nigeria have gone through civil war that almost wiped out the whole tribe of Igbo. If at all Nigerians are encouraged to pick up guns now, don't expect the Igbo people to join in the battle; not after their horrible experience in the civil war that is still affecting them up till now.

30

Secondly, the Hausas who have more people in the government than any other tribes normally favour their people in the Northern part of the country in many ways. In essence, the Hausas are not likely going to join in the civil war. In any case, no Hausa would spearhead any civil war in Nigeria because it is their people that are in the government. They would rather go on suffering than to have the power shifted to the south. So we are left with the Yorubas to fight the military along with few minority groups. If they try that, they would be digging their own graves and that of their children.'

'Why do you think the Hausas would prefer suffering to having the power shifted to the south?' Christie asked, trying to find out if she has facts that could substantiate her argument.

'Well, I came across a shocking revelation in the newspapers shortly before I came here. A political activist claimed that the Hausas are doing what the colonialists told them to do by holding on to political power by all means. He said that the colonialists told the northerners that the Southerners are the one having economic powers in the country. To a large extent, that's true. If the northerners let go off the political powers, they are doomed. Although there is no proof of the claim that the colonialists taught them that but considering the way the Northerners were determined to keep the political power to themselves even when it is obvious that it is not in their best interest, I'm forced to believe that there may be some elements of truths in the claim of the activist.'

'I don't think they need anyone to tell them they have to keep the political power,' Linda said. 'They can figure out the need by themselves.'

'My father did not think that the Hausas are as smart as that.'

'With due respect, I think uncle is biased. He never hides it from everyone, including me that he dislikes the Hausas whenever he's telling us about what is happening in the country. He always addresses them as animals because they were the ones mostly in the military, ruling.'

'Not that he dislikes the Hausas. He only hates the ones in the government with passion. He sees them as the ones destroying Nigerians,' Mary explained. She added with a chuckle, 'he always said that the fools in the government are much more dangerous than the armed robbers that are shooting at everybody in the streets.'

Linda and her mother laughed. 'I think he's right in that regards,' Christie said.

'Still, I don't believe a whole tribe of Hausas are so dumb,' Linda

31

argued. 'There are some Nigerians in this country, including the Hausas that are so resourceful and valuable that the US government cannot afford to let them go back to Nigeria.'

'That makes sense,' Mary agreed. 'It leaves us with the notion that if Nigerians think another civil war is the solution to the problem in the country, they would have gone into it. Don't you think?'

'There are lots of differences between being bold and being smart,' Linda said, not willing to accept defeat.

'You really think Nigerians are cowards because they did not go into civil war? To start with, who are they supposed to fight with?'

Linda did not want her argument to sound weak. So she said, 'who was fighting who in the civil war? The civil war in Nigeria, from what I gather in the history of the country, was politically motivated.'

'Whatever the motive,' Mary said, 'they still went into war.'

'Tell us who was fighting who,' Koya who had been following the trend of the discussion told Mary.

'Actually, I don't know what caused the civil war,' Mary admitted. 'But I think, as Linda pointed out, the war was politically motivated,' Mary said; giving Linda room to still present her points. 'There was power tussle between military officers shortly after the independence.'

'The military had always been in power?' Koya asked.

'Nigerians hardly practices democratic government since independence in 1960. The military overthrows the government each time she tried it. You know, when a country is having leadership problems, social and economic developments become almost impossible. The civil war was supposed to be a way to reconcile the ambitious leaders but instead it became a horrible experience which the people are not ready to go through again. The generation that went through it have a lot of bad stories to tell their children. When my father related the story to me, I used to thank God I was not born then. Only those who have gone through it will appreciate the fact that war should be the last option to consider in solving a problem. It really affects Nigerians even up till now. You only know when it starts. You can never predict when it will end. You can never tell what it will cost you. If the country had not gone through the civil war then, they would never have known the price of war. If the people did not know, the chances are that there would have been war by now.'

'I think Nigerians are bold and smart,' Koya said suddenly with pride.

'That's because you are a Nigerian,' Linda told him.

'He may be right,' Christie who was obviously enjoying their discussion said. 'Let him explain why he thinks so.'

Koya shrugged. 'I guess cowards never go into war in the first place.'

'The only reason the people did not want to fight as I can infer from your explanations is because they did not want to pay another price of war. Consider the situation in South African. The people had been fighting apartheid system for so long yet they never surrender. Why can't Nigerians do the same if they are so bold?' Linda said.

'The battle in South Africa is quite different from the battle in Nigeria,' Mary said; wondering when she would get her points. 'South Africans are fighting the apartheid system while Nigerians are fighting the military system of government. The difference, if you don't notice it, is that one race is fighting the other while the other is fighting his people that are ruling them with the use of military weapons. In South Africa, the blacks are fighting the white for not only ruling in their country but also oppressing them. There is a number of reasons Nigerians cannot fight the military. One of them is that Nigerians are reasonable enough to note that war is not always the solution to such peculiar problems. Secondly, it is a suicide mission for civilians to decide to fight the military government that is armed with the weapons that are used to protect the nation. You go back to your history book about your country again. You will see more reasons why Nigeria has to go into civil war then. From all the facts available, the country did all she could to prevent it.'

The chat and the argument were endless. Right from there, they began to enjoy Mary's company. She was willing to educate her cousins and their mother about what was happening in Nigeria. Before anyone knew it, even Linda who was a little controversial had to admit that she was ill informed about her country. When they got to the house where Christie lived with her children, Mary was immediately made to feel at home. She was taken to each room, including the room that had been prepared for her to stay; Christie's and Leke's bedroom. Until recently when his business had taken so much of his time, he frequently flew from New York to spend some time with his family.

They had a dinner before they began to chat endlessly. Mary talked so much about what she found very pleasant about America that everybody wondered how she could understand that much within the short time she has spent in the country.

'Would you like to live in Chicago?' Linda asked suddenly. Everybody looked at Mary. Obviously, she just expressed the desire of everyone in the house.

She hesitated for a while. She preferred New York to staying with them in Chicago. The main reason was that she has more freedom down there. 'But I've started my school down there,' she said.

'Your uncle can easily change the school,' Christie said.

'If he wouldn't disapprove it,' Mary said, trying not to give them the impression that she liked New York better, 'why not?'

'I'll talk to him about it,' Christie said.

That almost changed Mary's pleasant expression into disappointments.

Through out her stay in Chicago, Mary concealed her feelings about the idea of living with them. But then she needed not to worry. She knew what to tell her uncle about the idea of living in Chicago.

After spending the whole weekend with her cousins and their mother, enjoying most of the time, she flew back to New York.

* * * *

'You didn't tell me how you find Chicago,' Leke told Mary as they took their meal in the evening of the day she got back to New York.

'I enjoyed the place very much,' she said. It was a good opportunity to let her uncle know that she liked it more in New York. 'But I enjoy staying here.'

'Why?' Leke asked, amused. 'You like being a free girl down here?'

She smiled and nodded vigorously. 'Besides, I have a lot of friends in the school. I don't want to loose them.'

'I understand,' Leke said. 'Your cousins and their mother called me on the phone when you left Chicago. They all want you to live with them.'

'What did you tell them?'

'I told them I would think about it. I had the feelings you won't like to live there as much as you like it here.'

'They asked if I would live with them,' she said. 'I didn't want them to feel I don't like to stay with them. So I said I would love to if you approve of it.'

'You don't have to worry about that any more. I'll tell them I need you here.'

'Oh, thanks, uncle.'

After the dinner, Mary cleared the table and went to wash the dishes. She later went to the sitting room where her uncle was reading the newspaper.

'I forgot to tell you,' Leke said, turning the newspaper to another page. 'Someone called you yesternight. She said she's Comfort Olumbe or something like that.'

Mary frowned. She didn't know anyone with that name but the family name sounds like that of Charles.

'Is she a Nigerian?'

'I should be asking you,' he said. He glanced at her briefly. 'The name sounds Nigerian but she sounded American to.' He looked at her again. She looked thoughtful. 'You don't seem to know who the person is, do you?'

'No.'

'Then how did she get our telephone number?'

'I think one of my classmates gave it to her.'

'I see.' He continued reading the newspaper.

The following day, Mary met Thomas in the school during the recess. She asked him of the person called Comfort Olumbe.

'Oh,' Thomas said, 'she's Charles sister.'

'I guess as much,' she said. 'Why does she have to call me?'

'Her brother must have told her to call you or something.'

'Why?' Mary was irritated a little.

'You can ask him,' Thomas said, looking hard at her. 'Boy,' he told himself, 'she is beautiful.' He did not blame Charles for being so attracted to her. He wondered if she was aware that he was deeply in love with her. If not, she would soon notice. He knew Charles would not give up on her until he had succeeded getting into her life. Although Charles was decent and very modest but he knew he would scheme a way for her to play into his hands. He never hide it from him from the first time they met that he would go to any extent to possess her. He wondered how she would react when he expressed his love for her. From what he observed about Mary, she seemed to be a very interactive type of girl though she considered herself more matured than most of them. In any case, Charles could handle her. He had met many beautiful girls that were ready to do anything just to get his attention. So no matter how matured Mary thought she was, Charles would get into her life because he truly loved her. He had never seen a girl driving so crazy since he knew him. He had no doubt that he was in love with her but the question he was not able to answer was if Mary cared at all for him. The way she felt irritated that Comfort called her did not indicate that she liked him as much as he did.

'I wish he wouldn't have to call or tell anyone to call me again,' she said.

'Do you really mean that?' he asked quickly. 'I thought you've become friends.'

Mary regretted what she said. 'I wish he or his sister wouldn't have to call when my uncle is around.'

'You tell him whatever is in your mind. He'll probably tell you his.'

* * * *

Charles managed to get Mary's approval to enter the house after meeting for a few more times. This was really an indication that her determination to resist all his advances to possess her was growing weaker each time they met. They had met few weeks after she had complained to Thomas about the telephone call his sister made while she was away to Chicago. He explained to her that he was the one that actually made the call but he has to give the phone to Comfort when her uncle picked it. Being a Nigerian, he knew how her uncle might react to the idea of having male friends. Many Nigerian parents frowned at the idea of keeping opposite sex as friends. He did not want him to get the impression that she was playing around with boys.

Charles looked round the sitting room. He was very impressed by the luxuries he found inside. 'Your uncle must be wealthy,' he remarked. 'What does he do?'

'Why do you want to know?' she asked, not bordering to offer him anything.

He glanced at her. When he saw the disapproving looks on her face, he dropped his stare and said, 'I'm sorry I asked.'

Mary waved indifferently. 'He's into exporting business, auto deal, air travel and cruise tours.'

'I see,' he said quietly. All the while, he was standing.

'What can I offer you?' she asked, trying to be friendlier. Though she was almost sure of what he was up to, she regretted treating him with suspicions. With the way she was beginning to feel about him over the few weeks, she was afraid he might succeed with what he has in mind. Her mother had warned her in Nigeria against getting involved with boys. Even then, Charles seemed so different from all the boys she knew. He seemed so gentle and understanding.

'I'm Okay.'

'Are you sure?'

He nodded vigorously, trying to hide his frustrations.

She looked at him for a moment before she asked, 'are you

offended?'

He was silent. He shrugged.

'You don't understand me, do you?'

'I'm not sure I do,' he replied in a quiet voice. He walked closer to her slowly and added in a whisper. 'There are things I say or do that seem to offend you. I don't know why. Do I still look like a bad boy that means you any harm?'

'Remember what I told you about dating. I don't want dates. I don't play games of whatever kind with any boy. I have to erect the wall between us because I don't trust your feelings for me.'

Charles who was aware of the fact that she was very intelligent through their previous conversations could sense her fear at once. She was afraid of him. That was why she was trying to put up a strong resistance that was too easy for him to break. Somehow intelligent people were always easy for him to handle.

'Supposing the boy you're trying to resist is going to end up as your husband,' he said, trying to play the fool so that he could get her. If she would not give him the chance to express his feelings for her as a gentleman, he might as well express it as a fool. After all, one of the best ways to capture an intelligent girl like her was to play the fool.

'Two things are wrong with what you just said now,' she said after a brief hesitation. 'One of them is: I'm not trying to resist anyone. Secondly, I've not come to America to pick a husband. I've come to build my career and future.'

There was another silence. It was so uncomfortable that Charles shifted from his position, walking pass her.

'Can I at least sit down?' he asked.

'Be my guest.' She gestured to the settee in front of her.

There was another uncomfortable silence. They looked at each other for a while. She refused to look away and he was determined to play the man. In Africa, man was superior, no matter how intelligent the woman was. But then, the whole thing was turning into a cat and mouse game as she refused to admit inferiority. If the cat did not get the mouse, it would loose its mind. If he could not get Mary to be his girlfriend, he would never be the same again.

'Mary,' he said, breaking the silence as he took his seat. 'I've learnt never to pretend. I'm a plain person. It's easy for people who are not even as intelligent as you to read my thoughts and feelings. That may be a weak point but, at least, it is an advantage to those I'm dealing with; including someone that's going to be my wife. You said a while ago that you don't trust my feelings for you. That proves that that it's hard to hide from you even if I tried to. So I won't try to hide again. I'll tell you the obvious truth. I'm in love with you.'

She laughed.

'You can choose to be amused, baby, but that's just the plain truth. If that's not true, I wouldn't have gone this far with you.'

'I knew it. I knew all along that that's what you had in mind,' she said. 'By the way, what do you know about love?'

'Love has to do with deep feelings.'

'Do you think that kind of deep feelings exist within our age groups?'

'Mary, I'm almost twenty years old. Many people who are below that age are married both in this country and in Nigeria.'

'Are you saying a twenty years old guy can pick a sixteen year old girl who wants to build her career for marriage?'

'We are not talking of marriage yet. We are talking about love. What I'm saying is that be sincere enough to tell me if I have a chance to come into your life. Tell me you love me if you do,' he said. Then he asked softly, 'Mary, do you love me?'

'I don't know what love is,' she said, indifferently. 'So I don't.'

'I think you do,' he said. 'I'll show you.' He took the major risk to trash things out once and for all by trying to kiss her. He stood up, grabbed her firmly and forced a kiss on her lips.

She tightened her lips and struggled to break loose from him but he was too strong for her. After a few minutes of struggle she began to relax. Slowly, she started responding to his passionate kiss. Although she did not know how to kiss, she opened her mouth slightly and let his tongue messaged hers. She relaxed in his arms in total submission.

Charles was dazed by his success to have her in his arms. Her soft lips and tender body made his head exploded with passion.

After a long passionate kiss, he released her and whispered, 'I love, Mary.'

Mary was silent, looking thoughtful. She did not quite understand what was happening to her. She had never been so close to any man since she was born. So it was impossible to know if what she was feeling was real love or not. She, however, knew for sure that she was very comfortable with Charles. He may be very possessive but she liked him. She liked everything about him including the way he felt about her.

Charles felt the passion of love pricking his heart the more as he looked at her. He would do or give away anything to marry this girl, not only because she was very beautiful and intelligent but also because she was very descent. He was almost like a dirty piece of rag in comparison with what she was made up of. 'It does not matter if you don't know how love feels,' he said, holding her hands gently. 'At least, you can tell me if you like me.'

'I like you very much, Charles,' she said. 'But you went too far. Nobody has ever kissed or touched me like that.'

'I know,' he whispered.

'The way you kissed me shows you're not new in this type of game, are you?'

'You are the first and the only one I have ever felt like this for.'

'You mean you have never fallen in love before?'

He shook his head.

There was silence. He looked at her thoughtful face. He might be looking at her with the eyes of love but he thought all her expressions made her very beautiful.

'I was afraid it would result into this,' she said with serious tone. 'That's why I didn't want to encourage you getting close to me.' Her voice became softer as she added, 'I don't know how you did it but you have got me on a very soft spot. I don't know I have this spot until now.'

'What you call soft spot is actually love.'

'I don't know. Whatever it is, I don't want you to take advantage of it. If you do, I'll consider you an enemy. I want you to promise me that you will not take advantage of it.'

'I won't.'

'Promise?'

'Yeah.' He asked almost immediately, 'since you have this soft spot for me, would you consider me as your future partner?'

She smiled. 'You talk like the secondary school guys back in Nigeria.'

'I had all my elementary and secondary education in Nigeria before coming to this country.'

'I see.'

'Since you understand the language even though it is used in the secondary schools in Nigeria, would you answer the question?'

'I don't know, Charles,' she said, moving away. 'I have my career to think of right now. Besides, it's going to be long before I think of anything like that.'

'It may not be as long as you think. The future begins from now. It begins with what we agree to do now.'

He smiled at her silently. 'You are going to say yes.'

'Don't push your luck too far,' she replied, looking at him.

He fixed his gaze on her, still smiling. He looked handsome with the smiles.

Feeling uncomfortable with the way he looked at her, she looked away and said, 'As a Nigerian, it's wrong to think of marriage at the age of sixteen except, of course, if that person has no focus in life.'

'I don't want you to mix things up, Mary.' He said. 'I'm a focused person and I have a career I'm building. I don't want you to get the impression that I don't know what I'm doing. In fact, I'm making this proposal to you for three good reasons. One of them is to make you understand that I don't want stuff like lovers but serious minded youths who want to build their future together. Secondly, I want us to plan our lives together with the mind that we are meant for each other as husband and wife. And lastly, I love you. I want to concentrate on you and you alone.'

Mary was thoughtful for a long time, wondering if what he said was reasonable enough for her to accept his proposal or not. She went to sit down on the long couch, still thinking. Even then, she thought, no guy would make a proposal like that without being genuinely focused and serious.

He went to sit beside her, holding her hands.

'It doesn't make things right,' she said.

'Think about it, sweetheart,' he said quietly. He was almost certain he had won her heart completely.

'I don't know much about you,' she said. 'So I cannot accept your proposal right away.'

'Okay,' he said. 'Let's start from the basis - friendship and see what that would lead us to.'

She smiled. 'I really appreciate that. At least, it showed you are considerate. That's one of the best things I like in a person.'

He stood up to go, smiling. 'I have to go. I hope to take you to one of the parks around soon.'

'How soon?'

'This weekend perhaps,' he said. 'I'll call you later and inform you the actual time and where to pick you.'

She nodded, smiling at him.

'You're an angel, Mary. Bye,' he said, smiling and waving to her as he made his way out of the house.

'See you again.'

When he got into the street, he jumped up and cried, 'phew! I got her at last.'

CHAPTER FOUR

Mary was restless as usual whenever she was having a serious thought about her future. It was barely a week since Charles has forcefully entered her life. She would never forget how he kissed her, proposing to be her husband in future. Even though the issue of future marriage was still very strange to her but she could not help admitting to herself that she loved the idea. Although she did not tell anyone what was happening between the two of them, let alone admitting it to someone that she loved his proposal about marriage yet she felt the need to share the feeling with someone she could trust. She was almost sure Charles would not tell anyone. The little she observed about him showed he was a very secretive person. In fact, he cautioned her not to let anyone knew about their plan together. He had said, 'let's work things out secretly and give the people the surprises in our success.' Charles was always full of ideas. Sometimes she found it difficult to follow the trend of his thoughts. Even though there was still a lot to know about him and his family, she has practically agreed to be part of his plans and big ideas. He was a positive thinker and that was what she needed to flow with him. He believed he could build skyscrapers if he wanted to. There was no one who lived in Nigeria during the reign of the military before coming to America without changing from negative to positive attitude. America was full of golden opportunities which many of the citizens could not see. The condition in Nigeria had made most people alert mentally but very handicap in all areas of life. So Charles, like herself who lived most of her life in Nigeria, was like a lame person who could now walk. He would love to go places and make best use of his legs and other parts of the body. Many Nigerians were exceptionally intelligent and brilliant, not because they were created with special potentials but because the condition in the country always forced the people to make use of their heads whether positively or negatively. It was a pity many Nigerians were forced to use their heads negatively.

Mary was glad that Charles was using his head positively to make the best out of life. She had no doubt, going by what he planed; he was going to be successful together with her. She, however, needed to find more things about him. She wanted to know everything about him, including his family before she could wholly follow his plans. So she was going to start finding that out each time they went out together. With that thought and decision, she went to sleep and even dreamt that both of them were living together in a very beautiful house as husband and wife.

The following day after school hours, Thomas brought her a sealed small note from Charles. The note only informed her that Charles would be so occupied in the school that he may not see her for about two weeks. He promised to call her on the phone that week.

Mary called her parents in Nigeria when she returned from school. They lived in Ibadan, a city that was eighty kilometers away from Sagamu, their hometown.

It was the second time she would call them since she got to America. The first time was when she got into the country. It was almost unbelievable that she could stay so long without hearing from them. She was so close to her parents, especially her mother that she expressed herself freely with them. They were very loving and disciplined parents. As their only child, she was given the best of all the things they could afford. If not for the fact that they trusted her uncle to take proper care of her, they would probably retain her in Nigeria until she completed her tertiary education. Mary could still recall how they had spent so much time deliberating on whether to let her come to America or not. Her father who was not doting as her mother said, 'look, woman, this child may not have another chance to leave the country as easily as this. With the way things are going on here, Nigeria may start receiving sanctions from other countries. The implication of that is that more terrible things may begin to happen right now. The way fundamental human rights are being violated is making the outside world angry with the government. The people would be the ones to suffer the wrath. Remember if two elephants fight, it is the grass and those on the grass that suffer. We don't know where we are going. So let's give this girl a chance to build her future and career in America. If it is well with her there, it'll be well with us.' When eventually it was agreed that she should come to America, her mother sat her down and counseled her. She told her to always remember who she was and where she was coming from. The counsel did not end there. The day she was due to fly to America, she tearfully preached moral values to her. She had to promise her that she would be very careful. No doubt, she loved her parents very much

42

and she would never do anything to hurt them.

Her mother was the one that picked the telephone after ringing for a few seconds. 'Hello, mum!' She said.

'Who's this?'

'Mary.'

'Mary! My baby!' Her mother cried excitedly. 'How are you?'

'I'm just fine, mum,' she said.

'Why are you just calling?'

'The school takes so much of my time,' she lied. She had to find an excuse to avoid giving her the impression that she was not homesick. Really, she would have missed her parents, especially her mother if not for the excitement she found in America.

'So how's the school?'

'Very great,' she said quickly. I love every bit of it.'

'You must be careful down there. America is so far away, you know.'

'Oh, not again,' Mary thought aloud as it appeared as if her mother was about to deliver a sermon about what to do and what not to do. 'Be careful of the boys,' she could imagine her saying. 'Don't make bad friends. Face your studies. Don't attend to stranger…'

'You just need to be careful down there and all will be well.' That was all her mother said before she changed the topic. 'When you finish your secondary school down there, you'll go to the university and become a doctor or an engineer or … what?'

Her mother was obviously thinking the way many Nigerian mothers did. They were always dreaming of various types of professions that were prestigious in the country for their children instead of thinking of their area of interest. They took pride in telling their friends that they have engineers, doctors and lawyers as children.

'Mum,' Mary said before her mother was completely carried away in her dream. 'I'm yet to figure out what I want to become. There's still time to think about that.' She paused for her reaction. When she was silent, she asked, 'where is daddy?'

'Oow,' she said as if she just remembered to tell her. 'He went for the landlords' association meetings at Mokola.'

'When he comes,' she said, 'tell him I called.' To cheer her up, she sang, 'mum, I just call to say I love you!'

She laughed wholeheartedly. 'I love you too. Always try to call us. I'm sure your uncle would not mind.'

'I'll try as much as I can.'

'Bye, dear.'

'Good bye, mum.' Mary cut the line and called Bola almost

immediately.

"Hello,' she said immediately the phone was picked.

'Hello.' It was a female's voice but it did not sound like Bola's.

'I'll like to speak to Bola.'

'Who's speaking?'

'I'm Mary Toba,' she said. 'I'm calling from New York.' She could imagine how the person would react. To many people in Nigeria, especially those in the category of suffering masses, those who were overseas belonged to a very privileged class. Even then, those who were considered rich still believed they could be richer if they could find their way out of the country. Being in the privileged class, she did not expect Bola's family to think the life in America was a big issue but from the telephone conversation she had had with her, she still desired to be in America. Bola's father was a big time contractor. He made so much money from the contracts he got from the government that he could afford to feed all the families in his state. That was always the condition in Nigeria. While most people could hardly afford two meals a day, many were having so much that even the dogs in their houses would be irritated by the food which an average person in the country needed to survive. Mary and her friends had always criticized Bola's father even though she was a generous girl. She always distinguished herself from her father. Apart from being very generous, Bola was naturally kind and very considerate. She was always going against all the leaders in the country. Unlike most of the children of some political leaders in the school who were proud and conscious of their positions, she was humble and friendly. That was one of the reasons why many students liked her.

'Please, hold on a minute,' the lady who sounded like her elder sister or mother said. A moment later, Bola was on the line.

'How are you, Mary?' Bola said cheerfully.

'I'm fine,' she replied. 'How about you?'

'I'm doing fine too.'

They soon started discussing various things until Mary told her about Charles.

'Don't tell me you're in love, Mary.'

'I think I am but I'm still trying to get to know more about this guy.'

'Guess what,' Bola said. 'We are in the same boat.'

'Who's the guy?'

'He's the son of the minister of commerce and industry,' Bola said reluctantly. 'I met him at the birthday party of General Abdullah's daughter at Federal Palace Hotel.'

'I never know you can go to a place like that, let alone falling in love with the son of a military leader.'

'My father compelled me to go,' she said. 'And I couldn't help falling in love with this guy…' She paused. Mary could imagine what was happening. 'It sounds as if someone is listening to our conversation through the extension phone.'

'I guess as much, 'Mary said.

'I better check it out.' There was silence for while before she returned. 'It was my younger sister. She wanted to use the phone. I told her I'm receiving international call.'

'I see.'

'This guy is called Niyi. He seems so nice and caring. He's so different from all the guys I have known. So I kind of gave in to his demand to be his girlfriend.'

'How are you so sure he's not pretending?'

'We didn't just start off like that. We started as friends.'

'I see,' Mary said. 'Your father knows about him.'

'Are you kidding?' Bola screamed. 'Would you allow your father to know about your relationship with the guy down there?'

'You need to point a gun at my head before I can tell him.'

Bola laughed. They chatted for a few more minutes before she dropped the telephone. She knew her uncle was going to frown at her when he saw the telephone bill.

* * * *

The day was bright as Charles and Mary sat on a park bench, taking some snacks and talking. Mary was trying to get as much information about Charles as she could by going out with him nearly every weekend.

'My father and mother came from Ondo,' Charles said, trying to fulfil Mary's desire to know more about him and his family. 'There were three children including me in the family. My father didn't love my mother after the birth of three of us. Because…' He looked blankly at the meat pie he was holding. 'I'm embarrassed to tell you this.'

'Tell me,' Mary said quietly.

'My mother was cheating on my father.'

'I see,' she said, holding him. 'I won't cheat on you if we get married.'

'Ouch! That hurts.'

'What hurts?'

'What you just said now.'

'I expect that to make you happy,' she replied.

'On the contrary, it cast doubt in me that I may end up losing you.'

'I wish I understand what you mean.'

'By using the word "if", you give me the impression that you're not sure we'll get married.'

'I don't really mean to make you doubt my sincerity in our plans together,' she said. 'But the truth is anything can happen to our relationship or either of us. You and I may decide to change our minds.'

He looked at her with rigid face. 'Please, don't say that again. It hurts the more to think you're not going to be mine after we've gone this far.'

'We've not really gone far.'

'I see,' he said quietly.

There was a brief silence. Then she said, 'Okay, we've gone far.'

He looked at her but he said nothing.

'You've gone deep inside my life, lover boy. Does that make you happy?'

He smiled. 'If you really want to hit me hard I mean very hard, just make me feel I may end up losing you. To think of losing you is to think of losing my mind.'

She smiled at him. 'I'm hoping to end up as your wife though; the fact still remains that things may change for good or bad.'

'For good or bad, promise me you'll be mine and I'll be yours.'

'I can't.'

'Why not?'

'That's what people who are getting married use to say to the priest,' she said with laughter. 'The only thing I can say is what I have said. I'm hoping to be your wife.'

He put down his drink on the bench slowly and looked at her. He looked frustrated but Mary could not possibly change her words. She was not the type that gave her words on what she did not have the power to control. Anybody could change and decisions could change. Nothing was really permanent, including some so-called-marital vows. So why should she put herself in unnecessary bondage of vows when she knew he or she might change?

'So I've been wasting my time on you.'

'I didn't say that.'

'Then what are you saying?' he asked, looking disappointed. 'All the while I've been thinking and planning about our lives together.'

'Remember the song the students normally sing down in Nigeria?'

she said, trying to make him get over his feelings.

'I don't think this is the time you should remind me of any song.'

'I'll sing it to you anyway,' she said, singing:

> **Wherever you go**
> **Wherever you be**
> **Do not say "yes"**
> **When you mean to say "no"**

Charles was so hurt by the song that he had to forcefully resist the temptation to get up and leave. This girl was telling him she didn't mean to say yes to his plan all these months after all she had said to him as indications that she was his already.

'I have another version of the song,' she said, smiling and pretending as if she was completely ignorant of the way he was feeling.

> **Whatever you do**
> **Whatever you say**
> **Always remember**
> **Only God will decide.**

He looked at her, a bit relieved. 'You're pulling my leg, aren't you?'

'No,' she replied quickly. 'I'm not. I'm only trying to let you see that you're too possessive perhaps like your father.'

He frowned at her. 'Why do you say that?'

'You always like to get what you want. You are thinking of yourself alone.'

'Oh, come on, Mary. You know I'm not selfish. I love sharing my things with people.'

'Really? You can share me with another guy?'

'You're not a commodity to be shared with anyone.'

'You're jealous.'

'Yeah. I can say I am but that is justified.'

'If you see me with another guy, you'll gun him down?'

He tried in vain to hide his amusement. After a moment, he burst out laughing. 'You really think I'll kill a guy because of a girl.'

'That may be an exaggeration but I know you'll do something close to that.'

'All right. Yes,' he said. 'What's the point?

'The point is you've proved it in so many ways that you're possessive like your father.'

'I wish you don't have to compare our relationship with that of my

47

parents. They are quite different. In any case, what would you expect a man whose wife is flirting around to do? I really hate what my mother did. What my father did never proved that he is possessive. If there is anything it proves, it is genuine love.'

'You really think it did not prove jealousy?' she asked quickly.

'What difference does it make? The feeling of jealousy is a proof of love.'

'You'll have to prove to me that the feeling of jealousy is a proof of love.'

'How on earth am I supposed to prove that?'

'We may see the proof if you complete the story about your parents.'

He took a deep breath. He wondered what she had in mind. He looked thoughtful for a while as he recalled what went wrong between his parents. It suddenly began to occur to him that the conclusion of the story about his parents would prove him wrong rather than to buttress the notion that jealousy was a proof of true love.

He looked her and shook his head. He was beginning to have more respects for her intelligence. 'I think I'm afraid of you, Mary.'

'Why?' she asked.

'You're a witch.'

She giggled. 'Tell me again.'

'On a more serious note,' she said after a while. 'Tell me about your parents.'

He heaved a sigh before he continued, 'my father could have killed my mother when he caught her with another man. You may be right to think that my father was possessive of my mother. It's as if he had the mind to break up with her but just because he felt the need to defend his pride, he broke up with her. My mother got married to another man before he came to this country to set up another family.'

'You can now see that jealousy is not a proof of love. The proof of love is actually forgiveness. If your father truly loves your mother, he'll forgive her. If your mother was made to see her fault and how much your father was hurt, she could decide to turn over a new leaf.'

'Are you saying my father could have put up with attitude like that? You don't mean that, do you? If at all he tolerated the adultery, his family will disown him.'

'That's frightening. Your family is as possessive as that?'

'Mary, you're not talking like an African. If you are, you'll have known how serious adultery is in African. A man can kill if he sees another man sleeping with his wife and the law will justify him if he

48

relies on defense of provocation. I shouldn't be telling you this.'

'You have a point but I still maintain it that the proof of true love is not jealousy but forgiveness.'

'I know if my mother is repentant, my father might have forgiven her.'

'With what you said about your family, I doubt if she stood any chance to be forgiven and accepted as a wife of your father.'

'That may be true but my father is considerate. He may put us, the children into considerations.'

'Then it was not really your father's fault to break up with her,' she said.

'I don't think it is,' Charles said. 'To tell you the truth, I don't appreciate my mother. She was always thinking of herself and how to enjoy her life without assuming the responsibility of a mother. She never regretted what she did until it was too late. My father who worked with the U.A.C then came in contact with an investor who engineered his coming to America where he met my step mother.'

'Do you have a sister?'

'Yes,' he said. 'I have a sister and a brother,' he replied. 'I'm the eldest. My sister is older than my brother. Both of them are still in Nigeria.'

'Why are they still there?'

'My mother and her family in Ondo did not want them to leave the country. Besides, my father did not want to take up more responsibilities with the ones he already has here. His family here is taking too much of his income. I already have three stepbrothers and a stepsister.'

'How did you come here?'

'It was a tug-of-war, really,' Charles said with a smile. 'First, I had to get in touch with my father which was very hard to do. You know how expensive it is to make international call in Nigeria. I saved every kobo I had to make phone calls. I have to make a lot of promises to my father before he could consider giving me a chance. When he eventually agreed to get me down here, he had to talk with my stepmother about it. My stepmother is one intolerant black American who cannot bear to share my father with anyone, not even his children in Nigeria. He almost changed his mind after he discussed it with his wife. It was my cry on the phone that made him to reconsider it. I will never forget what I told him. I said, "dad, I never blamed you for deserting us. It was my mother's fault. She is to be blamed but if you don't get me down to America after having gone this far with you, I'll never forgive you. I've

49

spent all my earnings to get this far. Now you want to walk out of me."
He told me he would think about it. He had another discussion with my
stepmother about me. She was determined to stop me from coming
but thank God for my persuasive skills. I appealed to my father's
emotion over and over again. When she saw that I have a way of
persuading him, she almost stopped him from talking to me. The last
time I spoke to him before he decided to get me down without her
knowledge really proved that if you really need a thing, you can get it if
you don't give up trying to get it. I said to him, "no matter what you think
about me, my mother and my step mother; I am still your son. But I
want you to think of what it means to me when I need you most and you
turn me down for whatever reason. I can only say I'll be a good boy if
you get me to the country. It is the future that will prove that you have
made the right or wrong decisions. Dad, I need you now more than
ever. You brought me into this world. I did not choose you as my father
and you did not choose me as your son. God did. I did not choose my
mother and family. God did. I did not choose Nigeria as my country but
because you are a Nigerian, I am a Nigerian. If any sane person were
to choose a country, do you think he will choose Nigeria?" Boy, my
father was really touched. He said, "all right, son. You win. I'll get you
down here. But you have to promise me that you will be a messenger
boy to my wife if I do." Of course, I made more promises than that and I
did all I could to fulfil it. I have to play the fool since it was important that
I win the heart of my stepmother. You know, a lot of things depend on
my being here. I planned to bring my younger ones down here as soon
as I graduate in the college. So I cannot afford to let her hate me for
anything. Guess what, I won her heart - completely. She became very
fond of me. Contrary to expectation, it was my father that finds me
burdensome. In fact, he was always looking for reasons to stop paying
for my needs in the school. It was my stepmother that often assists me
financially. Of course, I didn't do anything to her except to do what she
likes. That made her loves me very much. I don't have to border my
father much for what I need. I'll simply tell her what I need and she
made provision for me to get it. I made all her children fall in love with
me. I do a lot of domestic work without being told. You see, I use to tell
people there is always a door to everybody's heart. The problem is
finding the door.' He smilingly pulled her nose and said, 'the door to
your heart was difficult to find but I found it and I entered into your life.'

Mary smiled. She could not bring herself to deny it. She didn't want
to create the impression again that she did not love him. In fact the little
she discovered more about him made her readily surrendered all to

him if at all she had not surrendered to him.

She surprised him when she drew closer to him. He quickly cuddled her before she changed her mind. She laid her head on his shoulder.

'Mary,' he said quietly, fondling with her hands, 'tell me if you'll like to marry me.'

'Charles,' she said in the same tone, 'we are too young.'

'We are not,' he said. 'In about five year's time, it's going to be a different story. It is better we begin to plan what will be executed in five years time from now than to wait till then. In between, we'll have knocked off all obstacles.'

'You believe so much in plans, don't you?'

'A man without plans is like a man without sight or vision. A lot depends on what you plan to be or to do. If you plan to build a castle in the air and work towards it, you will end up building a mansion in the city. I studied the lives of many successful people who ventured into impossible things. I discovered that they are people who knew what they were doing. They were focused and faithful to the cause of their mission in life.'

She looked up at his face. His handsome face showed serious expression. She smiled at him and asked, 'do you really plan to build a castle in the air?'

'Mary, I'm serious.'

'I know,' she said, kissing his cheek. 'I know but don't think I'll support you in building a castle in the air.' Both of them laughed. 'But I'll build a home with you.'

'At last, I got the confirmation I need. You'll be my wife,' he said, feeling greatly in love. He cuddled her more tightly. 'I love you so much, Mary.'

'I love you too.'

The cuddle changed into caressing and kissing, which went on for some time. With that, caressing and fondling with her breasts became a normal thing each time they were together until it resulted into love making right in her room one day. She lost her virginity that day and that marked the beginning of her getting involved in having sex with Charles. Just as she was completing her high school education, she got pregnant. She never knew she was pregnant until the baby was three months old. In between that time, she got an admission to study accountancy at New York University. Her uncle told her to see the doctor when she complained to him that she was not feeling fine. The doctor needed not to carry out any test before he told her she was pregnant. She became so perplex that it took her time to decide doing what she had been preaching against. She told the doctor that she would like to abort the pregnancy without anyone knowing about it. It was going to cost her a lot of money to remove a three-month-old pregnancy secretly. She told the doctor to give her few days to raise the money. She called Charles on the phone and told him to meet her at home.

They met in the evening. She tearfully told him she was pregnant.

Charles looked stunned. 'You're sure this is not a joke.'

'Do I look as if I'm joking?' she screamed at him. 'You expect me to joke with a thing like that?'

'How can you be so sure?'

'I've seen the doctor. I'm three months pregnant.'

He shook his head thoughtfully and muttered, 'oh, my God! If my father gets to know this, I'll be out of college. He may even send me out of the country.'

Mary looked at him. From what he had told her and from the way he looked, she did not need to be told that the pregnancy would ruin his life completely. That was why they have to get rid of the pregnancy. 'I'm going to have the same problem too,' she said. 'So the only way out is abortion.'

'Mary,' he said gently, 'I can't take that risk, not with a girl I want to marry.'

She was touched by his concern. It proved that he really loved her. For him to be ready to stake everything he has in America, including his career and plans to bring his brothers and sister who were counting on him to get out of Nigeria just to protect her was something very touching. If he was ready to do that for her, she was also ready to do anything to protect him, including taking the risk to abort the pregnancy. Still in tears, she ran into his arms and held him tightly. He was so emotionally uplifted that he felt tears wetting his eyes. He forced it back and pulled away, thinking of what to do. He was in a critical situation and something has to be done fast.

She said quietly, 'what's wrong in abortion?'

'Mary, abortion is not an option. So don't give me that as the only option we have. Three months pregnancy is dangerous to abort.'

'That's in Nigeria where you have many quack doctors,' she said. 'The doctor assured me that he'll get rid of the pregnancy without any problem. All it'll cost us is money.'

He looked at her with hope. 'You've discussed it with a doctor already?'

'Yes. He can do it secretly. He said it would cost me a lot.'

'How much would it cost?' he asked reluctantly. Actually, he hated the idea of abortion but he has to consider it because she seemed convinced that was the only way out.

* * * *

Lucy was one of the few neighbours Leke related with when he first moved to the apartment. She was a pleasant woman of about sixty, tall and always good looking despite her age. She was from Norway. She was married to an American about thirty-five years ago before her husband died of lung cancer. Lucy had been living alone since the death of her husband. Her two sons who came to see her once in a while lived in Florida and Arizona respectively.

Lucy who had learnt to mind her business sometimes observed that Mary used to take some friends home. Since none of them seemed rowdy, she did not particularly take keen interest in them until she began to notice slight symptom that Mary was pregnant. So she felt obliged to let Leke, her uncle to know what she noticed in his niece. Since she knew he always came home late, she waited in her room until she heard the sound of his car driving to his premises.

While driving in, Leke observed that the light in Lucy's sitting room was on. This was quite unusual. He thought of going to greet her. Just before he decided against it, Lucy opened the door and beckoned on him to come.

Leke parked the car in front of his house and went to her. He greeted her. He was about to make some old jokes when she said, 'I've been waiting for you to return.'

'What's wrong?' he asked eagerly.

'It's about your niece.'

'What about her?'

She opened the door wider for him to enter. 'Come on in.'

Leke entered the sitting room that was as old-fashioned looking as he always knew it to be. She led him to a seat and asked, 'can I get you some coffee?'

'I've been taking coffee since morning,' he said. 'Please, just tell me what you want to tell me.'

'Well, I know this is none of my business but I feel I have to tell you what is going on when you're not at home.'

'Okay,' he said, looking eager to know what the problem was.

53

After a brief silence, she said, 'I think your niece is pregnant.'

Leke frowned. 'Y-you are sure you're not making some mistakes?'

'I am a mother and a grand mother,' she said with a rueful smile 'So I know the symptom anytime I see one.'

Leke looked somewhat confused. "Could this really be?" he asked himself. Was it possible for the girl he trusted so much to get involved with a boy, let alone getting pregnant? No, he told himself, it couldn't be. He would have to confirm that tomorrow by taking her to the hospital before he could believe it.

'I guess she's probably mixing up with some friends that are not good influence.'

'All right,' Leke said, standing up. 'Thank you very much. I'll see to that.'

When he got to his bed to sleep, he could not keep his mind away from the issue. He thought of what he would do if he found out it was true. He could not tell yet. He was, however, certain that he would feel betrayed. The pregnancy could destroy all the plans he had for her. In fact, her father would be mad at him for giving her so much freedom. After concluding what he would do, he fell asleep.

The following day after breakfast, he told Mary to get ready to follow him to the office to meet someone.

Mary who was expecting Charles to bring the rest of the money for the abortion looked reluctant. She asked, 'who is the person?'

'He's a friend of your father,' he lied. He was trying to hide his suspicion that was growing stronger. 'He has a message from your parents.'

'Uncle, I ... em don't feel well. I need a rest.'

'I thought you went to the hospital the other day,' he said.

'Yes, I ... em... I was told to come back.'

Leke could see that she was not telling the truth. She was not good at telling lies anyway. He pretended to believe her and said, 'all right, I'll take you to hospital.'

'The appointment is not in the morning.'

'Perhaps you're not sure of what's wrong with you. If you're really sick, you will go to the hospital right away with or without appointment.' He could see it on her face that she was frightened even though she tried to conceal it with her innocent expression. To make her feel relieved that he did not suspect anything, he said, 'I'll drop you at the hospital. You can wait to see the doctor. I'll see you in the evening.'

Mary looked relieved. She would have the ample time to get away from the hospital, contact Charles and get rid of the pregnancy at the hospital she has scheduled to get rid of it before he returned. If she knew Leke was planning to stay with her until she was confirmed pregnant or not, she would never feel so relieved.

It was when they got to the hospital that Mary discovered that Leke had already suspected that she was pregnant. Without her knowing it, he asked the doctor what was wrong with her. He confirmed that she was pregnant. Leke called his office from the hospital and informed his secretary that he would be late. Then he took Mary back home. All the while, Mary was stiff with fright. She knew she was in a big trouble that would affect everything about her life as well as Charles'.

'Mary,' Leke said when they entered the sitting room, trying to control his temper, 'the doctor said you are pregnant. Do you have any explanation to that?'

'No, sir,' Mary said quietly.

'No what!' Leke roared angrily. 'You're not pregnant or the pregnancy just got in there?'

Mary began to shiver with fright. She had never seen him looking so infuriated. The expression on his face was similar to that of her father.

Leke was really in the mood to beat her out of her senses. He muttered, 'what were you planning to do?' he asked as if he was more shocked to think of it. 'You planned to get rid of three months pregnancy on your own - with pills or what? How do you expect to get rid of three-month pregnancy without me knowing it or you probably think you'll give birth to the child without anyone knowing it? Whatever you think, you're crazy to think of it.' He glared steadily at her as she looked down on the floor with guilty and fright. 'Now, tell me who is responsible.'

That was the greatest part of the problem. Telling him would get Charles into serious trouble that would affect his careers and his plans for his brothers and sister. She would rather swallow the shit alone than to get him involved. After all he was ready to protect her too. She was silent.

'You're wasting my time, young lady. Who is responsible?'

There was no response. Leke became so furious that she slapped her on the face. She screamed with pain and said in hysterical sobs, 'please, uncle…' She was really frightened. She did not know what next would happen. If her uncle who was too nice to be seen looking so angry could react like this, she knew her father would tear her into pieces if he got hold of her. She hoped fervently that he would not decide that he would tell her father.

55

Her helpless looks and sobs made him relax. He said, 'your refusal to tell me who is responsible for the pregnancy will get you deeper into the mess you created for me and yourself.' He was silent for a while before he continued, 'let me tell you the implication if you don't tell me who is responsible for that pregnancy. You're going out there and cater for yourself instead of me to cater for you while you are in the college. Even then, that will depends on what your father says. I can't keep a pregnant girl under my roof. So you better count the cost. I'll give you time to think about it.' Then he left for his office.

Mary threw herself on the settee and began to cry. She had no idea how long she had cried before Charles came to see her with some money as scheduled. He was agitated when he met her crying. 'What's wrong?' he asked in whisper.

'It's the pregnancy,' she told him.

'Why?' he asked. 'I've got all the money you said I should get.'

'It's too late.'

'What?'

'My uncle has discovered I'm pregnant,' she said in sobs. He took me to the hospital to confirm it.'

'Oh, my God,' Charles said. He quickly composed himself, knowing fully well that his reaction would determine if she would feel more perplexed. 'We'll keep the baby. Is that it?'

'It's going to affect both of us.'

'I know,' he said quickly. 'It doesn't matter. So long we are together. Together we can still gather what is left for us and continue with our lives. After all, we can always come back after a set back.'

'My uncle said he can't keep a pregnant girl under his roof.'

'Ooow, I see,' he said thoughtfully. 'I guess I have to find a place for you.'

'The problem is much more than that, Charles. Can't you understand?'

'Whatever the problem, we have to find a solution,' he said, trying his best not to feel hopeless about the whole thing. 'We must remain focused if we have to get over this. Problem cannot defeat a man. It is lack of hope that defeats a man. There's no argument that we have a problem but the main problem is how we feel about it. Believe me, Mary, we'll find a way out.'

She looked at him with fresh hope. He was really a man of courage. That was always the difference between the attributes of a man and a woman. A woman needed a man that would see a big problem as nothing. While the woman always saw the cloud, the man always saw the beautiful shape of the cloud. While the woman was easily frightened by the storm, the man was always thinking of the life jacket they would need to get out of the boat. Now, she knew she really have to depend on his ability to decide. 'What shall we do now?' she asked. 'My uncle wants to know who is responsible for the pregnancy but I've made up my mind not to tell him.'

'Tell him I am,' he said. 'I'll see him if he would allow me to.'

'Have you considered the consequences?'

'I don't want to think of the consequences right now. What is vital to me is you, Mary. I don't care about other things.'

'I do if you don't. There are far too many important things at stake,' she said softly. She knew he was getting irrational for thinking only of her.

'I'll soon be in the final year now,' he said. 'If my father cannot take care of my education, I'll survive somehow. I need the degree to get a job that will fetch me enough to take care of you.'

'Supposing your father decides to send you back to Nigeria despite how much he has spent on you, what are you going to do? Do you think he cannot do that? Come on, Charles, be sensible. We cannot afford to risk everything we plan by making anyone know you're responsible for the pregnancy.'

'Are you sure the worst that can happen on your side is to be kicked out of the house?'

'Yeah,' she replied. 'Even then I doubt if my uncle can do that to me.'

'You don't foresee him sending you back to Nigeria, do you?'

'With what he had said, I don't foresee that.'

'How do you think he plans to handle the problem?'

'I don't know yet.'

'Would he tell your father?'

'I don't think so.'

'Why do you think he won't?'

'He would be blamed for what happened. He is a little afraid of my father. He fears what he can do or say.'

'Your father is as tough as that?'

'Yeah. He's feared and respected in the entire Toba family.'

'So we can count on our luck that he would handle the problem by himself. If the problem gets out of hand, you would have to tell him I'm responsible for the pregnancy. Perhaps he can help us out.'

'All right.'

While they were having the discussion in the house, Leke was calling Mary's father in Nigeria. He felt he had no option but to inform him of what has happened. He considered Mary's refusal to tell him who was responsible for her pregnancy more grievous than her involvement with sex. She not only disappointed him but also ruined the plan he had for her. If she had told him who was responsible for the pregnancy, he could still sweep the whole mess under the carpet by deferring her admission until she gave birth to the child. Her parents would get to know she has become a mother much later, perhaps after she graduated from the College. By then, the pain would not be as much it was now.

When he told her father on the phone, his reaction was quite unexpected.

'Leke,' Tomi, Mary's father said, 'you really disappointed me. I gave you the only child I have the only product of my marriage, the one you know I can never release to anyone else and the one I have tried to groom in my own way. You gave her enough freedom to make her get involved with boys.'

'Egbon mi, I tried my best... I didn't know she could do that ... I could have vouched that she was not messing around. I'm very sorry...'

'Why didn't you hand over to Christie when you know you're too busy to monitor her?'

Leke knew he had to offer him a good reason he retained her in New York even when she told him to transfer her to the school in Chicago otherwise he would put the whole blame on him. 'For one, she was already in the school which she said she loved. Secondly, I needed her to help me with few things in the house.'

'Who's responsible?'

He took a deep breath, thinking. If he could get through the question he would be free from him but he doubted if he would ever get through it. He said gently, expecting a bombshell, 'she refused to tell me.'

There was silence. Leke had known his brother long enough to guess his feelings. No doubt, the silence was an indication that he was boiling inside. 'See what I mean,' Tomi said angrily. 'She refused to tell you and you did nothing about that. You cannot even beat silly and bastard out of her! If you have beaten her to the extent of rushing her to the hospital for refusing to tell you, that would have been better than telling me this.'

'Egbon mi, this is America. I mean if I do a thing like that here I'll wind up in jail.'

'All right then,' he said very calmly. That was another indication that he boiling the more. 'If America would not allow you to tear her into pieces for bringing open disgrace to us, send her back to me in Nigeria now! I'll do it myself.' The line went dead. He dropped the telephone slowly and thoughtfully. He was really stunned that he could make such a decision although he didn't need to be. He knew that his brother was very tough. In fact, he was feared and respected by every member of the family including their late parents. Anyone that tried to cross his path whenever he was trying to put things right always have himself to blame. Without being told, he knew his brother was very angry at him just as he had predicted. He had not quite told the truth when he said he tried his best. In fact, his wife would point accusing finger at him when she heard Mary was pregnant. She had pressed him so hard to make her live in Chicago with her before she completed her high school but he had refused.

He silently picked the phone again and dialled some numbers. After a brief moment, he said; 'hello, Jon. This is Leke….I'm fine. I need a reservation in your airline for my niece. She's going to Nigeria…I know there's no direct flight to Nigeria… I want it as soon as possible… Okay, I'll wait. Thanks.'

He dropped the phone again and leaned backward on his chair. He tried to keep himself busy with some work on his table while waiting for Jon to call but he was so concerned about Mary that he could not concentrate on something else.

He stood up and went to stay by the window, looking thoughtfully and blankly at some people that were moving busily in the street. He thought of how things have gone wrong. It began with the thought that he should not take away the freedom Mary had been enjoying just because he loved the girl. He had over pampered her. Now the consequence of indulging her in such freedom gave everybody the right to blame him. He did not do what was right at the right time because he thought she was matured and sound enough to do what was right without being told. Really, he had no reason to believe she was involved with a man. She was good at doing domestic work. Her result that made her qualified to study accountancy was excellent. How could he suspect a girl like that to be involved in sex? He felt really bad about it. He had always spent time with her on Sundays especially to find out what she would like to be. The girl had high hope and expectations in life. She even told him that when she became an accountant, she would contribute her management skill into his business. No doubt, she had the drive and the zeal to excel in whatever she planned to do. But now, she had forfeited all that. He knew that the moment she landed in Nigeria, her father would not give her a second chance in America. No matter what, her father was going to be tough and difficult to persuade. To him, anybody that forfeited the rare opportunity of proving his worth in life did deserve the second chance…

The telephone rang, jerking him out of his thoughts. He picked it up at once. It was Jon. 'Hello… You can make the reservation to get her to London…You can help me get her the transit…When is the British Airline taking off from here? …That's less than 36 hours from now… I'll take it…I'll send her particulars to you.'

He got home much earlier than usual after making arrangement for Mary's travelling to Nigeria. She was lying on the settee, thinking of the trend of her life until the time he returned that evening. Already, she knew she had messed up. If she had been told when coming from Nigeria that her life was going to be in this kind of mess, she would never believe it. But now, it was now messed up and, as Charles had made her realized, she would have to gather what was left in the pieces of her shattered life and see what she could still achieve.

She stood up quickly from the settee when her uncle entered. She greeted her by kneeling down. He only waved and took his seat. He was too sad to say a word for a moment. When she saw him feeling so unhappy, she was moved to tears. She had really frustrated him in his efforts to help her dream come true. She summoned all her efforts to control her emotion, saying to herself, 'there's no use crying over split milk.' All she needed to know before she knew which step to take was his stand about the issue. Was he going to kick her out into the street or take her to Chicago or what? She consoled herself by thinking her father did not need to know about the pregnancy before he decided what to do. She concluded that since her father was in Nigeria, he was going to handle the issue the way he deemed necessary. No doubt, he would help her cover the mess. Her father may get to know about it long after the matter had died and buried.

'Mary,' Leke said, 'you not only betrayed me, you also broke my heart. After all I tried to do to help you realize your dream; pregnancy is the result you'll give to me. Do you have any idea how much I've invested on you? What do you make out of the investment? Pregnancy! I never believe you can do a thing like this to me.'

'I'm sorry, sir,' Mary said quietly.

'You better be because your father wants you in Nigeria.'

She looked stunned. She stammered, 'y-y-you t-t-told him, uncle?'

60

'You left me with no choice. You didn't tell me who is responsible for the pregnancy. You know what it means to have a bastard in the family, don't you?'

Mary's hands fidgeted as she asked, 'w-what's he g-going to do with me?'

'That's for him to figure out.'

'You're supposed to make decisions about things that concern me.'

'That's what I thought until you decided not to tell who impregnated you. The decision to go back to Nigeria may not be the best but you have to realise that this is your fault. Your father made that decision and that's final.'

'Y-you could p-persuade him to…'

His voice was very harsh as he said, 'you have the audacity to tell me to persuade him to change his mind after you got me too into the mess. You never expect it to result into this when you were sleeping around with boys. Up till now I found it hard to believe that you're so promiscuous.'

'I'm sorry….' She said in a whisper.

'You've been scheduled to fly to London within 36 hours by the British Airways. You'll be handed over to Nigerian Airways that will take you to Lagos. I don't know what your father plans to do but he wants me to send you to him right away. I'm sorry. That's the life you have chosen.' He stood up and went to his room, feeling very unhappy. He wished his brother would trust him in the way he hoped to handle the issue but he obviously didn't. He did not blame him really. The whole fault was Mary's. If she had at least told him who was responsible for her pregnancy, she still stood a chance to stay in America. He wondered why she did not tell him even when things seemed so critical. She was probably hiding the man that impregnated her because she feared he would deny it or she was sleeping around with so many boys that she was not sure who was responsible. In either case, she compounded the problem by not telling him. He hoped she understood why he had to tell her father and why she had to be sent back to Nigeria without achieving her dreams.

Mary did not know how she got to her bed. Her mind was full as she thought of what she was leaving behind. She had never thought the consequence of what she has done would be this bad. Even though she was certain that her uncle would not have told her father about the pregnancy if she had told him about Charles, she never regretted not telling him. She could not risk telling him and get Charles into serious trouble. She only wished she could reverse everything and rectify all the mistakes she and Charles have made. But the situation could not be reversed. So she had to pay for her mistakes by going back to Nigeria where she did not know what she would face, let alone knowing how to start. It did not really matter. She was ready to pay for her mistakes with her career and dreams. She was sure of one thing. Her love and Charles' for each other would find way for them in the midst of the problem. All she needed to do was to wait for God of love to find the way. What she was more concerned about was how to escape the wrath of her father. Nigeria was going to be a real hell for her if she got there. She could not afford to face her father. It would be a nightmare unless she ran away. Her conscience prevented her from thinking of trying to run away from her uncle. So she did not even think of it. According to him, she has let him down. She has done more than enough things that broke his heart. She would not run away in America because she would never be at peace with her conscience if she did. She would rather run away when she got to Nigeria than to run from him. If not for the fact that she would be hurt too if she hurt him again, the best thing to do in her desperate condition would be to run away before she was kicked out of America. The fact still remained that she would do everything not to face the furious and threatening expressions of her father. She did not need anyone to tell her that her father would nearly kill her when she landed in Nigeria. No! She screamed to herself. Come what may, she would not face her father, the family terror. He would stop at nothing but to make her regret her mistakes for the rest of her life. Only her mother could rescue her from him once he bounced on her. Even then she was not sure if her mother would make any attempt to rescue her from him. She would feel betrayed as well. Well, she thought, concluding, she would run away from the airport in Nigeria. She would call Bola to pick her in the airport and take her to her home. She would later inform her uncle what she had done. No one would see her again unless he talked to her father to forgive her and give her a second chance in America. Satisfied with her plans, she went to sleep and even dreamt that she gave birth to a boy. She never saw the boy as he grew up in the dream until he was about fifteen years old, looking exactly like Charles. She could not tell in the dream if she eventually got married to Charles but she knew it would come to pass come what may.

CHAPTER FIVE

Mary remembered the first time she was leaving Nigeria for America as she sat in the plane that was taking off from London to Nigeria. It was now two days since she left New York. She did not have the chance to say goodbye to Charles because, all the while her uncle was making arrangements for her flight, he was busy in the school. He had told her on the day before her uncle discovered that she was pregnant that he would be very busy in the school. Consequently and coincidentally, the day she left the country was the day she expected him to meet her in the house and find solution to the problem. None of them expected that things would turn out this way. By now Charles would be worried sick. He must be trying to find out what has happened.

She would have enjoyed her brief stay in London if not for the thought of what was ahead of her in Nigeria. She would have taken the opportunity of the delay of the flight to study the life in London through the programs on the television in the hotel but she was so sorrowful and concerned about how to carry out her plans that she could not think of anything else. In fact, she could not enjoy the delicacies that were served through out. She thought of how she was going to teach her father one or two lessons when she got to Nigeria. When she landed, she would call Bola who has agreed to help on the phone in the airport. She would disappear and throw everybody into a panic. She would hold her family for ransom and call her uncle. She would make demand and dictate her terms and conditions to him. She would tell him that no one would see her unless she was given a second chance in America. Since her primary aim for running from her parents was to get a second chance in America, she would get it. By the time her family spent a week looking for her, she would have driven them frenzy enough to give her the chance. After all, it was not a big deal in America for a sixteen-year-old girl to be pregnant. It was mainly in Africa that importance was attached to family values as if the lives of everybody depended on it. Being a pregnant girl or even a mother did not mean she could not achieve anything in life again. She wished her father had the American mentality. If he had, he would not handle the case of pregnancy with hammer and chisel by asking her uncle to send her back to Nigeria. If he thought she would allow his rash decision to distort her dreams, she was going to prove him wrong. She was going to let him understand the need to compromise when so many things were at stake. Compromise did not mean weakness in anyway. On the contrary, it was sometimes necessary when there were other things to put into considerations. Every principle that did not give room for compromise when there was need would do more harm than good. Many parents often failed to understand the positions of their children when they were under pressure. They did understand why or how their children got into a particular situation. They would use the yardstick which their parents used to guide to direct them, forgetting the fact that they were two different worlds with different ways of thinking. When their differences began to surface, open conflicts between children and their parents became the result. The youths began to revolt. Their parents began to wonder what went wrong with their children. Each person was faced with situations that were attributed to the people in his generation, his level of understanding, exposure, situations and even genetic factors. If any parent tried to enslave his children with his principles, he would have his house full of rebellious youths. Many youths sometimes defied their parents because they were misunderstood. For the first time, she was really going to be unruly to her parents.

She took a deep breath and heaved a sigh when it was announced that they were left with thirty minutes to land in Nigeria. She was feeling so sorrowful and upset that it took her great efforts to compose herself. She needed all the motivation she could give herself. So she began to encourage herself by reminding herself of some motivating words of Charles. He always said that problem was not a problem until it blurred one's ability to see solution. To him, problem was simply a test of strength. As the saying went, if she fainted in the time of trouble, her strength was small. She was going to prove it to everybody that her strength was not small by staying cool and collected as she registered her grievances through rebellion.

The plane landed in Nigeria at last. The first thing Mary did after she was through with the immigrations was to change some of the dollar she brought with her into naira. She found a telephone and dialed Bola's number.

'Hello,' she said as soon as the phone was picked. 'Please, can I speak to Bola?'

Few minutes later, she was talking with Bola.

'How are you, Mary?'

'I'm fine,' Mary replied quickly. 'I'm calling from the airport right now.'

'Which airport?'

'Muritala Airport, off course.'

'You mean you're in Nigeria?'

'Yes,' she said impatiently. Her parents may be around to take her home. 'I really can't talk much now. I want you to come and pick me up at the airport. I'm staying with you for at least a week.'

'How about your parents?'

'Don't worry about them right now. Just come and pick me up at the airport right away. I'll explain everything to you when we see.'

'You'll have to give me five minutes. I need to confirm if any car is available. If there's none, you'll have to take a taxi. Can you find your way down here?'

'I'm not sure. That's why I want you to come and pick me.'

'I might have to give you the address if I don't get a car or I come to you at the airport. We'll take a taxi when I get there. In any case, I want you to call me in five minutes time, would you?'

'Okay,' Mary said and dropped the phone. She found a place to wait. Every second that dragged by made her more impatient. Five minutes was barely over when she called Bola again. Her sister informed her that she was already on her way to the airport. She felt a little relieved. She knew could rely on her.

She took her luggage and went to wait at the place where either of them would easily spot the other when coming. Even then, she risked being spotted by her parents in the place if they have come for her at the airport.

She waited for about twenty minutes before Bola parked the car and walked to her. They hugged each other, exchanging pleasantries before they took the luggage. Within some minutes they were driving away from the airport.

* * * *

Leke was talking on the phone with his business associate in London about the shipment of some items from US to South Africa. After they have exchanged the information required on various

65

business transactions, Leke asked, 'by the way has the plane that is scheduled to take my niece and other passengers to Nigeria arrived?'

'I thought I told you she's gone about thirty hours ago.'

'You didn't tell me that,' Leke said. 'You told me the plane was delayed.'

'I'm sorry I didn't tell you,' the man in London said. 'Another plane took them to Nigeria. She should be home by now.'

'All right, I'll call Nigeria to confirm if she's down there.'

About thirty minutes later, he was talking with Mary's father in Nigeria.

'I was told the plane took off from London about thirty hours ago,' he informed his brother. 'So Mary ought to have been in Nigeria by now.'

'You didn't tell me when the plane took off. I would have gone to pick her at the airport.'

'I was just informed that it was another plane that took the passenger to Nigeria.'

'She's not here yet,' Tomi said. 'If the plane had landed in Nigeria, I'm sure she'll find her way home or at the very least, she would have called to inform us.'

Leke was a little worried. The journey between London and Nigeria was not expected to last more than six hour except the plane stopped over in another country. 'I'm sure she'll soon be home,' he told his brother. 'Please, call me as soon as she gets there.'

'All right.'

He dropped the telephone and began to think. He was almost sure that the decision to send Mary back to Nigeria was not the best. What he would have done if her father had given him the chance to handle the situation was to find out who was responsible for the pregnancy, at least to protect the family dignity. Once he found that out, he would arrange with the family of the would-be-father about how to take care of Mary until she gave birth to the baby. Once she gave birth, she would continue building her career. But then his brother has a way of doing things. He did not know how he would feel keeping a pregnant daughter under his roof. He was such a man of dignity that he would do anything to put wrong things right. Well, he thought, only time would tell how he would handle the situation. He only pitied Mary who was obviously going to face a lot of problems. He would not be surprised if her father beat her blue and black.

He heaved a sigh, trying to think of other things but his mind was still on Mary's issue. It was really a disgraceful thing that one of the family members was going to give birth to a bastard. He really could not blame his brother for overreacting to it. He would never tolerate anyone who was not even related to him to have a child out of wedlock let alone thinking of his own daughter giving birth to a child that would not have a father.

He forcefully brushed aside the thoughts about Mary and focused his mind to the files to be treated on his table.

* * * *

Bola looked at Mary for a long time as she told her all that happened before she was told to come back to Nigeria. When she finished telling her everything, there was long thoughtful silence. Bola was wondering how she managed to get herself in such mess and how she hoped to get the second chance by not going to her parents. Mary on the other hand was thinking of the injustice, which her father planned to subject her into.

They were in the guest room in one of the buildings that belonged to Bola's father. There were eight flats in the compound, apart from the duplex, which her parents occupied. Bola and her elder sister occupied one of the flats. All the rooms, including the guest room where Mary lodged were well furnished. The entire compound was very beautiful and inviting.

'Mary,' Bola said, breaking the long silence, 'I respect your guts a lot but I don't expect you to get so involved with a guy to the extent that you would be having casual sex with him.'

'I don't need to be condemned again, please,' Mary said, looking sober. 'I already regretted it.'

'All right,' Bola said quickly. 'I'm sorry. I just feel part of the help I must render is to tell you the truth.' She went to sit beside her before she asked, 'why didn't you tell your uncle who was responsible?'

'Like I told you, it's going to affect a lot of things, including his younger ones that were counting on him to get them down to the States.'

'But it's affecting you a lot.'

'Obviously, it is. But I'm willing to give what it takes not shatter other people's hope.'

'The price is too much, Mary. Think of the psychological effect on your parents, especially your mother. I don't think anyone in your family deserve what you are going to make them go through.'

'They are still going to know but I'll give Charles the time to

67

complete his studies before I tell them.'

'What if Charles give himself up to your uncle? He can do that if he really loves you as you make me understand. Don't you think?'

'He may do that but I'll rather not think of that.'

'If he does that, what would you have achieved by not telling him from the onset?'

Mary looked indifferent though she was silent.

'To be honest with you, I really don't appreciate the way you're handling the matter. You were forced to leave the country that offers you a great deal of opportunities because you're pregnant. Instead of you to tell your uncle who was responsible for the pregnancy, you didn't. When you're forced to come to Nigeria, you're running away from your parents. You'll achieve nothing but to compound the problem. It's like you're moving from one error right into another. You can't solve one problem by creating another.'

'Bola, I know exactly what I'm doing.'

'I hope you do. If you don't, when the repercussion comes, you will cry. I won't be there to cry with you.'

'You see, all I'm trying to let my family; especially my father to realize is that I'm no longer a baby. If I made mistake, treating me like one is definitely not the way to rectify it. My uncle is so full of understanding that he would have covered up the whole thing when he sees the need.'

'Why didn't he cover it up?'

'I told you. It's because I didn't tell him who was responsible for the pregnancy.'

'You don't seem to get the point that you cannot rectify an error with another error.'

'Well, I see your point. My own point is that the approach of my father to correct the error is wrong. My uncle confirmed that. If not for the love and respect I have for my uncle, I won't get missing here. I'd have run away in New York.'

'It makes no difference to me. Getting missing here or in New York is all about getting your family into a state of confusion. Someone will be blamed for that. Guess who. It's the same uncle you love and respect.'

'I plan to call him and let him know what's on my mind.'

'You expect him to help you, don't you?'

'Yeah. If not for my father that instructed him to sent me back here, he would have done all he could to help me in spite of the fact that I disappointed him. He's so nice and gentle. I wish he's my father. If he is, I won't have this problem.' She added almost with annoyance, 'my father is so stern and authoritative that everybody in the family is afraid to challenge him.'

'That's unfair, Mary. Your father is equally good. At least, you're always proud of him. Just because this has happened does not mean he's not nice, you know.'

'I feel bad to think of it,' she replied. 'It's like he wants to live my life for me. I need my freedom.'

'The freedom your uncle gave you is what resulted into this.'

Mary was thoughtful for a moment, thinking she was taking sides with her father. She did not blame her. She had always painted her father to be a perfect man before her friends when they were in school without letting anyone know his character flaws.

As if reading her mind, Bola said, 'I'm not against you, you know. I'm just telling you the plain truth.'

She sighed and said, 'may be you're right. May be not. If you know how much this guy and I love each other, perhaps you'll understand.'

'That does not give you moral justification to get involved in sex and it does not give you any reason to blame your father for being so hard on you. Any good parent can react the way he is reacting.'

Mary looked at another side, hiding her hurt feelings. It looked as if nobody understood her. Bola put her arm round her and whispered, 'Mary, you are always my best friend despite the fact that we were far away. The last thing I would do is to take side with you when I know you're wrong.'

'I still believe there's a purpose why I'm in this condition,' she said.

'Don't tell me you're becoming religious.'

'Somehow,' Mary replied. 'At least, I dreamt that I gave birth to a boy that looked like his father the day I was told I'll be coming back to Nigeria.'

'I see, but I think you dreamt that probably because you were thinking of it.'

'May be and may be not.'

'So,' Bola said, getting more serious, 'what do you plan to do now?'

'Like I told you, I'm staying here for at least a week if you don't have the mind to kick me out as I was kicked out of America.'

Bola chuckled. 'I don't think anyone kicked you out and I don't think anyone will. It is you going against yourself by taking wrong steps.'

'I'll do things in my own way and damn the consequence.'

'That's one of the things I know you for - heady. You're always doing things in your own way.'

She looked at her. 'You think that's funny?'

'Tell me what's funny in what's happening to you now. I have a friend that is dear to me in America. She is kicked out. What's going to make me laugh in that?' She shrugged before she said. 'Anyway, tell me what you expect to be the result of your action.'

'I'll call my uncle and inform him that I'm not going home. What he says would determine the next step I'll take.

* * * *

Leke just finished talking to Mary's father who called to inform him that Mary was yet to show up in Nigeria. He has gone to confirm at the airport if the plane from London has arrived. He was told it arrived about thirty hours ago. Invariably, Mary ought to have been in the country. He had to calm his brother down, telling him that Mary could have missed the plane. He promised to contact his business associate in London to find out where she was.

He was still wondering where Mary was when the telephone rang. When he picked it up, the caller turned out to be Mary.

'Where on earth are you?' Leke yelled at her. 'Everybody's worried sick about you.'

'I'm already in Nigeria, uncle.'

'What do you mean?' Leke said. 'Your father just called to tell me you are not there.'

'I did not go home when I got to Nigeria,' Mary said. 'I don't think he or anyone is going to see me for a long time.'

Leke frowned but he managed to ask, 'why? What's wrong with you?'

'Uncle,' Mary said, 'I never have problem with you. That's why I obeyed you by coming to Nigeria. But if you think I'm going to face my father when he's so mad at me, you're wrong.'

'You can't do that, Mary!'

'I can and I will,' she replied. 'Nobody wants to give me a breathing space.' Suddenly, she burst into emotional sobs. 'I don't need to be treated like this before I regret my mistake. I don't have to be denied another chance because of the gravity of what I have done...'

Leke did not know he loved the girl this much until he began to feel deep emotion overcoming him. 'Mary,' he said quietly. She noted deep regret in his voice. 'You know how much I love you, don't you?'

'I know,' Mary replied. 'That's why I call to let you know I'm okay. I

70

don't want to betray you by running away in America. I would never have come back to Nigeria if you were handling the situation the way my father is handling it.'

'Mary, if you don't go back home, you're going to hurt me much more than your parents because all the blame would be on me.'

'I'll think about it,' she said. 'I'll call you tomorrow.'

'Wait a minute…'

'Uncle, there's nothing wrong in the way you handled me. The problem is that you don't understand why I have to keep the person responsible for the pregnancy a secret. I'm not a bad girl, you know that.'

'Good girls don't run from home.'

'I'm just staying away from condemnation from everybody.'

'You can't handle things like this, Mary.'

'Considering what I expect from my father, I'm left with no choice. You can tell him that you've heard from me but I'm not going home until I get the assurance that nobody is going to hurt me. Secondly, I must be given the second chance in America. Those are the only things I need from you before anyone can see me.'

'I'll tell him not to hurt you,' Leke said. 'But I can't guarantee the second condition.'

'The second condition is much more important to me than the first one.'

'You know I'm willing to give you the second chance but…'

'I know he's the problem, uncle. If you want me to go home, you'll have to do all you can to make him accept the two conditions. At the very least, he has to accept the last condition.'

'You'll have to promise me that you'll go home if I try to persuade him to accept the conditions.'

'I can't until I know what he says. I'll call you tomorrow and find out what he says.'

'As for me,' he said, 'I'll give you the second chance but you know your father is in the position to make the final decision.'

'You can talk to him.'

'I'll do the best I can.'

She said in a shaky voice, 'thank you, uncle. I know I can count on you. I'm really going to miss you. I'll call you tomorrow.'

'I'll be expecting the call. Take care of yourself.'

When he dropped the telephone, he sighed. He was thoughtful for a long time, thinking of how to handle her father. After he had found a way to persuade him, he picked the telephone again and called Mary's father. The phone was picked immediately as if he had been expecting the call.

'Egbon mi,' Leke said, 'Mary just called me now.'

'What about her?' he asked anxiously.

'She's already in Nigeria,' Leke said cautiously. 'She said she won't go home because you're going to hurt her.'

'It's your fault!' Tomi roared angrily.

'I know,' he said quietly, 'but, please, don't make me regret trying to build the career of a girl I consider my own daughter. Besides, putting all the blame on me would not solve the problem.'

Tomi calmed down and said, 'okay, what do we do now?'

'She said she'll call me tomorrow,' Leke said, relieved that things were going the way he figured them out. 'The reason she'll call is to know if we'll fulfil the two conditions she attached to her coming home.'

'What? She is attaching conditions to her coming home. What has America turned this girl into? She is another thing entirely.'

'Egbon mi, this girl is afraid of you.'

'Why would she not? She knew the gravity of the crime she has committed. That's why she is afraid. Now tell me the conditions.'

'She wants assurance that you'll not hurt her when she comes home.'

'If she thinks she would go away with the mess she has got us into, tell her she is daydreaming! When I get hold of her I'm going to skin her alive!'

'Do you want me to tell her that?'

'Must you do that? Just tell her I'll fulfil all the conditions. When she gets here, we'll trash things out - perhaps never mind.'

'Egbon mi, I don't want you to handle things this way.'

'You don't tell me how to handle things! You don't know how to handle the girl in America. That's the reason she's in Nigeria. So don't try to teach me how to handle her in Nigeria.'

'We must not be so hard on her. It'll complicate the matter.'

'The matter is already complicated. She got pregnant while in school and she refused to tell you who is responsible. As if that was not bad enough, she ran from home. Let's see how long she'll run before she gives up.'

'Egbon mi, I'm begging you in the name of God and of the family. Let's not drive her into more mistakes.'

'What other mistakes could be as bad as the ones she has made?'

'Supposing - we just want to suppose that she hurts herself. We can't rule that out. She already regretted what she has done. She told me she is running from condemnation from everybody.'

'If she regretted what she has done, she'll tell you who is responsible for her pregnancy.'

From the tone of his voice, Leke noted that he was getting softened. He said, 'I need an assurance that you won't hurt her when she comes home.'

Tomi was silent for a while. 'Okay.'

'Do I take that as a promise that you'll not do anything to her?'

'Okay, okay, I'll try as much as I can not to touch her. What else does she want?'

'She wants to be given the second chance in America.'

'She won't get that one, no matter what you say. She would go to school here with her baby on her back.'

'If you don't grant her the two requests, you won't see her.'

'Must you tell her I won't grant them?'

'Mary is no longer a child. Besides, she is now more sophisticated than you think. If she is lured back home without doing what she wants, she would run away again. Please, I want you to do this for me. I love this child. I know you love her too.'

'Do you think we are helping her if we don't allow her to feel the gravity of what she has done?'

'She already regretted it.'

There was a long silence before he said in sober reflection. 'Let's do it this way. If she tells us who is responsible for the pregnancy, we'll fulfil the two conditions. If she has done that in the first place, I wouldn't have asked you to send her here. Tell her to come home. We'll see how we can straighten things out.'

'I'll call again as soon as she calls tomorrow.'

* * * *

Charles sat down outside his home, feeling unhappy. It was getting to evening, the time he was planning to go to Mary at home to see her, making eleventh time he would attempt to see her. He could not stand what was happening any longer. He had been calling and going to the place for days, trying to see Mary without success. He could not quite guess what could have happened. Since he had told her to let her uncle know he was responsible for her pregnancy, the worst he expected to happen to her was to be kicked out of the house. He had prepared for the worst by arranging how she would stay with Comfort's friend in Madison Avenue, which was just about five kilometers from where he stayed; pending the time he would find permanent solution to the problem.

After trying to resolve the mystery about her disappearance, he decided that he must go and wait until the time she or her uncle would show up in the house. He would get to the bottom of the problem and trash it out once and for all. If he had to risk giving up what he and Mary were unwilling to sacrifice, he would. He would tell her uncle what was happening. He felt that was better than having no clue of what was happening or waiting for nothing to happen. The thought that Mary's uncle had probably decided to get rid of the pregnancy and then keep her away from him was so strong that he could not think of anything else. He could have sent her to Chicago where her cousins and their mother lived just to keep her away from him. If that was what happened, coupled with the fact that Mary refused to call him or drop a message for him, then the chances were that she no longer cared about his feelings for her. If that was what happened, he would soon become an emotional wreck. The implication of that was that everything about his life would go wrong. He hoped he was wrong in his thoughts. The only way to know what was actually happening to Mary was to see her or her uncle.

He stood up all of a sudden. 'No,' he told himself aloud. 'Mary must not be taken from him.' He would do anything to see her and find out what was happening. He went to the motorbike, which he borrowed from one of his friends that lived in the neighbourhood and rode it to Leke's house. He parked the bike somewhere and waited, hopping to see anyone going into the apartment.

Leke came at the usual time, feeling exhausted. He parked the car in the garage. As he was going into the house, Charles who had been watching him from a distance in the semi darkness; expecting to see Mary; went to him. He greeted him by prostrating. 'Good evening, sir,' he said.

Leke looked at him, a little startled. By his accent and the way he greeted him, he could see that he was a Nigerian. 'Hello,' he said. 'Can I help you?'

'My name is Charles Olumbe.'

'Olumbe....' Leke was thoughtful, trying to recall where he heard the name. 'That name sound familiar sort of. Do I know you?'

'I don't think so.'

'Then who are you?'

'I'm not sure if you'll be pleased to know me.' He fell on his kneels,

74

closing his eyes and clutching his hands together as if he was expecting him to hit him. He said, 'I'm Mary's boyfriend and I'm responsible for her pregnancy.'

There was a long uncomfortable silence between them. Contrary to what Charles expected, Leke was staring at him with awe. He knew it took a lot of courage, especially when he knew the implication for a young man with African background to make that kind of confession. There were many young men who impregnated schoolgirls in Nigeria, denying that they ever had anything to do with them for the fear of facing the serious consequences. Often times, then men ended their academic careers and took up a job to fend for the girls who would automatically become their wives. The early marriage often resulted into rigorous struggle since the-would-be-parents were supposed to be dependant.

'Stand up and let's go inside,' Leke said, breaking the long silence.

'Thank you, sir,' Charles said; standing.

When they settled down in the sitting room, Leke said, 'do you know the implication of what you did?'

Charles looked down with guilt. 'I do, sir.'

Leke shook his head. 'I don't think you do.' He paused. 'Did you tell Mary not to tell me who is responsible for the pregnancy?'

'No, sir,' he replied. 'In fact I told her to tell you if she has to but I guess she didn't tell you because she knew a lot of things would be affected.'

'Such as?'

He smiled ruefully. 'I'll be out of college if my father gets to know.'

'You're in the College?'

'Yes, sir.'

'If her father were to be here,' Leke said, looking hard at him, 'he could break your neck for this.'

'I know I deserve whatever comes out of this. I just want to appeal to you to tamper justice with mercy.' He fell on his face once again and added, 'I beg of you, sir. I know I don't deserve to be treated with mercy.'

'You can sit down.'

He obeyed.

Leke stood up and began to pace round the sitting room, thinking of how to handle the situation. He wished he knew what the young man wanted to achieve by coming to make such confession and he wished he knew what his brother was planning to do about Mary's pregnancy. At least, he was sure of one thing. His brother would never think of aborting the pregnancy.

'Since when have you been involved with Mary?'

'About three weeks after she came to America.'

'You've been messing around with my niece…'

Charles went on his kneels quickly. 'I'm….'

'Are you such a bad boy? You turned Mary into a bad girl too.'

'I'm not a bad boy really, sir. And Mary is… is not a bad girl either. She was a… a virgin when I met her. That's the more reason I love her…' He knew he was being foolish but he certainly did not know what else to say or how to appeal to him. He was uncomfortable in the way he looked at him. He added more foolishly, 'we actually planned to get married as soon as she finishes her school.'

Leke eyed him silently. If not for the way he had appealed to him in the first instance, he would have considered him weird or insane to think he could get his cooperation through that. 'You never put your plans into consideration when the two of you were messing around, did you?'

He was silent, looking down with guilt. There were tears in his eyes when he looked up at him, saying; 'I'm really sorry, sir.'

He asked, 'where are your parents?'

'My father is here in New York,' he replied. 'My mother is in Nigeria.'

'You have a step mother?'

'Yes, sir. She and my father with the children lived together.'

'What about you?'

'I stay mostly in the campus.'

'What do you study in the college?'

'Engineering - civil engineering. I'll soon graduate.'

'So your academic career is that smooth,' he said. 'But you never allow my niece to have a smooth career.'

'I…' He stop shot, knowing fully well that he might get angry if he said it was a mistake. 'I'm sorry, sir. I want her to have a smooth career too. We can make things rights if we are given another chance.'

'Both of you are asking for another chance,' Leke said, irritated. 'Do you know what it cost her father and me to give her the chance you just blew off with your sexual malpractices? Why not go out there and work for the money you would need to get a second chance? That will make you appreciate the cost of giving her another chance.'

More tears rolled down Charles' eyes. 'I've messed up.' He looked hopefully at him. 'I can work on part time. I know I can't get you much but it may do something to assist. If I have to start all over again to help her build hers, I'll do that.'

Leke was really touched. He asked, 'and why would you want to do that?'

'It's because I love her, sir. I want to marry her if you give us the chance.'

It was becoming more difficult for Leke to be hard on the young man. His tears, actions and words proved that he not only regretted what he had done but also showed that he really cared for Mary. He must be a charmer. Obviously they were very much in love. Mary proved her love for him by hiding him from the family and he just proved his with all he was saying. Well, he concluded, the strength of the love for each would see them through. If the second chance was what would give them the push they needed to get on with their lives, why could he not give it to them and be at peace with his conscience?

'You can sit down,' Leke told him. He slowly sat down again on the edge of the chair. 'Your father must know about this if you want me to help you. Do you care if he knows?'

'No, sir,' he replied quickly.

'I want you to count the cost before you reply. He might get you out of College according to what you said.'

'I know the cost, sir,' he said. 'It's going to affect my plans. It'll also affect my younger ones that are counting on me to get them here from Nigeria. My father can even get me out of America.'

'Are you ready to pay that price?'

'So long Mary and I are together.'

Leke wanted to know if he was really serious about it. He stood up to get a biro and a sheet of paper in his brief case. He went to hand them over to him. 'You can write the name and the address of your father on that paper. I would need to find time to see and talk with him.'

Without hesitating, he wrote them and gave it to him.

Leke took and read it. He went to sit down opposite him before he said, 'you're not going to see Mary until she had given birth to the baby.' The expression on his face was asking why. 'Her father told me to send her to Nigeria since she wouldn't tell me who was responsible.'

Charles leaned backward in helpless gesture. "Oh, my God," he thought aloud.

'Perhaps if she had told me who was responsible for the pregnancy, her father would have asked me to handle the situation.' He paused for a while, thinking whether to tell him she ran away or not. He decided not to, knowing fully well that it would upset him the more.

'S-she was trying to protect … oh no… Did her father hurt her?'

Leke was reluctant to answer him.

'Please, tell me. She told me he would not take it lightly with her. Please, tell me, sir. Did her father hurt her? I won't forgive myself if he did.'

'Are you sure you want to hear this?'

He nodded vigorously.

He shrugged. 'Mary did not go to her father in Nigeria.'

'Oh, my God!' Charles muttered. 'Why?'

'She was holding her father and me to a ransom. She wanted us to promise her that she'll not be hurt. She also wants to be given the second chance to build her career in America.'

'Oh, my God! Why did I do this?'

'You don't have to worry.' Leke said. 'I'll sort things out but I can't guarantee you'll see her before she has given birth to the child.'

Looking dejected, Charles stood up to go. 'I'll see you again, sir,' he said in a whisper.

'You're welcome anytime,' Leke said. 'I hope you have not changed your mind about me coming to see you father.'

'Oh, no, sir,' he said quickly. 'When do you want to see him?'

'I want to ensure Mary gets back to her parents first. She promised to call me tomorrow.'

'Please, sir, tell her to call me at home,' Charles said. 'I'll persuade her to go back home.'

'I will.'

Charles later left the place with his head full of different thoughts.

CHAPTER SIX

'Uncle, y-you mean Charles came to make confession to you?' Mary was saying in the telephone boot.

'It was foolish of you to think the truth will not come out,' her uncle replied. 'Now listen. I've talked to your father about the conditions you gave us. He gave a counter condition. He wants to know whose child you're carrying. Since Charles has showed up, his condition is fulfilled. It was hard for him but he promised to comply.'

'How are you going to assure me that he'll comply?'

'You have my word, Mary. Besides, you have no choice but to believe that he would comply except if you want to betray me again.'

'What are you going to do with Charles?'

'I want to ensure that you go home first before I go to see his father and tell him what happened.'

'Yy-you are going to tell his father?'

'Of course, I am,' Leke replied. 'He's a Nigerian and we are Nigerians. So we have to handle the matter in the Nigeria way. The reason your father wants to know him is to find out who his family is and to resolve the issue of the father of the child. All these are in the bid to save the face of the family here and in Nigeria. Apart from that, I've reached a compromise with Charles. He seemed to be a very considerate young man. He wants me tell his father and get you back. He says you planned to get married. Perhaps with the untimely pregnancy of yours, you may end up getting married. So don't ruin the plan to get you back here by not going back to your parents.'

'Alright,' Mary said, 'I'll go back tomorrow morning.'

'I want you to go back now.'

'It's night down here, uncle. It's too late to go home from here.'

'Okay,' he sighed. 'I'll tell your father to expect you tomorrow. Charles wants you to call him.'

'I'll call him later.'

* * * *

79

It was night in the city of Ibadan in Oyo State that Tomi Toba and his wife waited in the sitting room for the telephone to ring anytime. The couple had been feeling restless since they were told that their only daughter, Mary had run away from home.

Tomi Toba who was known as double T in his college days was a reasonably good looking man in his early fifties. He was light in complexion, fairly tall and slender. His wife Ayanfe was a beautiful woman in her mid forties. She was plump although she was slim before she got married. Both of them were nice people. In fact they were attracted to each other by the virtues they found in each other. Tomi was a very studious man who loved to get involved in informed debate though some of his attributes were conflicting. He captivated Ayanfe when he just completed his ordinary national diploma in electrical engineering. He was posted out for an industrial training in the Electrical Corporation of Nigeria. The officer he was attached with was a nice and gentleman who gave him the privilege to visit him at home. Ayanfe who was then in what was now called Junior Secondary School was living with the officer. Ayanfe was a relation to his wife. Tomi often visited the officer and became attracted to Ayanfe. The first day they would really get close was the time she was struggling to solve a problem in Mathematics. By then, nobody was at home except the children who were playing in front of the house. When he entered the sitting room that day, she was alone; looking frustrated. He greeted her briefly and asked, 'you don't look happy. What's wrong?'

'It's this mathematical problem. I can't remember the formula that was used to solve it in the class.' He offered to help her and later got acquainted with her. They soon started meeting secretly even after he left the electrical corporation. Ayanfe even at that age could not help falling in love with his personalities. He was so loving and caring. Above all, he was so intelligent that he knew when to take decisions, when to be firm and when to be soft. His intelligence and other attributes earned him the leadership position in his family even before his parents died of old age. The way he handled the future of his brothers and his sisters had placed them in comfortable positions. He had sacrificed so much for them that they were always willing to do anything for him. When he first worked in an electrical company, most of his income went into paying their school fees and buying things they would need. All his brothers and sisters gave him the respect of their father for his prominent role in the family. Indeed, he saw them as his children. He could give them a command and all would obey. Everybody in his family would rather carry out his orders even if it were

80

wrong than to disobey him. Anyone that disobeyed him was always regarded as a rebel in the family. Anyone that fought with him was actually fighting all the members in the family. Whenever Ayanfe wanted to tease him, she would address him as the commander-in-chief of the family forces. She always share with her friends how one of his brothers kicked his wife with the children out of their house in Lagos where they lived. The woman went to them in Ibadan with the children late in the night. Tomi was so furious that he picked the telephone and said, 'Mayowa, you know you're in trouble! Your wife is here with me.' Mayowa was a very intolerant man, an attribute which Tomi himself possessed. He tried to explain what happened but he never listened. He commanded him to see him in Ibadan first thing in the morning. Of course, he came in the morning the following day. Tomi said without asking why he sent his family out of the house, 'I find you guilty no matter what. Do you know why? It is because there is no way you can justify the way you sent your family out late at night.' Mayowa tried to explain that it was not late when he told them to leave. 'Don't you try to tell me anything! By now, I shouldn't be telling you how to run your home. Even if your wife does anything wrong, you feel the only way you can deal with the situation is to send her out with the children? If our father have sent our mother out of the house with you, me and other children the way you did; you think things would not go wrong? Now take your family and get out. If you cannot solve your problem, keep it to yourself. Don't let it extend to this place.' Mayowa had taken his family without anyone knowing what actually happened. As long as Tomi was alive, everybody in the family knew they still have a stern leader because he had a firm grip over every member.

The couple waited a long time with Ayanfe getting sleepy and bored as the time dragged by slowly. She did not even understand why her husband was making so much fuss out of their daughter's pregnancy. After all it was not big news that a teenager got pregnant. It was happening in every nook and cranny of Nigeria. He was the only one insisting that a thing like that should not happen to him. He was a disciplinarian that frowned at things like that.

When she first heard the news that Mary was pregnant, she had mixed feelings. She was both disappointed and glad that at least they were going to have another child in the family. As the proverb said, no one was expected to get angry because one of his things was doubled. She was only bordered about Mary's welfare since there was no one that could possibly look after her. She had tried as much as she could to pacify her husband who overreacted when he heard the news. He had growled and foamed, threatening to squeeze the life out of Mary when he set his eyes on her. When his brother told him Mary ran from home because she feared he would hurt her, it became very necessary to compromise with what he had in mind. The shame of having a pregnant daughter who was supposed to be in school was enough to make him decided dealing with her in a way she would live to remember for the rest of her life. Until Mary held everyone for a ransom, he had determined that she would live in Nigeria and struggle like other girls of her age. The life in America was doing more harm to her than good. So it was a lot difficult to say if he really would give her a second chance though his brother persuaded him of the need to be considerate.

At last, the telephone ran. Tomi jumped on his feet and went to grab it. 'Hello.' It was Leke. 'Yes, what's the news?'

'She said she is coming home tomorrow. I told her to come right away but she said she's far from home. She didn't tell me where she is but I think she's probably in Lagos.'

'All right,' Tomi said, almost feeling angry afresh but he forced himself t say, 'thank you.'

'The other good news is that the young man that was responsible for her condition came to confess to me. He's a Nigerian. He's still in college - I mean university. Well, I don't know how you'll feel about this but he said he wants to marry her when both of them complete their education.'

'Leke,' Tomi said, 'do you know exactly what you are saying? Mary is still a teenager. How could she be thinking of marriage at that age?'

Ayanfe who was listening reminded him, 'I was a teenager when you proposed to me!'

He looked at her. She was smiling at him. That really performed the wonder. He returned the smile faintly.

'Whose voice is that?' Leke asked.

'That's her mother,' Tomi said. With pressure from both sides, he knew he was going to compromise with his stiff principles.

'So what do I do now?' Leke asked.

'Do what you think is right,' he replied.

Leke paused for sometime, an indication that he was a little surprised to hear that. 'I… I'll do all I can because, even if you feel I am negligent about her, she's still my baby girl. Already, I'm beginning to miss her down here.'

'We'll discuss how she'll return to you when she comes. Meanwhile, do all you can to see the boy's parents and tell them Mary is carrying their grand child.'

'From what the boy told me, his mother is down there in Nigeria.'

'How about his father?'

'He's here in New York. I'll see him as soon as I can and get back to you.'

'All right. Good bye.'

* * * *

It was bright Saturday morning when Leke drove to Charles's home as he agreed with him. He had told him that was the best time to see his father at home. He got to the place and parked in front of the house. He got down from his car and went to press the doorbell. It was Comfort, one of Charles's two step sisters that came to open the door. Charles had already informed her of what was happening. She was the most co-operative and understanding of all that lived in the house. Charles who has gone to stay with one of his friends nearby had told her to come for him when the need came. Although he was not afraid of the way his father would react to the situation but he was quite uncomfortable with the way things might turn out to be. He was counting on Mary's uncle to handle his father. He would likely try his patience and tolerance but if he proved to be matured, he hoped, he might be able to handle him.

'You're welcome, sir,' Comfort said in America accent but adopting Nigerian form of greeting by kneeling down.

Leke was impressed. He wished his children could be that courteous. 'Thank you,' he said as she allowed him inside. 'Can you by chance be the person called Comfort?'

'Yes, sir.'

'I guess as much,' he said. 'I'm sure you know my niece, Mary.'

'Yes, sir.'

He stepped into the sitting room. It was not well furnished as he expected. There was nothing modern or new in the sitting room but the place was neat and tidy. Charles had already told him his family belonged to the second-class citizens in America. So he did not hope they would be financially comfortable or secured. Charles told him his family always find it difficult to pay their bills, including the essential ones.

'I've come to see your father,' Leke said. 'Is he around?'

'I'll call him right away, sir.' She left and came back a moment later

83

with him.

Charles' father was a tall man. He has some features like Charles even though age and stress seemed to be taking their toll on his good looks. He was not quite educated or sophisticated but he was a reasonable man who was dedicated to his job because it brought in the money to feed his family.

'Good morning, sir,' Leke said. He made his tone sounded Nigerian to give him a clue of his background.

Simodu as Charles' father was called before coming to America nodded his welcome. He said, 'good morning. Can I help you, please?'

'I come to have a very serious discussion with you about your son, Charles,' he said courteously.

'You sound like a Nigerian,' Simodu said. 'Are you a Nigerian?'

'Yes,' Leke replied.

Simodu gestured him to sit down while he sat opposite him on an ancient looking sofa, not suspecting anything. He asked, 'what is it about?'

'Well, it is about Charles and my niece called Mary.'

Simodu frowned, looking expectantly at him. 'I'm listening,' he said.

'They were having an affair,' Leke said. 'And it resulted into pregnancy.' He paused for his reaction. He was expressionless but he was almost boiling inside. 'I told Mary's father who happens to be my brother in Nigeria about it. We were trying to find out who was responsible for the pregnancy when Charles came to confess to me that he was the one.'

Simodu was silent for long time, struggling not to burst out in rage.

'I have to send Mary back to Nigeria because she did not want to give out Charles. Whatever the reason for trying to hide him from us is not the issue now. The issue now is Charles is going to be a father. You, his father must be informed of this.'

It took Simodu several minutes before he could find something to say. When he did, it was not what Leke really want to hear. 'I suppose you want my approval to let him go to Nigeria and set up a home with your niece?'

'No.'

'What the hell do you want then?' Simodu's voice was harsh.

Leke pretended to be offended. He said, 'excuse me.'

To his relief, Simodu softened his stiff looks. He seemed to realize that he was talking to the stranger that might turned out to be his in-law in future. Nigerians attached a lot of importance to the way in- laws were treated. 'I'm sorry,' he said, 'but I have to let you know that I am frustrated and very angry. In fact I'm in the mood to break the boy's neck. If he's going to start off his life that way, I'll give him the chance.'

'That's the serious discussion I want to have with you,' Leke said gently.

'Please, I don't want you to tell me what to do.'

'I'm not here to tell you what to do, sir,' Leke said politely. He knew he had to let him see he was not the only one grieved. 'But I have to let you know how my brother is feeling in Nigeria.'

Simodu resisted the temptation to say he did not care about what anyone felt. If anyone was involved in sexual misdeeds, he or she should bear the consequence. After all they were in a free country - free would where no one had to be bugged with what was expected of him as the father of the would-be-father. If they were in Nigeria, he could be forced to succumb to pressure from the family. The case was different in America. No one has the right to come into his house and remind him of what was expected of him to do in a situation like this.

He stood up to go. 'I wish I am in the mood to hear more but I'm not.'

'That's not the best you can do, sir,' Leke said, standing up. When he did not respond, he said in an angry voice, 'supposing it was my boy that impregnated your daughter, Comfort, would you walk out of me like that if I come to resolve things amicably?'

Simodu paused for a while before he looked at him.

He lowered his voice as he said, 'I understand how you feel. It's really frustrating. I feel bad too. The reason I feel bad is because it cost me several thousands of dollars to get Mary down to this country to get trained as an accountant. She was yet to accept the offer of admission before she was sent her back to Nigeria. The pregnancy is setting her back. But here you are with your boy, about to graduate. He doesn't have to carry the pregnancy but when the child is born, he or she would by called by your name. ' He sighed and said gently, 'I'm sorry but you have to know that you're not the only one frustrated. I am. We are the ones at the suffering end. My brother and the girl's mother are frustrated too. It brings setback in everything we planned for her.'

Simodu went to sit down. He robbed his head thoughtfully.

Leke sat down again. 'We've got to help these kids. We must not allow what has happened to affect their careers.'

'It's not easy for me to imagine the boy I could have vouched for proving to be so irresponsible.'

'I understand how you feel.'

'No,' he said firmly. 'I don't think you do. I spent a lot of money that could have made life better for us in this house, hoping that one day he

85

would reciprocate all we have sacrificed for him as we normally do in Nigeria. B-but … oh, my God.'

'He can still do what you expect from him. You can't give up on him now.'

'By the way,' Simodu said as if it just occurred to him, 'where is the son of a bitch?'

Comfort who was out of sight all the while, listening to them came out to inform him that he was with one of his friends nearby.

'Go, get him here now!' Simodu roared.

Comfort hurried to go and call him.

Although Simodu looked as if he was still foaming with frustration as the two men waited in silence, he was actually the good and the ills of his son becoming a father. Leke was also was wrapped in deep thoughts, thinking of how to get more of his co-operation. Simodu thought of various ways to deal with Charles in a way he would never forget but he could not quite guess how. If not for the gentleman that won his respect through the matured way he handled the matter, the boy would be sent back to Nigeria to be with the girl he impregnated or be left to fend for himself.

Comfort came back with Charles about ten minutes later. He half prostrated himself before Leke, saying, 'good morning, sir.'

Simodu could see that he already recognized him as his father-in-law through the gesture of deep respect he accorded to him.

'Good morning, Charles,' Leke said. 'Where have you been?'

'I went to see one of my friends.'

'Now, young man,' Simodu said, 'how come about the pregnancy of the girl that was supposed to be in school?'

Charles looked on the ground with guilt. 'I'm sorry, dad.'

'You're sorry?' Simodu said, getting angry afresh.

'If I may come in, sir,' Leke said, trying to avoid wasting time by going back to what they have discussed. 'I don't think….'

'Are you saying I should give him a pat for what he did?' Simodu asked. He did not seem as if he wanted him to feel the gravity of what he has done. 'How am I supposed to know he had not been sleeping around with other girls?'

'Oh, no, sir,' Charles said quietly.

'Would you shut?' he bellowed at him. 'If not for this gentleman here, you know what would have happened to you for what you did.' Suddenly he added in a roar. 'Get missing before I loose my temper!'

Charles hurried out of the room.

Simodu looked at Leke. 'You really have to forgive me for this. May be we should call it another day before I say things I'll have to apologize for later.'

'I understand,' Leke said, standing up. 'I'll find time to see you again.'

He surprised him when he saw him to the door. He even offered his hand in handshakes and muttered that he was welcome anytime.

* * * *

Mary laid on the long sofa, pretending to be sleeping as her father took the key of his car, ready to go out with her mother.

It was now two days since she returned home and, despite all he had said that really hurt her beyond measure, he was still bent at making her to feel the full gravity of what she has done.

When she agreed with her uncle to come, after giving them her conditions, she had gone to her parents who were waiting for her the following day with her things in the taxicab she had hired from Lagos. Her parents who saw her coming did not even welcome her home, let alone helping her with the luggage she had brought. Her mother simply opened the door for her and nodded at her. She would never forget the looks of her father when she entered the house.

He had calmly asked her to sit down after she dropped her things. He began to shoot rich collection of arrows of insults at her. 'You're a big disgrace to the entire nuclear family of Toba. You are big embarrassment to me. You knew your crime and in the course of dogging the penalty, you committed another crime. You ran from home and had the guts to attach conditions to your coming home. You must have considered yourself a smart girl for holding everybody to a ransom but I tell you: you're not as smart as you think. If you want to play games, fine! I'll play it with you but you must remember that there are rules for every game. You have succeeded making me to promise my brother that I won't touch you and I'll give you the second chance. But I did not promise him that we would take the child from you when you're going back. If at all I'll permit your mother to take the child from you, he or she must be at least six years old.' He had read the confusion on her face and smiled. 'You can now see that you're not as smart as you think. If you're thinking of running away again, the door is not yet closed.' She had looked tearfully at her mother who was standing behind him, trying to find out if she was as harsh as he was. She placed her hand of her bosom, indicating that she wanted her to calm down. Her expression did not indicate anything and she almost concluded that they were crucifying her together. 'And if you're thinking of dumping the child at our feet when he or she is born, I'll be obliged to take him to the motherless home. You know this proverb very well: if a child is wise enough to kill himself, the mother would be wise enough to bury him. We did everything within our abilities to give you proper home training but you just proved it to us that all your knowledge and intelligence lay between your thighs. A man was able to go through them and messed up everything we ever invested in you. I'll see how you're going to make up for all you are going to lose and I'll like to see you repairing the damages you've caused everybody.' She had burst out crying suddenly. 'You better save that crocodile's tears of yours for the real time to cry. The real time to cry is not now. It is when you start nursing the baby, the time you'll begin to have sleepless nights. A few months of stress will make you appreciate why you must not spread your thighs for any man if you are not prepared to be a mother.'

He had left her with her mother who all along had been pretending to be on his side. She never knew she felt any sympathy for her even when she gave her a sigh that she should calm down until they were left alone. She said in a soft voice, 'Mary, I want you to understand that everybody is disappointed. Your father's pride is wounded. You are our only child. He feels he has the duty to train you properly. Remember that it was him that said you should be given an opportunity in America. With the way we have brought you up, he has the confidence that nothing would go wrong with you. It was like he misjudged you. You really wounded him. He has the right to do whatever he says he would do.'

She had looked at her tearfully but hopefully. 'He's not going to do what he says, is he? It's not going to take that long before he let me go back to America, is it?'

'I really don't know but we are going to do something about that. If we have to call your uncle in America to talk to him, we'll do that. Right now I don't want him to feel I'm not on his side. Just take things as they are right now. With time, he'll calm down and we'll be able to find a better way of putting things right.'

'Thank you, mum.'

She later asked her few things about her condition. After that, there was nothing more. She had hoped to find refuge in her counsel but the constant presence of her father prevented her from having any serious discussion with her. So she had to keep to herself most of the time, thinking of how things would end. She wondered if the situation would not be so critical if she had not run from home when she came back to Nigeria. She tried to motivate herself but, this time, she could not find anything to hang on. To make things more hopeless for her, there was no message from either Charles or her uncle in America. If her father had physically tortured her for what she did to the family that would have been better than all she was going through psychologically. She suspected all along that she might not outsmart him. He was too tough for her to handle. Just as her mother had suggested, the only person that could handle him if at all there was anyone that could talk to him was her uncle. Though he was younger than her father, he seemed to have a way of dealing with him and making him do what he wanted. Her only hope therefore was to use him to appeal to him to change his mind about staying in Nigeria until the child was six years old. She could not possibly wait that long before she went to continue her education in the States. If for any reason she was compelled to wait that long, she would go crazy real crazy. She wondered how long she would have to wait before she knew what exactly to expect. She was really running out of patience. 'God,' she constantly cried, 'if you are there, do something!'

Her parents were going out. As usual, they never tell her where they were going and when they would be back. She guessed it through the previous discussion that they were planning to go to a burial ceremony. A few minutes after Tomi had taken the car keys, Ayanfe came out; dressed in the attire she normally wore to special occasions. She looked at Mary and said, 'you better go and sleep in your room.'

'Let's go, woman!' Tomi said curtly as if he was irritated that she conversed with her.

Mary looked at her parents. Her mother was staring at her while her father was checking his wristwatch. Suddenly, she burst into hysterical sobs.

Tomi and Ayanfe exchanged glances. Not finding anything to say, Tomi left the sitting room and went downstairs to the place he parked his car.

Ayanfe looked at Mary, not sure of what to do or say. Actually, it was not her wish to treat her only child that way but her husband felt that was the only way they could make her see the pain and the shame she had brought into the family.

Mary continued to sob as her mother went to sit beside her. She pulled her to herself and hugged her. Mary who had longed for the hug felt so comfortable that she cuddled her tightly.

'Mum,' she sobbed, 'I can't stand this anymore. You have…to do something.'

'I tried to talk to him last night. He's still angry. I told him he's hurting you. He said you broke his heart, wounded his pride and shattered his dream.'

'I… don't need to be treated like this before I realize my mistake.'

'This condition should draw you closer to God.'

'God knows I regret what happened. I'm confused, mum. Don't you think it's better if I'm dead?'

'It's not that bad.'

'It's bad enough for me. Dad's heart has gone cold towards me. Mum, please, don't tell me your heart has gone cold as well. Tell me you still love me despite what has happened. I need someone that cares… Someone that understands what I'm going through.'

Ayanfe soon found herself crying as well. She managed to say, 'I promise you all will be well. Just hang on until your father calms down. You know we love you. That's the more reason he's trying to make you regret it.'

'I feel he's torturing because he's wounded, not because he wants me to learn from my mistake. It's like he's not ready to forgive me.'

'Like I said, your father is very hurt and frustrated,' her mother told her. 'Let him get over that before we can really sit down to iron things out. I'll not stop trying to appeal to him. You know he's hard but, with time, we'll bend him. If we'll have to use your uncle, we will. I will let him know how I feel as we go out now.'

'Thank you, mum,' she said.

'Just get yourself together and expect the best from us.'

She nodded. Her mother stood up and went to join Tomi who was downstairs, waiting in the car.

There was brief silence as Tomi drove the car.

'Darling, don't you think the girl have been through enough.'

'The girl's matter is not an issue to discuss.'

'She's our only child,' she said with emotion.

'As if I don't know!' he bellowed.

'The Yoruba adage says if we discipline a child with the right hand, we hug him with the left hand.'

'So you expect me to hug her for putting herself in the family way?'

'No. What I mean is that you've dealt with her enough. I have to let you know that you're hurting me too with the way you're treating her.'

'That makes many of us. She is hurt, you're hurt, and I'm hurt, Leke

90

is hurt. So many people will be hurt when they hear what she has done. Only one person caused these hurt feelings - Mary. She hurts everybody and you expect her to go away with it. I wish you know what you are saying.'

There was brief silence. She thought of what to say to calm him down. She really loved and respected her husband but there were times he was totally unreasonable in his dealings, especially when he was really frustrated. She said in a low voice, 'you have achieved your aim by making her regret what she did. Now she's beginning to see the way you are treating her as a torture.'

He looked at her briefly before he looked at the windscreen. 'How am I treating her that appears as if I'm torturing her? Did I beat her?'

'What you did was worse than that.'

'And what is it I did that's bad?'

'I'm not saying you did what is bad. Please, don't misunderstand me. You promised uncle Leke that you will give her a second chance.'

'Did I say I won't?' he shot at her.

'You did not tell him that you won't allow her to leave the country until after six years.'

'I don't need to tell him that, do I?'

'Your decision will hurt many people, including me.'

'You can say that to someone who really cares. I don't. I have only one child and I cannot handle her the way I like. Tell me: what do you think people I have influenced their lives to say when they hear that the only child I have is pregnant?'

'But it's not your fault.'

'How many people am I supposed to tell that it's not my fault?'

'Let me too ask you this, honey, must you allow the opinions of other people to influence you in the way you handle a sensitive issue like our daughter's case? This child has realized her fault. The way you're treating her is making her to feel death is a better option. She thinks you don't love her. She is turning into an emotional wreck. I cannot bear to see her like that though I never give her the impression that I feel this way.' Her voice was getting shaky with emotion. 'I'm sure brother Leke too cannot bear to see her like that.'

There was another silence. She studied his expression. She could see that she had succeeded appealing to his emotion. 'You know I never justified her involvement in sex but I want you to cast your mind to the time you met me. You could have taken advantage of my adolescent attitude and the love for you. You could have made love to me but you didn't. Even though I was a virgin then, you would have

91

succeeded impregnating me if you had wanted to. If you have impregnated me then while I was in school, would you have blamed me? If there is anything to blame, it is love. Most men like to express their love through sex. They are not as disciplined as you. So it's wrong to use what you would have done to judge others. These young ones are in love and they made the mistake of playing the game of married people. It's obvious they really love each other. Just because Mary got pregnant does not mean she is a bad girl. The man could have taken advantage of her adolescent attitude. From what uncle Leke said, she and the man plan to get married. We have to give them a chance to work out things as they plan. I'm willing to help her nurse the child if you permit me. All I want is for you to prove it to her that you still love her by giving her the chance. Have I made any sense to you, my love?'

He nodded slowly. There was a brief silence. She was looking at him fresh love and respect. She had made a very valid point. She knew he could see it. That was enough to make him compromise with his stiff principle.

'Would you promise her that you would let me have the child and let her go back to U.S when she gives birth?'

He said, 'I know how to put things right.'

She smiled. 'Thanks. I love you very much.'

He looked at her briefly and smiled. 'You have a way of digging into the past.'

'I cannot help thinking of how we met. I'm glad and proud that I married a man like you.'

When they returned from the burial ceremony, Tomi changed from his outfit and went to sit on the couch in the sitting room. By then, Mary who dreaded him had gone to her room as soon as she heard the sound of his car coming into the premises. He was in a better mood as he called his wife who also just finished changing her cloths. 'Let's talk to her now. You can call her.'

Ayanfe happily went to Mary's room and said, 'your father wants to see you.' She looked a little frightened. She asked quietly, 'why does he want to see me?'

'I've let him know how I feel about the way he treats you. I think he wants to tell you what we are going to do.'

'What do you plan to do, mum?'

'He will tell you.' She smiled. 'I'm sure it's what you want to hear. Come on, let's go. He's waiting.'

She left the room. Mary followed her almost immediately.

Ayanfe went to sit close to Tomi while Mary silently stood in front of them, looking at the rugged floor. The entire sitting was much more pleasant looking than when last she lived in the place. She was not able to notice the beautiful look because she was clouded with the problem she was going through.

'You must have considered me a very mean father, didn't you?'

'No, dad,' she whispered. Her eyes were getting soaked with tears.

'I really mean to be very hard on you if not for your mother and my brother, Leke. Do you why?'

She nodded.

'If you know the reason, tell me.'

'I disappointed you.'

'No. You broke my heart and hurt many people that really love you. You stained the name of the family and on top of that, you ran from home for days. You threw everybody in the state of confusion and you gave us conditions…'

Mary quickly went on her kneels and whispered again, 'I'm sorry, dad.'

'Do you really think I hate you?'

'No, dad.'

'Then why did you tell your mother that I don't love you?'

'Dad,' she said, sobbing. 'I was confused. I'm sorry. Please, forgive me.'

There was a brief silence before he said, 'tell me about the man that impregnated you.'

'He's… em ..a Nigeria.'

'I know that. Tell me what he plans to do with you before you start playing love together.'

'We plan to… em… get married as soon as we finish our studies.'

'You plan to get married and settle down in U.S, I suppose.'

'We have not decided where we want to settle yet but we feel America would be okay.'

He sighed. 'Your mother offered to help you nurse the child when you give birth. Leke told me you've been offered admission into the university there. I will tell him to defer it till next year. That will give you time to sort out things about the child.'

Mary felt so happy that she went to hug him, crying over his shoulder. He patted her gently on the back. She released him and went to hug her mother, saying, 'thank you, mum.'

CHAPTER SEVEN

Charles sat opposite Leke in the sitting room on Sunday afternoon. Leke had invited him to see him shortly after he and Mary's father have finalised their new plans. He wanted to communicate their intentions to Charles since he was anxious to know about the plan to bring Mary back.

'How is your family?' Leke asked after they have briefly discussed about his school.

'They are all fine. Thank you, sir,' Charles replied. 'I really don't know how to express my gratitude to you for the way you handled the issue with my father.'

'It's okay,' Leke replied with a wave. 'I hope he's getting used to the idea of becoming a grand father very soon.'

Charles chuckled. 'I really don't know if he is.'

'Did he discuss about it?'

'Yes. He talked about it the day you came to see him.'

'What did he say?'

'He said if not for you, I would have been out of College and back to my old wretched life in Nigeria.' He chuckled again as he added, 'I know he would have thought of a way he could hit me where it hurts but I guess he could not find any because of all you said to him. I'm sure he just figured it out that I could justify the investments he is making on me. So he probably considers me as the evil he would have to tolerate. Besides, my step mother influenced him to give me the cooperation I need from him.'

'Mary's case is a little different.'

'What happened?' Charles asked eagerly.

'Well, her father gave her a hell of time for a few days until her mother talked with him. Contrary to what we decided before Mary went to them, he insisted that the child must be at least six years old before he allows her to come back although he told me he just wanted her to regret what she did. The truth is my brother could do what he said. He's as tough as that.'

'Mary told me he's a disciplinarian,' Charles said. 'I hope the word is not strong.'

'Well, it's not. More so, that's a fact. He's a very principled man. He could be hard on anyone. But I tell you he is a very simple person to deal with if you understand him. When you get to know him deep inside, he's a very loving person. I wouldn't have gone to the University if not for him. He has invested so much in all his siblings that it's almost impossible for any member of the family to dislike or disrespect him. He has to borrow a lot of money before he could get me down here. I would never forget what he told me at the airport when I was about to board the plane. I said I'd send the money the borrowed as soon I get some money. He said he'd pay it. He growled at me as if he was angry that I was leaving the country, "at least, I don't have to border my head about you any more. If you mess up down there, you're on your own. I'll pretend as if I don't know anything about your travelling. If you succeed, however, I will be proud to be part of your success." As tough as people think he is, he's a gem. He's so smart that the family always relies on his foresight and sense of judgement. I've had to consult him from here for counsel and sometimes instructions.'

Charles wanted to say he observed that Mary exhibited similar level of understanding but he decided against it and said, 'I'll be proud to have a man like that as my father-in-law.'

'When you get to know him closely, you will always like to be around him. The only thing that makes him so tough is forcing people to always do the right thing. He feels no right thinking people have any option but to do the right thing. He's fond of quoting the proverb that says if you possess two evil weapons, you'll harm yourself with one of them. He believes everybody lives in a glasshouse. So no one has any reason to throw stone if he wants to keep his glasshouse. Mandela is his mentor. He quotes a lot of his sayings like "true freedom is when you truly forgive those who wrong you." He has a way of reasoning which is sometimes out of the regular run. You can't argue with him on what he stands for and defeat him.'

Leke told him more about Mary's father before Leke introduced what Charles was eager to hear. 'Now, Charles,' he said on a more serious tone, 'tell me in details what you have in mind to do before and after Mary has given birth to the baby. Right now, my concern is about her admission into the University which I trying my best to differ till next year. Forget the idea about Mary bringing the child here, let alone to nurse him down here.'

Charles was silent. He had all along thought he would persuade him to bring Mary down immediately. He was hoping her uncle would allow her to give birth to the child in New York even while she was still in school. Although he did not know how it would work out but he believed they could find a way out. He could not see the problem of nursing a baby and at the same time going to school because he was dying to see her. Obviously, he was not in the position to make or influence any decision. He had no option but to count on the decision of Mary's family. He wished it would be in his favour.

'Sir,' he said, 'I had thought Mary would come back right away.'

'She has no reason to come for now,' Leke said quickly. 'If she comes back now, who is going to look after her and the child? You? What'd be the basis of going to school when she has a baby to nurse? The only sensible thing to do is for her to give birth to the child before coming. Her mother will help you look after the child.'

'Her mother would look after the child?'

'Who else can better look after him?' He paused for a while before he said, 'what we really have to focus on right now is Mary's future and yours. You can't do anything about the child. You can't even think of bringing him here because both of you are still dependents on your parents. It is when you start working that you can think of bringing the child to this country. You get the point?'

'I get it, sir.' From the look of things, Charles could see that they have made a sound decision.

'Now tell me what you have in mind.'

'I'll look for job as soon as I complete my studies,' Charles said. 'I would like to assist in Mary's education.'

'Don't worry about that,' Leke said. 'What I want to know is your plan about your marriage with her. Is that not what you mean the other day you told me you want to marry her?'

'That's what I mean, sir,' Charles said quickly.

'Tell me how and when you want to do that. I want to know where I can come in.'

'I want to get a job as soon I complete my studies,' Charles said. 'I'll do that so that I can get enough money to start my own business.'

'You'll like to start your own business?' Leke said, looking interested.

Charles nodded.

'I like that. What kind of business?'

'Constructions, real estate, stocks and things like that. That's what Mary and I planned to do when she graduates. While she's in school, I'll work to gather some money, experience and possibly connections.'

Leke looked impressed. He was beginning to realise that he has a focus. Only stupid people who came to U.S from Nigeria would not be focused anyway. The condition in the home country was challenging enough to create the drive for success in any right thinking Nigerian. Mary has the drive to achieve success in America. That was possibly the reason she craved for the second chance. 'What makes you think you can own a business like that, especially in a country that is not yours.'

'I've got what it takes to accomplish much more. All I need is to acquire relevant information and skill. Then I'll simply go out there and get what I need.'

'What about the money?' Leke asked, thrilled by his confidence. 'Where does it come from?'

'It's one of the reasons I'll like to work. Really, I don't see money as an obstacle in setting up my business. If there's any obstacle at all, it has to do with the way I see things. If only I can see in mind what I want, I know I can get it. If I don't see it, I won't get it. I believe the adage that says: once there's a will, there's a way. Besides, I've come to realise in this country that if I can distinguish myself with my skill and experience, I can always get what I want with what I have to offer. If I don't have anything to offer, I would not be different from the destitute in the street even if the country is paved with gold.'

Leke was silent for a while. He smiled and then nodded. 'I like your guts and confidence. It will definitely see you to the top. I can see that you're smarter than I thought. You've really got what it takes to get you what you want. It's not easy to realize dreams in America unless you have the unusual strength and determination. I faced a lot of things down here but now I'm more or less above the status of an average American. Some guys make a few thousands of dollars and then decide that it's time to show to people that they are wealthy. Nearly everything they have is on mortgage. When you see them in posh cars, expensive wristwatches, big chains and stuff like that, you think they are moneybags. They don't really have anything. All they put on is bluff. Let the banks decide who's rich and who is a debtor. I don't want you to be like that. I can see that you're not. You seem to know what you are doing. That's all I need to know before I continue to give you my full cooperation and support.'

'Thank you so much, sir.'

'For now, where do you need me in your plans?'

'I want you to bring Mary back to U.S as soon as you can, please. It really matters to me. It'll help to concentrate on what I'm doing.'

'Like I told you, you won't see Mary until she has delivered the baby. That's the time her father can release her to me again. The only thing you can hope for is her parents' cooperation. I'll tell them all I've discovered about you and your plans together. You can call her anytime. Her parents will see you as their future son in law. You understand?'

Charles nodded quietly.

'Mary will come soon after she has given birth. She'll go straight to the College. When the two of you get married, the child will join you. How about that?'

Charles smiled and said, 'I like that, sir. Thank you.'

* * * *

'You really mean my uncle went to see your father twice?' Mary asked on the phone, talking to Charles. It was the first time they were going to hear each other's voice since she arrived in Nigeria. Both of them were very happy to be reconciled after weeks of anxiety to hear from each other.

'Yes, love. The first time he saw my father was when he went to tell him of your condition. He handled my father so well that it was incredible that my father did not even say much that could hurt me. He did not even threaten me. He only said that if not for your uncle, I would have been sent to Nigeria to come and take care of you. You wont believe this but when he went to see him the second time, he received him as his in-law!'

'Wao! That's incredible!'

'He made my father accept all the plans we have.'

'What are the plans?' Mary asked anxiously.

'The one your family has made about us, of course. Actually, the whole plan is based on what we want. I communicated our intentions to your uncle when we had a discussion about the plans. That's the time he told me your father did not take it lightly with you.'

'Yeah,' Mary said quickly, feeling the need to defend her father for his action. 'He actually punished me psychologically just to make me regret what happened. It was later I realized that I really broke his heart just as the incident broke my uncle's. Anyway, that's over. Right now, my parents were eager that I give birth and get back to school in New York University.'

'Are they aware that we planned to get married.'

'Of course, yes. My uncle told them. That was one of the

strategies he used to get my father's cooperation.'

'He told my father too,' Charles said. 'I think you have the most wonderful uncle in the world. If I can afford to disappoint anybody in the world, I can never afford to disappoint him. He has done so much to help us and rectify our wrongs that I would rather disappoint the whole world than to disappoint him. I'm going to share him with you. Do you mind?' he asked and added with laughter, 'if you mind, you can go to the international high court.'

She laughed. 'I'm glad you've taken him as yours.'

'I'll be calling you from time to time but we are actually going to see each other after you give birth to the baby. I can't wait till then.'

'Me too.'

'Uncle told me to call my mother in Ondo state and tell her to come and see you down there. He has given me your residential address. I'll call and tell her everything as soon as possible. Please, tell your parents to expect my mother anytime.'

'Oh, Charles, I'm so happy.'

'You can tell your parents about her. I can now understand why you wanted to know so much about my family.'

'I never know this is going to happen to us so soon,' she said.

'Yes, I know,' he said. 'At least, it was good that I told you so much about her before now. So don't expect the best care from her. Expect the best from your parents. When you come back to New York, expect the best from me, not even from uncle.'

'Are you sure you can give something better than what he's giving us?'

'No matter what he's given you, he can't give you a baby; can he?'

'That's a terrible joke, Charles!' she screamed, laughing. 'Besides, I don't need any baby from you until we get married. The one you gave me put me into big trouble. When I get back, I'm going to steer clear of you.'

He laughed. 'I know I'm terrible but I'm not stupid. At least, I also know better than playing around with you. The mistake we made is adding a year to the time you're to complete your school. That's terrible enough. I promise you I won't play that game again, not until we are ready for another child.'

'Now you're talking like a gentleman. I'm going to see to it that you don't play that game with anyone.'

'That's my jealous girl!'

'Tell me I have no right to be jealous and I'll bang this phone.'

'You have every right to be jealous but you don't have any reason to. You know I don't have anyone except you and I'll never have anyone.' There was brief silence. 'Does that make you feel better now?'

'Yeah.'

'I love you, Mary.'

'I love you too.'

* * * *

Mary eventually gave birth to a baby boy just as she had expected few months later. He looked so much like his father that she could not help saying to her mother who was with her through out the childbirth, 'he's the carbon copy of his father.' The picture of the baby was sent to Charles and his family in New York. Charles' father named the boy as Tokunbo, which literarily meant that he was brought from overseas.

It was three months after that she gave birth that Mary found her way back to U.S. She resumed straight into the university to study accounting. Charles began working when he graduated as he planned. He started to save money for his private business, buying and selling stocks. Leke not only encouraged him by giving him a lot of financial support but also invested on Mary who was also involved in stock market though she was still in school. The dreams of the intending couple seemed very fantastic but they had the hope and determination that kept them going at an incredibly high pace. They took risks that often resulted into giant steps or minor breakthroughs. Barely a year after Charles started working, he had set up a small construction company that was getting some contracts through giant companies.

Meanwhile, Tokunbo was growing into a very active boy. His grand parents, especially Tomi who initially was embarrassed that Mary came up with unexpected pregnancy became so fond of the child that he doted on him. The boy really gave his grand parents, especially Ayanfe a hell of time. If he was not pulling one thing in the sitting room, he would craw to the kitchen; scattering the place. They have to remove so many things that could injure him in the house because they fear he could pull or push any thing his hand could reach. On the whole, he was pampered and spoilt beyond limit. It was as if the couple has nothing else to care for except him. One day, an incident occurred that made the couple went frenzy. Ayanfe was

100

pressing some cloths on the table while the boy was sleeping on the couch. As she went to see what she was cooking in the kitchen, the boy woke up. Out of curiosity, the little boy went to the table, pulled the pressing iron by the cord. The pressing iron fell from the table and landed on his left leg. He screamed with pain. As he pulled his leg away, the pressing iron rolled to his right ankle. Before Ayanfe could get to the place, he was already injured. He was rushed to the hospital. He was immediately treated but the scars were indelible.

Mary who was then in the second year in the college was informed. She was so eager to know the condition of the boy that she requested for the photographs of the boy, the parts of his body that was injured. The photographs were taken and sent to her after the bandage had been removed. Apart from the scars on left leg and right ankle, the boy was perfectly okay. So Mary and Charles did not feel there was anything to worry about.

About a year later, he was registered and placed in the custody of a nanny who ran a day care service. An incident that completely changed the destiny of the boy occurred at the place. Three men waited in a car, looking for the opportunity to steal seven children, which they would need for rituals. Stealing human beings, especially children to make sacrifices either to make quick and easy money or to appease to demons was a very common occurrence then. The men have stolen five children already, remaining two more to get. So they looked around the streets in Ibadan and came to the place the nanny used as baby care centre. The job of taking care of little children was usually a tedious job, especially where there were few hands available. So people who were engaged in such business or activities are always very careful and vigilant.

There were more children than the ones the nanny could possibly handle. So while she was rocking a baby to sleep, about five children who were playing ball in the compound she used as the children care centre went out of the place without her noticing. Before she could know it, the men in the car had grabbed two boys which included Tokunbo. Within few minutes, they were gone.

As soon as the boys were found missing, the nanny raised an alarm. She took to the street and began to scream for help. Within a short time, the whole street was in chaos. The parents of the children were informed. Ayanfe who ran a shop in the market in another area became frantic when she was told Tokunbo had been stolen. She started acting like a mad woman. She rushed to the children care centre where she found a lot of people, still looking for the children.

When it dawned on everybody that they would never see the children again, Ayanfe ran into a nearby Church, and began to roll in front of the altar, screaming. 'Lord! Don't let them kill my baby! He's all the joy I have got.' She wept, screamed and prayed for long time.

Meanwhile, the men have taken the children away through Lagos-Ibadan expressway, bypassing Sagamu, Tomi's hometown. After driving for a long time, they turned to a bushy area that led to a shrine. By then, the two children who had been drugged were already asleep. It took them about forty more minutes, driving through the bushy road before they could get to the shrine where a witch doctor was waiting to receive them. The children woke up immediately the car stopped. The environment was soon filled with their cries.

The witch doctor, an old looking man in his late sixties went to examine the children. He was decked with red and pure white cloths and fetish items that always made every child that was brought to him frightened. Instead of feeling frightened, Tokunbo curiously touched one of the fetish items. The witch doctor looked puzzled when nothing happened to the boy as he expected. He glanced at the men and said, 'where do you get this child from?'

'We brought him from Ibadan,' one of the men replied.

'He's a strange boy. He was supposed to pass out when he touched the charm but he didn't. That's an indication that he's different from all others. So we can't use him.'

The men exchanged glances. 'Why not?' one of them asked.

'Are you deaf? He's different from others. He's not going to be acceptable by the demons,' he replied. 'If at all he does not pose a problem to the entire rituals, he can spoil the juju medicine.'

'So what do we do?' the second man asked.

'Take him back and bring another child.'

'I'm sure you're not asking us to take the child to where we picked him from. By now, the police would be looking for him. If we are caught with him, we'll be in trouble.'

'You can take him to anywhere you like but I don't want to see him in this place. Go and bring another child,' the witch doctor said with finality. 'Bring the other child to me.' He went into a small hut that was within the reach of the shrine. The other child was taken into the hut. He did not resist the man that took him inside. The inside of the hut was horrible to look at. It was full of the dried animals, herbs and human parts like hearts, eyes, skulls and other things. The wall was marked with fetish items and human and animal skins.

The only child that could be used as ritual was added to the other

102

five that were already in the hut, dumbly and innocently waiting for the time they would be slaughtered.

The men took Tokunbo in the car and drove out of the bush. They drove through the express way again. They drove through Sagamu and bye passed the town. They finally turned to another town called Illisan. When they were getting to where there were lots of people, the car stopped. They put down the boy who had along been quiet, looking round the strange environment. As soon as they put the boy down, the men drove away.

The boy began to wonder about the street. A woman who was coming from a chemist shop nearby saw the boy. She was a short woman with dark complexion in her mid-forties. She looked homely and kind. She was attracted to the boy roaming the front of the shop. He was well dressed and good-looking. He looked very tired, if not very hungry. She looked round the area, expecting to see his mother or guardian but no one took any notice of him. Then she concluded that no one was probably with him. She wondered how a sane person would leave a child to wonder round the town all alone, especially in the environment and generation that were characterized with so much evil.

She went to him with the polythene bag containing all the items she had bought at the chemist shop. She stooped to talk with him. 'How are you, my boy?' she said but the boy was yet to learn how to make any intelligent statement except to say, 'momma….' Still filled with awe and compassion, she looked around again for the mother. No one was taking any interest in them. She looked back at the boy. He was pulling the bag she was holding, an indication that he was probably looking for something to eat.

The woman opened the bag and allowed him to take what he wanted. He took a pack of digestive biscuit inside. The woman helped him tore the wrapper and gave him a piece. The boy grabbed it and began to eat it hungrily. He soon finished eating it. She gave him more and more until he consumed he whole pack. Then the woman knew she really has to look for the parent of the boy.

* * * *

The nanny looked at the pills on the table and the suicide notes she had written, thinking of the consequence of the children that were stolen in her care at the baby care centre. Everybody was blaming her for not being so careful enough even though most people knew the rate at which human beings, including adults were being stolen even right in their homes was unbelievably high. Many parents knew she was dedicated and hardworking. A lot of them so much trusted her with their children that they never entertain fear once they were with her at the baby care centre.

She would not have ventured into the work if not for the serious economic problem in the country. She was forced into the job when she was laid off at the company where she worked as a sales representative. The company was running at a loss. So the management decided to lay off some workers, including her. Her husband soon became one of the victims of the economic crunch that was forcing companies to either fold up or to lay off their workers when he was also retrenched in his place of work, making the family to live in poverty. Since they needed a good source of income before they could survive, she told her husband that she would like to establish the baby care centre through which she could provide and fend for the family including their two children. It took time before they could raise enough money for the business but she managed to establish the baby care centre. It was a fairly good business. At least, her family was able to get enough to feed on. She had run the baby care centre for almost two years, doing all she could to make it grow before the evil men struck her in the place she would not be able to recover. The news about the two children that were stolen in her care had attracted a lot of attention, including the government officials and the police. They were always coming to interrogate her, making her to feel that running a business like that was a serious crime. Some of them, in the bid to make money out of her plight, convinced her that the consequence of not registering the centre with the government; let alone providing adequate infrastructures and security carried jail sentence. With the pressure and talks, most of which could be attributed to either the bribery or corruption that were rampant in the country or jealousy of her rivals in the business. Many of her rivals envied her for doing so well within a short time. They could not understand how she could get so many children within two years while those who had been in the business for as long as five years were still struggling to get half the number of the children in her care. The truth was that the nanny was not just dedicated to the job but also jovial with everybody. She genuinely loved children. Their parents not only knew that but also convinced others of her love for children. As children naturally found it easy to recognize those who loved them, they always flocked round her, calling her their mummy or aunty.

She read the suicide note for the last time as she was about to take the pills that would end her life:

I am sorry I have to take my life, not because I want to arouse pity but because I cannot stand the pressure any more. People are saying things that really hurt me. Even if I do not end it up now, the pressure will gradually choke me to death. If anyone cares, he could help me with my two children. I am sorry I have to do this.

She wished she could write something more meaningful but at least, she thought, she has passed the message to the world of evil, animosity and jealousy.

She took the pills and swallowed them with some water. She leaned on her back, waiting for death to come.

* * * *

Tokunbo had slept over the shoulder of the woman since she started looking for his parents. After all her efforts to find his parents proved fruitless, she decided to do what people advised her to do. Most of them told her she would never find the parents because it was not unusual for mothers, especially those who dropped out of school as a result of unwanted pregnancy, to drop their babies in the street and vanished into thin air. She argued that the boy could not have been dumped in the street like that. He was a two year old child, well dressed, well fed and healthy looking. One woman told her to continue looking for the parent whom she was sure would not be found. If she could not find him or her, it was better for her to take the boy to the motherless children home or take him as hers. Taking him to the police was a waste of time if at all it was not risky. Someone who was not related to the child could claim him from the police if he or she has enough money to give to the officers.

The woman was somewhat sorrowful that she could not find the boy's parents or relation. She found it hard to understand how a sane mother could drop a two-year-old child and drop out of sight just like that. From the boy's appearance, he did not look as if he was from a home that was characterized by poverty that was prevalent in the country. She knew she might not be able to provide for all the things he must have been enjoying at home but at least she could do all she could to look after him instead of taking the risk of giving away the boy to someone she was not sure was related to him. Her heart was really broken and captivated by the child's helpless condition. He probably had been walking aimlessly for hours before she found him. She has no choice but to take the child as hers. The only problem was how to persuade her husband to accept the child as one of their children or nephew.

A few hours after trying unsuccessfully to find his parents, she took the boy to her home in Ikenne, a town that was close to where she found him.

She lived in a two bedroom flat with her husband and their two male children. The family were comfortable in the house which the husband inherited from his father. Even though they were not wealthy, they lived in peace, love and with mutual understanding. It was hard to find wealthy people these days anyway. So the wealth of people was actually the joy and peace in their homes. Even then, those who could be considered wealthy were either fraudulent government workers or those who made money through dubious means or crimes.

The family of Kujor, as they were called, were nice, hard-working and honest people. They were respected in the town for their roles in the development of the town. How Sunsomade, the woman that found Tokunbo in the street met her husband, Sesan, was not like the ways most couples met in the modern days. It was during a funny traditional festival called Jabajaba, the time the males would hold canes and begin to flog each other to impress the females. Most, if not all the males would have worn extra cloths underneath, so as not to feel any pain when flogging each other. Whenever two men were flogging each other, many ladies who were still singles would stand by and watch. In most cases, no one gave up until their canes were completely destroyed. A man who desired to woe a lady could impress her that day. It was an ideal time to prove to her that he was a man. All he needed to do was to go with another man to where the lady lived and flog each other in her presence. The act often times indicated to the lady that one of the men was interested in her. In other to find out who, she would be on the look out for the man that would walk to her and ask, 'how do you find the show?' If she was interested in him, she would say, 'it's wonderful.' If she was not, she would say, 'you're clumsy' or 'I've seen a better show.' If the answer was the latter, the man would understand that she either eyed another man or she was engaged to someone else.

Sesan had a friend popularly known as Igbameji, which literarily meant two calabashes. Igbameji was given that name because he loved drinking two calabashes of palm wine at the same time. Igbameji intended to woo Sunsomade's cousin called Ayobami. She and Sunsomade lived with their parents in the family house then. At that time most extended families in the town lived together in compounds or extended houses that were built with mud. They often contained many people though they were usually not durable like the modern houses.

Sesan went to Sunsomade's family house with Igbameji. It was at that time that Sesan spotted Sunsomade. He decided that he was going to woo a girl too. The two boys had flogged each other endlessly until an old man who was the family head told them to find another place to fight.

'We are not fighting, Baba,' Igbameji had said.

'Then why are you flogging each other as if you have both lost your minds?'

'We have not lost our minds. We are celebrating Jabajaba festival,' Sesan had replied.

The old man who was quite familiar with the motive behind such game continued, 'is this the only place you can celebrate the festival?'

The boys had looked at each other. Igbameji said, 'we love to celebrate the festival everywhere.'

'I know what you kids are up to. There are so many girls living here. Which one of them has gotten so much into your heads that you decided to flogged each other like mad people?'

The boys burst out laughing.

'Better go and injure yourself in your houses, you hooligans. If you wound yourselves there, people would say we place a spell on you in this house. They would not understand that it is one of the girls here that is driving you crazy!'

They knew the old man could frustrate their efforts in getting the girls they were planning to woo. They whispered to each other and reached an agreement. Igbameji said, 'Baba, can we buy you some palm wine?'

The old man looked a little surprised at the offer. He said quickly before the boys changed their minds, 'that's good. That's what you should have done in the first place instead of flogging each other like mad people.'

It was while drinking the palm wine that the elderly man gave them the chance to talk with the girls. The boys later in the year succeeded in getting married to the girls they came to impress.

Tokunbo was still sleeping when Sunsomade got home. She laid him on a sofa and went to do some domestic chores. It was in the evening that her husband returned home. She did not wait for him to ask what Tokunbo was doing in the house before she told him what happened.

'The parents could be looking for him and nobody knows where he comes from,' Sunsomade said. 'I have a feeling that her mother dropped her at Illisan and disappeared. I tried all I could to find his parents but I couldn't.'

'You think keeping him is the safest thing?'

'There's no where we can take the boy.'

'We can take him to the motherless home.'

'No,' she said quickly. 'I don't like the idea at all.'

'Why not?'

'Someone else who is not related to him can go and claim him.'

'What is the difference?' Sesan asked. 'You're not related to him, are you?'

'My conscience would not permit me to give him away like that. Besides, I love the boy... Please let's keep him…'

'You have to do what I say, woman. How can you think of keeping another person's child in this house without expecting trouble or evil talk in the town?'

'I've tried to look for the parents,' Sunsomade said, kneeling down. 'We'll give everybody the impression that he's one of the children of my brother that lives in Ghana. I mean the one that has never been home for ages.'

Sesan sighed and looked thoughtfully at the boy. That moment, something that felt like compassion gripped his heart. He said quietly, 'but…'

'Let's suppose he's one of our boys that got lost like that, what would you do?' Sunsomade pressed, appealing to him. She sensed his feelings.

'Have you counted the cost of…?'

She burst out crying unexpectedly.

'All right, all right,' he said. 'What's his name?'

'I don't know. But we'll call him Nicholas Folusho.'

'Nicholas?'

She nodded.

'How do you come about that name?'

'Folusho, as you know is my maiden name. That's the surname of my brother. I love the other name, Nicholas. It's my former boss' name at King's Way Shopping Centre in those days, remember?'

'All right. Where's my food?'

She quickly went to get it for him, knowing fully well that that meant he had consented to accept him as one of their children.

* * * *

Charles Olumbe waited at the University library for Mary Tomi as the students walked leisurely to various departments. Although it was not unusual for Charles to come and see his fiancé in the school but this time around, an urgent message which he has to deliver to her compelled him to see her that day. Mary did not suspect that he had brought her a very bad news despite the long looks on his face. She, however, began to feel that something was wrong with him when; in the course of exchanging pleasantries; he was not as cheerful as he used to be and he was not so enthusiastic about the contracts he won when she asked him about his job.

'You don't sound particularly happy, Charles,' she asked, looking at him with concern. 'What's the matter?'

'Can you afford the time to follow me home?' he asked her after a brief pause. He came with a small car. His house was about fifteen kilometres away from the school. With what he was making already, he could afford a bigger car and a bigger house but he chose to be modest in everything he did so that he could have enough to invest in all the businesses he and Mary planned to establish together.

Mary saw the unusual invitation to his house as an indication that he has something very important to discuss. Both of them have decided to stay away from what could lead them into the mistake they have made in the past. The invitation to his house invariably made her more eager to know what has happened.

'Yeah,' she said slowly, looking reluctant.

'I'll tell you what happened when we get there.'

'You know I hate suspense. Can you at least give me a hint?'

'It's nothing so serious, depending on how you take it.'

Mary did not believe him that it was not serious. Nothing was ever so serious to him even if it was death of a loved one. Because she has no way of making him to give her the clue, she decided to wait until they got to his house.

Within thirty minutes, they were together in the house. It was so

109

well furnished that Mary always thought that there was nothing much to buy in the house when she became his full wife. He gave her some fruit drinks before he sat beside her on the couch. He looked at her remorsefully thinking of how to break the bad news to her.

It so happened that when Leke received the message that Tokunbo had been stolen from the nanny in Lagos, he had felt very unhappy. He did not know how to break the news to either Charles or Mary. He felt that Charles should be able to absorb the shock more than Mary. If he was able to break the news to Charles, he would leave the burden of breaking the news to Mary for him to bear. So he called him on the phone, asking him to meet him in his house. He diplomatically broke the bad news to him. Although Charles considered it a tragic loss, especially when he considered what he and Mary planned for the child when they got married but the main problem was not only how to bear the loss but also how to make Mary bear the pain of losing the child she bore with so much sorrow. He really felt bad about it but he knew there was nothing anyone could do about it. When he eventually got over it, he felt obliged to console Mary's parents whom he knew would be doing all they could to find the child in Nigeria. He called them that day and informed them that they should border less about him. He especially talked to Mary's mother who was still hysterical. Though he needed to be comforted, he managed to say; 'Mummy, don't hurt yourself because of one grand child. You still have many grand and great-grand children to look after.' So far the best comfort Mary's parents have ever received was that of Charles. Now he would need much more than that skill to handle Mary. He knew how much she loved and thought about the child. She had told him that the child would be brought to New York as soon as she graduated from the school.

He forced himself to smile at Mary as she looked at him expectantly with her intelligent and beautiful eyes. His hands went round her neck and rested on her shoulder. He whispered into her ears as he said gently, 'Mary; I love you very much.'

'Is that what you've brought me here to hear?'

'It's one of them.'

'Tell me what happened? I know something you're reluctant to tell me has happened. I want to know what it is and I want to know it now.'

'You can at least tell me you love me.'

'Okay, I love you.'

'Very much?'

'Charles, I'm running out of patience.'

There was a long thoughtful silence. He wished her uncle had not given him this type of assignment.

'Charles, whatever it is, you can tell me. Going by the looks on your face and the way you normally react to critical situations, I know what happened is bad enough. No matter how bad, you still have to tell me.'

'Promise me you'll not overreact.'

'I'll not. Even if I do, you are around to handle me.'

'Mary,' he said quietly. He could not keep it any longer. 'If not for your school, I would have taken you to the Church for marriage. That would have probably been the best solution to the problem.'

'You haven't told me what the problem is.'

'We've lost Tokunbo,' he said gently.

Mary looked at him as if she did not hear him. After a brief silence, she asked, 'you said what?'

'You promised me you'd not overreact.'

'You said we lost Tokunbo - our child?'

'Mary, you'll give birth to other children.'

'What happened to Tokunbo?'

This was one of the parts he was trying to avoid telling her. 'He got lost when he was with the nanny in Nigeria,'

'My child got missing? Do you know what you're saying?'

'Yes. Actually, they are still looking for him.'

She jumped on her feet. 'Oh, no! It can't be! It's not Tokunbo that's missing. Come on, tell me it's another child!'

'It's him. I've talked with your parents.'

Mary threw herself on the floor and began to cry hysterically. Charles stood up and went to pull her up, holding her tightly as she cried over his shoulder.

* * * *

It was now getting to a week since Tokunbo was found missing. Tomi and Ayanfe were still grieving over the lost of the boy despite all Charles had said to console them. Though Mary was still grieving over the child, she had called to inform them that she was getting over what people called tragedy in the family.

Later in the day, a teenage boy who was one of children of the nanny came to inform Tomi that his mother had made attempt to

111

commit suicide two days before.

He looked a little concerned in spite of his grief. 'Why did she want to kill herself?' he asked the boy who looked rather hopeless. 'We never blame her, did we?'

'No,' he lamented, 'but people are saying all sorts of evil thing against my family. One of my friends in the school told me that he heard that my mother took two of the children in her care to make rituals. Some women said she was the architect of the loss of the two children. The government is after her because the baby care centre was not registered.' He began to cry as he added, 'please, sir, we need you to say something to encourage my mother. She is about to loose her life unless…. I'm sorry I've come to you for help. I know how you're feeling about your grand child that is missing but there's no one else I can go to except you….' The boy began to cry.

'Where is she now,' he asked her.

'She's in the hospital.'

Tomi stood up immediately she said, 'let's go.'

He went to the hospital with the boy. The nanny was still lying on the bed. Her husband was with her. He has done so much to revive her after the suicide attempt. He spent a lot of money, most of which he borrowed from his friends and neighbours before he could get the service of a specialist hospital that saved her life. Tomi could see that the family was really going through traumatic period, which was similar to those whose children were missing.

The nanny's husband looked guilty when he saw Tomi. He was silent, looking on the floor. The nanny's eyes were soon filled with tears. She looked uncertain. She was not sure of what Tomi would say her. She did not really expect him to come. In fact, it was her son that took the initiative to call him for help. No one actually sent him.

With what the family must be going through, Tomi felt obliged to get the woman out of the trouble. He did not need to be told the psychological torture she must have been subjected to.

He went to pat her husband on the shoulder silently. He was so moved by the touch of love and understanding that he had to force back his tears. He quickly gave Tomi a chair beside the nanny who was sobbing silently when he walked closer to her.

'There are times we face a tough time,' Tomi began softly, 'but that should not force us to take our own lives. The reason is that many people would affected. A family man or woman, for instance, would need to put his or her family into considerations before he or she takes any action. For one, if it's a wrong step, someone would have to pay

112

for it. Secondly, I don't think God will spare anyone that takes his or her life. In the first place, you have no power to make any part of your body.' He was silent, thinking of what to say. He was not in a sound shape himself. Notwithstanding, he still has to let the family know that it was not the end of the world if anything evil happened to anyone. 'Although,' he continued after a brief pause, 'I'm very unhappy that our grand child is missing but did I or my wife blame you?'

'No,' the nanny replied tearfully. 'I... I thought you come ... to torture me.'

It was when she said that that he realized that she had not sent his son to him. He looked at the boy who looked away quickly. He looked back at her. 'You know better than to think that I will join others to persecute you. Let me tell you this. If I have another child, I'm still willing to entrust him into your care.'

Everybody was truly surprised to hear that.

'Well, I've not come to persecute you but to tell you that the attempt to kill yourself was a very foolish thing to do. Who would take care of your family if you end it up now? Come to think of it, is it not because of your family that you found yourself in the job that brought you into this mess? Anyway, I come to let you realize that you're fighting a battle just like everybody in the world. It will never end until you are dead. You must not let it overcome you. You don't win in the battle by running. You have to build the courage before you can overcome. If you build the courage, you will understand that battles are meant to be overcome. It is not meant to destroy you but to make you stronger.'

'The police and the government are treating me like a criminal,' she cried. 'Things look so hopeless. What you just said is the only hope I have ever get so far. People make me feel....'

'I'll get the police and the government officials off your back. You don't have to worry about what people say. Everybody is entitled to his own opinion. But don't let what they say or think affect you. People would definitely throw mud at you whether you like it or not but you don't have to let that push you into the grave. No doubt, you're in the heap of refuse. People are bound to bury you with all sorts of rubbish. It is you that will prove it to them that you're still alive by getting out of the mess. The measuring stick people use to access others is bad enough. If the secrets of those pointing accusing fingers at you are revealed, you'll be shocked. So they are not in the position to judge you with their opinions. It's true that you made a mistake by not getting enough hands to help you with the work but don't let anyone make you feel like a criminal because of that. You are not a criminal. You are a very responsible woman. I'll stand for you anywhere. Do you understand?'

Still filled with tears, she said quietly, 'yes, sir. Thank you so much. There's no way I could have survived this without all you said.'

He stood up and said, 'the credit goes to your son who came to inform me of what's happening.' He looked at her husband and smiled at him. 'If the battle is too much for your family, I'll advise you to take her to another place.' He turned to look at the nanny. 'I'll do all I can to get them off your back. Just brace yourself up. You're in the days of adversity. You must be strong before you can survive.' He looked thoughtful for a while. He was considering paying the hospital bill. 'Let me know when you are about to be discharged here. I'll see what I can do about the hospital bill.'

After leaving the hospital, he called various government officials he knew; requesting them to drop the case against the nanny. He later paid for the medical expenses that were incurred by the nanny in the hospital.

It was few months after the incident that the nanny's family relocated to her husband's home town where they began a new life there.

CHAPTER EIGHTEEN

The loss of their child made Charles and Mary to get married in New York immediately she graduated from the University. At first she worked with her uncle who encouraged her to take over the stock business which Charles had set up along with his Construction Company. Within the five years of their marriage, so many things have taken place. Three beautiful girls arrived and the financial status of the family was highly elevated. Charles who was very hardworking had turned the Construction Company into a substantially big one with annual turn over of about two million dollars. Mary's involvement in the stock market added immensely to the fortune of the family. They remained in New York, living in a very big house which Charles considered more of a liability than an asset despite their accumulated fortunes. Having made so much money, Charles was able to fulfil the promise he made to his younger ones in Nigeria. They have graduated from the college and now working in the country. The couple had been able to support their parents in Nigeria. Tomi and Ayanfe did not need to work for money again while Charles' mother who sometimes paid her in-laws visits now have more than enough to spend in Nigeria.

Meanwhile, Tokunbo who was now called Nicholas was so pampered that he grew into a spoilt and stubborn child. He was almost a terror among all his mates right from the time he started his elementary school education. Because of what he had been made to believe about his parents in Ghana and the way he was treated along side with Gbenga and Seyi, his supposed cousins, he had no reason to ask about his family. His fostered parents, especially Sesan who had grown exceedingly fond of him, seemed to know how to answer the vital questions about his identity even before he asked them. They would sometimes threaten him, each time he did something wrong, 'we'll send you back to Ghana where your parents live as if they have no relation.' One day, however, he has reason to tell them that he would like to go to his parents when he was beaten for causing problem in the town.

Nicholas shared the same room with Seyi who was a twenty-two year old tailor. Gbenga who was the elder child lived in a separate room. He was a twenty-four year old man. He was a local soap maker. Both men could not go further than secondary school education because, like many of the young people in the town then, they were not interested in tertiary education. Besides, tertiary education was quite expensive.

Seyi was always complaining to his parents about Nicholas who had grown into a very stubborn boy. They were so intolerant of each other that were always at each other's neck. Though Nicholas was at least six years younger than Seyi, he always treated him as if he was the big brother. Though Seyi was naturally cool headed but he soon found himself losing his gentle temperament because Nicholas never gave him a moment of peace in the house. Nicholas was the kind of boy that could drive any sane person out of his mind. He was a terror in the school, at home and in the town.

One day, Seyi burst into the sitting room and complained bitterly to his mother, 'Mummy, I can't stand this any more! I need my own room!'

'What's wrong?' Sunsomade who was ironing some cloths in the room asked.

'He performed an experiment with my bed sheet!' Seyi said, looking frustrated. 'I could kill that rogue for all he's been doing to me in this house.'

'What sort of experiment did he perform with your bed sheet?'

'He told me yesterday that his science teacher said the acid in a car battery could cause a lot of damages in so many items. He said he would like to know how it damages items. So today he poured some acid on my bed sheet and turned it into pieces of rags!'

'Call him here,' Sunsomade said, looking angry.

Seyi left and later brought Nicholas who was just a teenager yet looking like an intimidating bully.

'Seyi said you poured acid on his bed sheet,' Sunsomade said. 'Is that true?'

'That's not true!' Nicholas said in a loud voice.

'How come the bed sheet turned into rags overnight?' Seyi screamed at him.

'It's old and filthy,' Nicholas said in a hard voice. 'You never care for the bed sheet. There are bed bugs all over the bed and the cloths.'

'Liar!' Seyi screamed and grabbed his neck angrily. Nicholas pushed him roughly away.

'Stop that both of you!' Sunsomade screamed at them.

116

Seyi glared at him. Hissing, he began to walk away. 'You'll see what I'll do to you, you hooligan.'

'You heard him, Mummy. You heard him calling me hooligan.'

'You're a hooligan,' Seyi said; turning to give him a malicious smile. 'You don't belong to where normal people live. Boys like you live in the garage.'

That really hit Nicholas. 'You're an idiot.'

'Would you shut up, Nicholas?' Sunsomade bellowed at him. 'He's your senior, you know that.'

'You're taking side with him, Mummy.'

'You want me to take your side after what you did to him. Tell me, did you pour acid on his bed sheet?'

'No.'

'Tell me the truth!'

He was hesitant for a while as he said, 'em …. I didn't know he still needs the bed sheet. It has already become a rag when I poured little content on it.'

'Why were you denying it in the first place? Why didn't you pour the acid on your own bed sheet.'

'Mine is still good.'

Sunsonmade studied his face. He was a real tough boy. She wondered if his real parents were so tough. Until that moment, she never thought of his parents. No doubt, if they have been looking for him, they would have given up hope of ever finding him. Because of the way they treated him in the family, he did not even border about his parents whom he believed were still in Ghana. Whether they were dead or alive, he simply did not care. To be treated like a baby in the house was fair enough. In fact her husband was of the view that what attributed to his misbehaviour was the way he was handled. He was really spoilt rotten because they were still conscious of the fact that he was a lost child.

There was silence. 'And where did you get the acid?'

He was silent.

'Are you deaf? I said where did you get the acid?'

'I got it from one of my friends.'

'Where did your friend get it from?'

'He got it from his father's car.'

'Have you been going out with bad boys?'

'They are not bad boys. At least, they are not as bad as the one I'm living with.'

'Are you saying your cousin is bad?'

'I did not say that.'

'You don't have to.' There was a brief silence. 'Nicholas, why are you behaving like this? None of your parents behave like this.'

After a while she changed the subject and she asked him when he was going to sit for the General Certificate Examination. It was in a few months time.

'So what are you going to do after the exam? You know we can not afford to send you to the university.'

'I'll like to go to the university. I'll like to be an engineer.'

'You don't have to go to the university before you become an engineer,' Sunsomade said. 'You can learn the work in a company. By the way, what kind of engineer do you want to become.'

'Electrical or civil engineer,' Nicholas said.

'Why do you want to be an engineer?'

'I just like it.'

'I know of someone you can learn the work from.'

'No! I want to go to the university and learned the work.'

'Okay, you make sure you pass your final examination very well in the school.'

Nicholas could not pass the examination well enough. So his fostered parents used that as an excuse to hand him over as apprentice electrical engineer to Ben Janosi who owned an electrical engineering company in the town.

Ben began his career as an electrical engineer in Kaduna, one of the cities in the northern part of Nigeria. Like many electrical engineers in his class, he learnt the job through someone. Shortly after his apprenticeship, he worked as a join man with a reputable engineering company in the place. He was so good at the job that each time he attempted to quit the job and establish his own company, his wages were doubled. At last, after meeting Lade who bore him a boy and a girl, he resolved to quit. It was as if many people who knew he was good at his job were waiting for him to have his own company. He became a licensed electrical contractor in a few government establishments and numerous private companies. Within a relatively short time, he had become very prosperous. This aroused the envy of many of his peers who equally desired the same success. Lade who was a very intolerant woman picked quarrels with nearly everyone she suspected to be the enemy of her family. Things would have continued to be rosy for Ben if not for the religious riots that were common in the north at that time. Religion was a do-or-die affair in the area. In fact, the military government used it at times to divide and rule the people. Each time there was riot in the area, so many people; especially the successful southerners always became victims. Those who were envious of the successful people usually made it a suitable platform to express their burning desire to see them going down the drain. So the so-called-rioters usually destroyed and vandalized many properties, creating room for thieves to cart away goods. It was one of these riots, which almost cost him his children's lives that pointed him the way back home. He was away that day when all of a sudden some people took to the street and started burning houses. His house was almost burnt while his children, who were too young to know that they were supposed to flee the house, locked themselves inside. If not for the police that came to their rescue, his house and the children would have been burnt into ashes. He sold out the house which was the only landed property he has and one of his major equipments which would cost him a lot of money if he were to transport it to Ikenne, his home town. He brought three plots of land, built a bungalow and started the business there. Even though Ikenne is far from north, he still went there to serve most of his valuable customers. The money he made in the north and in other places pleased him much more than living in the midst of danger with his family.

Nicholas really made an impression on Ben when he first met him. Sesan at first introduced him as his wife's nephew.

Nicholas who was expected to be polite to an older person looked at Ben as if he was trying to access him if really he could train him to be an engineer.

'How are you, young man?' Ben said.

'Fine, thank you,' Nicholas said. 'How about you?'

Sesan shot a glance at him. 'Nicholas, how long do I have to teach you how to greet older people, especially the one that is old enough to be your father?'

'He asked me, "how are you?" Nicholas said. 'I thought the way I replied him is the normal way I should reply.'

Sesan stood up, looking annoyed. He pulled one of his ears. 'You're a disgrace!'

Ben smiled and said, 'it's okay, Sesan. He's just a boy.'

Sesan sat down again.

'How old are you?' Ben asked, looking at him calmly.

'Seventeen.'

'Anytime you want to talk to him, you say "sir"!' Sesan yelled at him.

'The boy looks tough,' Ben said, looking at Nicholas. Then he looked at Sesan. 'How do you cope with a boy like this?'

'He's a big problem. He's been giving us problem ever since he was a child.'

Ben smiled again. Somehow he liked the boy. He could not explain to himself why. Perhaps it was because he was tough too when he was his age. He remembered the time he was in the secondary school at Abeokuta, the capital town of Ogun state. He not only proved tough to his teachers but also a street fighter. There was a time a boy of his age was admitted into the school. Unknown to him, the boy was also a troublemaker. In fact, he was kicked out of his former school because he was so unruly and mean. He did not have the figure of a bully but he looked tough enough to intimidate anyone. While taking some snacks at the school canteen, Ben and his friends spotted him taking a bottle of soft drink. Ben was told to go and slap the boy on the face to prove a point to his friends. Ben went to the boy, looked at him and hit him straight on the face. The boy looked both confused and furious. He waited for a few seconds, looking at Ben as if he was expecting him to explain why he hit him. When he could not get any explanation, the boy took the bottle of the soft drink, went close to him and smashed it on his head. Ben passed out. He woke up in the hospital.

'He must be moving with the wrong set of people,' Ben told Sesan. He stood up from his chair and moved closer to him. 'Are you sure you want to learn this job?'

'Yes… sir.'

'Guess who I am.'

'I don't know.'

'I was once a lunatic just like you,' Ben said quietly; making Sesan to burst out into uncontrollable laughter. 'That's right. You can rightly call me lunatic Ben. I was once a violent psychiatric patient. So we both have something in common - insanity. So you have to decide now if you're willing to work with a mad man.'

Nicholas would have burst out laughing like Sesan who was still roaring with laughter if not for Ben who looked dead serious.

'The equation is balanced, don't you think? A mad boy wants to learn electrical engineering and he meets a mad man who is ready to teach him. They would get somewhere if only both of them pretend as if they were normal people. If they don't, either of them would end up in jail for killing the other or both of them end up in the hospital. So let's make a deal. Are you willing to pretend to be a normal person until you learn the job?'

Nicholas was silent.

'Answer me!' Ben bellowed at him.

'Yes, sir.'

'Okay,' he said. 'You can get out while I sort out things with your uncle.'

Nicholas left the small but well furnished office.

Ben went to sit down behind his executive table. Sesan stopped laughing when he sat down. 'So you were once a lunatic?' he asked with a chuckle.

'Sometimes you have to behave like one if you're dealing with a tough boy like him.'

'I can see that you can handle him,' Sesan said. He fell into the temptation to confide to him that he really did not know the boy's parents. He narrated how his wife found him in the street and how they have given him a wrong identity. 'I must confess to you that the way we, especially my wife brought him up made him so heady and spoilt. We really don't want to give him any reason why he should think of his parents.'

Ben who was attentive as he narrated the story about Nicholas to him shook his head thoughtfully. 'He must have been taken from somewhere that was not likely to be close to this area.'

'You may be right,' Sesan said. 'With the way things are now, we have to remain his parents.'

'Sooner or later, the boy would discover the truth about himself.'

'I have that feelings too but let's wait till then,' Sesan said. 'Anyway, what's going to be the arrangement for his apprenticeship?'

'We'll make the arrangement as soon as all papers including the form and the agreement are duly completed and signed,' Ben replied. 'I'll arrange how he'll live with other apprentices in their quarters.'

Within few weeks, the payment and arrangement for his accommodation and apprenticeship had been made. The first day Nicholas slept in the quarters, however, was the day other apprentices found him impossible to live with.

One of his roommates snored, making Nicholas restless while others were sound asleep. Suddenly, he stood up from the bed in irritation and shook the roommate. 'Wake up, pig!' he shouted at him.

The boy who was in his age group woke up with a start. 'What's the matter?'

'You're snoring like a pig. How do you expect me to sleep with a noise like that? If everybody can tolerate the noise, I can't! Let me sleep first before you sleep.'

The boy who was called Victor looked annoyed. 'You woke me up in the middle of the night because you want to be the first to sleep?'

'Yes, you swine!'

Victor probably did not know he was a very mischievous person. He punched him on the face. Nicholas pulled him down from the bed and began to beat him up. He would have seriously wounded him if not for the intervention of other apprentices in the room.

The matter was reported to Ben the following morning in the office. Nicholas and Victor were in the office with Danjuma, their supervisor.

Ben snorted when he heard what happened. He looked steadily at Nicholas. 'You must be really mad. You beat your roommate because he snores?'

'He first punched me on the face, sir,' Nicholas replied gently. Having witnessed how much his fostered uncle had invested in the apprenticeship and having been told that if he blew the chance he had been giving to be trained as an electrical engineer, nobody would be willing to invest anything on him again; he really tried very hard to hide his true colour.

'Shut up!' Ben flared up. 'This is your first day in this establishment and you're already proving to everybody that you're a hoodlum.' He walked to him as he looked on the floor, showing the expression of remorse. 'I told you I'm a violent psychiatric patient. Don't force me to prove that to you. Now listen, young man, if you behave like a lunatic here, I'll not only show you the kind of person I am but I'll also tell the boys to let you realize that every normal person has certain elements of insanity inside in him. If I tell them to beat you out of your senses, do you think you can handle them? I'll give you this as a warning. If you misbehave again, I'll not handle you back to your uncle. I'll deal with you myself. I'll make every minute of your life miserable. Have I made myself clear?'

'Yes, sir.'

'Now get out of here!' Nicholas left the room. Ben looked at Victor. 'Did you punch him in the face?'

'Yes, sir,' Victor replied. 'He made me angry. He woke me up and started calling me pig.'

Ben almost chuckled at the way he said it but he checked himself. 'You shouldn't have punched him first. You should have reported him. Anyway, sorry for what have happened.' He waved the boys away.

'I don't think we should keep the boy,' Danjuma said.

'We have to,' Ben replied. 'He's the nephew of my bosom friend. So I have to handle him like my son. Besides, I must confess to you that I like the boy.'

122

But that was not the end of Nicholas mischief. He developed the habit of disturbing everybody in the room with an ancient looking radio which he got from Sunsomade. He would deliberately turn the volume of the radio to the maximum each time it was time to sleep.

Victor who now hated and feared Nicholas since the day he beat him blocked his ears with a pillow, trying his best to endure him.

Another apprentice called Sola said, sitting on the edge of his bed, 'Nicholas, why must you make noise with that radio every time we want to sleep?'

Nicholas pretended as if he did not hear him.

'I'm talking to you, Nicholas!'

'Would you stop barking like a dog otherwise I'll break your empty head with this radio?'

Sola snatched his pillow and bed sheet and began to walk out of the room. 'I'm going to sleep at master Danjuma's room. I can't sleep under the same roof with an animal.'

Again, the matter was reported to Ben. Nicholas and all his roommates were brought before him in the office.

'I think it's time I show you how to behave unless you tell me why you have to disturb your roommates with your radio.'

'I didn't disturb them, sir.'

'He's always disturbing everybody,' Sola said. 'When he's not making noise with his archaic radio at night, he'll be drumming. He does all these on purpose just to make it impossible for us to live with him.'

Ben got up, removed his belt and told Nicholas to lie on the table. 'I'm going to give you twelve strokes.'

Nicholas who was used to being beaten like that in the school lay on the table with his face downward. Ben stroked him on the buttocks. Everybody was surprised that he did not even show the slightest sign of pain after the last stroke. Even Ben who panted a little just realised that he was more hardened than he thought.

'You're truly a he-goat,' Ben said. 'I jus need one more report about you before I know what to do with you.' He dismissed all of them with a wave of his hand.

Ben did receive another report that proved to him that Nicholas really took joy in seeing others feeling uncomfortable with him. He was obviously determined to take revenge on his roommates for reporting him. So he planned a way to deal with each one of them without making anyone to suspect him. He killed a wall gecko and laid it on the bed of one of the apprentices who was his chief persecutor, making it appeared as if it died there. He did not clean the bloodstain on the body of the little animal, which could easily prove that it was killed.

When the apprentice lay on the bed and found the dead gecko, he sprang up, wondering how it got to the place. He found the bloodstain, which instantly told him it was killed. He did not need to investigate who was behind it before he knew it was part of Nicholas' mischief.

The matter was reported to Ben again. Nicholas denied knowing anything about it.

'Geckoes sometimes die like that,' Ben told the apprentices. He almost believed Nicholas.

'This one was killed and laid on my bed, sir,' the apprentice said. 'I'm sure it's Nicholas that put it there. He doesn't like me because I don't like him. No one likes him. So I don't think I can live in the same room with him. It'll be a great favour if you allow me to live with master Danjuma.'

Ben looked at Nicholas as if he was thinking of what to do with him. 'People say you're an animal. You never attempt to prove them wrong even for once. Instead, you're behaving like one. I wish I could bring myself to break one of your legs. Perhaps that'll prove to you that you'll be at the losing end if you continue to behave like this. You know what I'm going to do now?' He stood up and went to look at his tough expression. 'You're going to live with me. You know my wife knows you're a sick boy. She knows how to take care of boys like you. Perhaps you don't know much about her. She's a no-nonsense woman. So if I were you, I'll not let her know that I have been to a madhouse. I'll behave like a normal person. If you behave like a mad boy in my house, my wife will prove to you that she is equally insane. I won't say more than that. A trial will convince you of the type of person she is. Now, go, pack your things and move down to my quarters. Do you understand?'

'Yes, sir, Nicholas said, not a bit moved by what he said.

Ben had a serious argument with Lade before she could permit Nicholas to live with them. She even pointed out that Nicholas might be more roguish than he thought. 'What if he's a thief?'

'The boy is not a thief,' Ben said. 'I can vouch for that.'

'You know Janet also live in this house,' Lade pointed out. 'What if he sneaks into her room and rapes her?'

'How can you imagine such evil against the boy just because you don't want him to stay in the house with us? He's not as bad as you're trying to paint him.'

'If he's not that bad, why can't he live with other apprentices? I can't

124

risk having him here. If anything happens, it's going to affect everybody. Besides, why do you have to go this far to accept the boy as an apprentice? If he's a ruffian, you can hand him back to his people.'

'The boy is a nephew of my childhood friend.'

'He's not even his son,' Lade said. She was a short light complexioned woman in her late thirties. She looked strong and very stern. She was the kind of woman that loved to always have her way. She was not only domineering but she also always ensured that her orders were carried out to the last letter. If Ben had not been tough enough, their marriage would have become history a long time ago. Everybody in the house, especially her two children knew better than crossing her part. In fact, when she was really angry, her victim always felt sorry. Her marriage with Ben was stormy at the early stage until he proved to her one day that he was the leader and the champion in the house. He beat her to the extent that she landed in the hospital for attempting to slap his face during an argument. Since that day, Lade knew better that to challenge his authority in the house.

'I want you to get this,' Ben said, about to remind her that he has the right to do what he liked without anyone intimidating or questioning him. 'The boy has become my responsibility. I'm obliged to do and give all I can to make the boy an electrical engineer. It is part of the deal I made with my friend. I hope I have made myself clear enough.'

'So this has to do with what you took from your friend, isn't it?' she asked, looking irritated.

'If that's all you can get from all I said, yes.'

'Have you considered what the boy can do to us?'

'The boy is not harmful,' Ben snapped at her. 'He's just going through the normal adolescent stage that...'

'You talk as if I've not raised children. Jim is about his age if not older.'

'You don't have to think of any evil, everything will be just fine,' Ben said and went into the small room to see if he could get him a bed in the place. There was one in the place. He called Lade who was outside the room, saying, 'you can tell Janet to arrange this place for him.'

Lade came to join him in the room, looking irritated. 'Don't think of it. You can't give him a room here.'

'Don't tell me you want him to live outside.'

'He can live in the pantry,' Lade said.

He looked at her for a while, thinking whether or not to exercise his authority. He felt he had done enough to bring the boy into the house.

125

Going extra mile would make her more hostile towards him when she saw him. He asked, 'can you tell one of your children to live in the pantry?'

'You can't compare the rogue with any of my children. Jim is a descent and very serious boy. He was not as old as him when he began his tertiary institution and Janet as you know is a very good Christian. So you can't compare any of them with him.'

'So all these were achieved through your efforts?'

'I trained my children. You know that.'

'You must have considered yourself a very perfect person.'

'I'm not perfect. No one is perfect but we know what to do and what not to do.'

There was a long thoughtful silence. Then Ben signed and shrugged. It was nobody's fault that Nicholas was being rejected everywhere. It was his attitude that subjected him into rejection.

Ben later took Nicholas to the pantry. His daughter, Janet had cleared the place for him. It was a small place though, it was big enough for him to use as a bedroom. A student bed, a table and a chair had been placed in the room. Janet who prepared the place for him had gone to the Church for Bible Studies before he brought his things.

Nicholas put his bag on the table and waited for Ben's instruction without even looking round at the place.

'How do you find this place?'

'I can manage it, sir.'

'Don't just manage it. Be grateful that we can still find a room for you. At least, you're on your own now. You'll find peace here if you want it. If you're looking for trouble, this is also the right place to get it. Just before you come, I had an argument with my wife. She didn't want you here. Don't give her reason to kick you out. If she kicks you out, I can't find another place for you.'

'I'm hated by many people, including those who don't even know me,' he said quietly.

'You have no reason to complain about anybody. Nobody hates you. You're the cause of your own problem. So you can't blame anyone for getting you to this place. Nobody can stand the way you behave. If not for your uncle who is my very good friend, I would have asked him to come and take you back when you had problem with other apprentices. You really have to do something about your character. Otherwise, you'll continue to have problem with everybody. Like I told you, you'll get both peace and trouble here. You can get into much more trouble than you think if you misbehave here. You do

126

whatever I or my wife tells you to do and eat whatever she gives you and everything will be just fine.'

When Janet returned from the Church in the evening, Lade went to her room to warn her about the bad boy her father had brought to live with them in the house as if she was not aware of the apprentice that was to live in the pantry. Janet was a fifteen-year-old girl who was yet to complete her secondary school. She has fair complexion like her mother but she has the height of her father who was a little bit tall. She has a very attractive face that was always full of captivating smiles and dimples.

'You have to be very careful with the boy,' Lade said. 'He may be a potential rapist.'

'What?' Janet looked surprised. She wondered if truly her father could bring a boy as bad as that into the house. But then, she didn't totally believe her mother. She has a way of making things sound very bad or ugly. In any case, she was sure nothing could hurt her. To her, the power of God was always backing her wherever she was.

'I mean it,' Lade said, looking serious. 'He's rejected by everybody in the quarters. I don't know why your father brought him here.'

Janet smiled at her mother with assurance. 'Mum, you know nothing can hurt me because the Bible says that even though I walk through the valley of shadow of death, I will fear no evil because the Lord is with me.'

'I know you believe so much in God,' Lade said impatiently. Although she knew Janet was not just a discipline girl but also a devoted Christian yet she could not help thinking that a boy like Nicholas go haywire one day and hurt her. 'So do I but God never wants us to be careless. You know you're a beautiful girl. So don't leave the door open. Don't stay alone with him in the house.'

'But, mum, why are you overprotective? Even if you try to protect me from him, how about the rough guys I meet everyday in the school, in the street everywhere? Anyway, I'll tell him about Jesus and pray for him. That's the best I can do for him instead of running from him.'

'I don't want you to have any conversation with him.'

'Why?'

'Why? It's because I'm telling you not to.'

'That'll be hard. If you feel so bad about the boy, I'll ask daddy about him.'

'No, don't tell your father anything. We already have an argument over him.'

'I'll assure you that there's no problem. The boy will either change if he's that bad or I'll kick him out of the house with prayer. Leave the matter to God, mum.'

Lade studied her daughter's face. Her opinions were always different from hers but she always admitted it to herself that she was a smart girl. Therefore, she was capable of taking care of herself. She said, 'you will be awarded a medal if you can influence a boy like that to change.'

It was in the evening the following day that Janet had the opportunity to converse with Nicholas who have made up his mind to keep to himself both at home and workshop. It appeared as if no one understood him and he didn't seem to care.

Janet was warming some rice on the cooking gas while Nicholas was listening to his radio as a presenter ran the commentaries on the past leaders. He started from the time the country got her independence, commenting on the past governments. He did not appear to have anything good to say about each of them. He commented that the first republic in 1979 was not really the people's choice but whom the incumbent government selected for them. The country did not enjoy the first republic for more than four years before the military government took over again. Now that the country could be said that she was practicing partial democratic system of government after decades, the commentator wondered what the difference was except that there was freedom of expression and there were rooms for pressure groups to compel the government to do what the people desired. On the whole, though the commentator did not seem to heed the changes since the country had changed again from the military to democratic government two years ago; a lot of things have improved. In spite of the fact that the havoc the military regime had wrecked on the political, social and economic sectors, which were still taking their toll on the people, the new government seemed to be putting so many things that could help the country in place. Nigeria, which has been set backward in many areas, was now trying to keep pace with the rest of the world in their quests for economic and technological advancement.

Nicholas was so deeply engrossed in the commentaries on the radio that he did not notice Janet standing by the door, looking at him with charming smiles.

'Hello, Nicholas,' Janet said, smiling more brightly.

Nicholas, whose attention was always hard to get, found himself looking admiringly at Janet. 'How do you know my name?'

'My father told me. I arranged this room for you.'

'I see. You must be Janet.'

'Yes,' she replied. She expected him to have heard about her. So she was not surprised he mentioned her name. 'I hope you'll like this place.'

'I have no choice but to like it.'

'You're forced to live here, I suppose.'

'Yes.'

'I'm sorry this is the best you could be offered.'

He smiled at her.

She returned the smile. 'I have some rice in the kitchen,' she said. 'It's too much for me. Would you like some?'

'Yes,' he said slowly. 'Thank you.'

'You can come to the kitchen and take it now,' she told him.

He stood up from the bed and followed her. Nicholas had never been so attracted to anyone and he had never been so well treated by any girl before. He did not seem to have any luck with anyone. In fact, for a charming girl who was superior to him in every sense to pay attention to him surprised him a little.

She smiled at him and gestured him to a stool. She dished the food on a silver plate, put a generous cut of fried meat on the food and gave it to him. She dished hers and went to lean against the kitchen cabinet, eating the food slowly and studying his face. He has the attractive looks and figure which many girls in her school could die for but that was not what made her pay him attention. What she actually wanted from him was a change of the attitude that made people disliked him. She did not need to be told that he was a tough boy but she saw it as her duty to change him with the word of God.

There was a long silence. Nicholas was eating the piece of meat as if he has never tasted anything so delicious while she continued to study him, thinking of how to address the issue of his manner.

He looked up and found her staring at him. 'You seem so nice, Janet.'

'Thank you.' She smiled. 'I wish people can say nice thing about you too.'

'You've heard some ugly things about me, haven't you?'

'I don't have to believe what people say.'

He continued eating.

She said, 'Nicholas....'

He looked at her again. She smiled at him. 'This is good,' he said, pointing at the remaining food. 'Did you cook it?'

'Yes,' she said. 'But my mother supervised the cooking.'

'I see,' he said. He threw the last piece of meat in his mouth and munched it.

'You're supposed to finish eating the rice before you eat the meat,' she told him with soft laughter.

'I'll eat everything if it makes you happy.'

'You really want to know how you can make me happy?'

He nodded, looking determined to do anything for her.

She saw the determination on his face. 'Are you sure you'll do it for me?'

'I will if I can.'

'You can, Nicholas,' she said softly. 'If you do it, I will be happy and I will remain your friend.'

With that statement, Nicholas looked more determined. 'I promise you I'll do it.'

'I want you to give your life to Christ and be a changed person.'

Nicholas looked thoughtful, wondering what she meant by giving his life to Christ and wondering what she had heard about him.

'Why do you say I should be a changed person?'

'I said you should be a changed person because the Bible says you must be born again. She went to open a drawer and brought out a Bible.' She showed it to him. 'This is the word of God that says you should be a changed person.' She flung through the pages of the Bible and said, 'I'll read the book of Romans chapter three verse twenty-three. It says, "for all have sinned and come short of the glory of God." Chapter ten verse nine and ten of the same book says, "if you confess with your mouth the Lord Jesus, and shall believe in your heart that God raised him from the dead, you shall be saved. For with the heart man believes unto righteousness; and with the mouth confession is made unto salvation."' She looked at him. 'You see, according to that place, everybody in this world is a sinner and we need Jesus to cleanse us of our sins. If anyone dies without giving his life to Christ, he would die again.'

Nicholas frowned, 'how can someone die again after he had died?'

Janet turned the Bible to another page and said, 'how a person can die again after he has died is explained in the book of Revelation chapter twenty-one verse eight. It says, "but the fearful and unbelieving, and the abominable, and murderers, and fornicators, and sorcerers, and idolaters and all liars, shall have their part in the lake which burns with fire and brimstone; which is the second death." Did you hear that? Second death?'

He nodded.

'We are all born to die in this world. Those who are not born-again I mean those who refuse to give their lives to Christ will die the second time by going to hell. Since we cannot do without committing sin, Jesus came to die for our sins. He rose from the dead and then gives us the Holy Spirit that will help us to live a holy life. No one needs to be taught how to commit sin because by our nature and practice we are sinners. Because of that, we all need Jesus. Only Jesus can make us a changed person. You cannot do it by yourself. That is why I want you to give your life to Jesus Christ who will make you a brand new person.'

There was a brief silence. Then Nicholas said, 'you know so much about the Bible. I wish I can know as much.'

'Jesus taught me everything I know through his Spirit. If you give your life to him, he will teach you too. We'll be studying the Bible together.'

Lade came into the kitchen unexpectedly. She frowned when she saw the silver plate with Nicholas. 'When did we start sharing the same plate in this house?'

Janet said, 'I gave it to him.'

'And why didn't you use his plate for him?'

'I didn't know there's a plate in particular for him,' Janet said. 'Besides I don't see why his plate should be different from ours.'

Lade snatched the plate from him, took a plastic plate and poured the food inside. Then she practically threw it on the table in front of him as if she was giving the food to a dog.

Nicholas was mad with rage and it showed on his face. He felt like bouncing on Lade and beating the hell out of her but Janet's guilty expression seemed to hold him bond on the stool. He stood up and went to his room.

'How dare you walk out of me like that!' Lade yelled. 'Come back here.'

'Mum, you're at fault if you ask me,' Janet said quietly.

'Well, I didn't ask you,' she said. 'So keep your mouth shut!' She turned to his direction. 'Nicholas!' He walked to his room. Nicholas slammed the door closed. 'It's not your fault. I don't know why Ben had to bring a ruffian into this house in the first place.' She stormed into the sitting room where Ben was watching the television. 'See what the ruffian apprentice has done.'

'What's wrong?' Ben asked without looking away from the television.

'Janet gave him some rice, using one of the plates we use in the house. I poured the food in another plate. The next thing he would do was to walk out of me. I thought he was going to beat me when I saw the looks on his face.'

'Did you hear yourself, Lade?' Ben asked, turning to look at her. 'I'm surprised all the boy did was to walk out of you.'

She pretended to be surprised. 'What exactly do you expect him to do? You expect him to beat me?'

Ben was silent. He was clearly not in the mood for argument.

'I can see what is happening. You brought the boy into this house to be used against me. See, see, I am prepared for him if that is his mission in this house. By the time I'm through with him, he'll wish he had not been born.'

'What has the boy done to warrant this hullabaloo?' Ben asked, losing his patience. 'Please, woman, don't get on my nerves. If you do, you'll get more than you bargain for.'

'You want to beat me, huh?' she asked. 'You can beat me if you want. It's not your first time. Let me tell you, somebody will pay for this.'

'Don't put words into my mouth, Lade,' Ben said gently. He could sense the trend of the discussion. 'I know you don't like the boy. You are finding an occasion to accuse him of causing the misunderstanding in the house. You're doing all you can to provoke him so that you will find a ground to get him out. Let me warn: you will fail because the boy is my boy, no matter what you feel about him. I've been mandated to stand as his father and I'm going to do just that.'

'I now see what's happening,' Lade said, glaring at him. 'I know you brought the boy here to scatter the family.'

'You probably don't know the kind of person you are. You've always been at loggerheads with many people, including your own children but I don't really blame you. The proverb says that if a woman stays too long in the matrimonial home, she turns into a witch.'

'What? You're calling me a witch because I'm trying to protect my matrimonial home!'

'If you don't want me to call you a witch, don't behave like one. Leave the boy alone!'

'The boy is taking over this house and you expect me to leave him alone?'

'What's your problem, woman?' Ben growled at her. 'If the boy does anything wrong, I'll deal with him. I don't see anything wrong in what he has done so far, going by what you said. If the boy is rude to you for trying to treat him like a dog in the house, I don't see why he should not react the way he did.'

'You mean if the boy had beaten me, this is the way you would have reacted?'

Ben did not say anything again. He continued to watch the television as if he was already through with her. Indeed, as far as he was concerned, he was through with her. He only needed to wait for the opportunity to prove it again that he was the boss in the house and whatever decision he had made was the final. If she liked, she could spit fire or spill into foams. Nicholas has come to stay in the house and there was nothing she could do about it.

'This house is already on fire,' she hissed, walking to her room.

'There is a fire fighter in the house,' Ben replied without looking at her. 'He's just waiting for the opportunity to prove how effective he is.'

'We shall see to that!'

Janet had gone to Nicholas's room, knocking the door gently. He didn't need to be told who was knocking before he opened the door. 'Nicholas, I'm sorry,' she said quietly and guiltily. 'I'm to be blamed for all these.'

'I can't see your fault,' he replied gently. He had no doubt that she had touched something in his life, which he could not explain. He was surprised that he reacted the way he did. No one could have treated him like a dog and gone away with it. Somehow, he felt obliged to please Janet though he was yet to promise her that he was ready to change into a good boy.

She said, 'I think it's the devil who does not like peace, love and joy to reign anywhere that caused all these.'

'Who's the devil now? Me or your mother who did not hide it from everyone that she hates me?'

'Nobody is the devil. He's a spirit that moves around looking whom to devour. He's fond of using people and situation against one another.'

'I see.'

There was a brief silence before she asked, 'would you like to be going to Church with me every Sunday?'

'Yes, if your father approves of my going out with you.'

'He would,' she said quickly. 'He likes you very much.'

'Yes, I know. If not for that I was supposed to be kicked out of this place. But that does not mean he trusts me going out with you.'

'People may have wrong impression about you but I don't think my father thinks you're that bad. Besides, he trusts my judgement.'

'How about your mother?'

'You don't have to worry about her,' she said promptly. 'What's

133

important is for you to make up your mind that you'll be going to Church with me. My brother and I used to go together whenever he's around.'

'Do your parents go to Church?'

'They use to go to the one across the street but not all the time.'

'Their Church is different from yours?'

'Yes?'

'Why?'s

'I like the Pentecostal. I mean the kind of place where the word of God is the central figure of everything the people do. A place like that is good for people who are just coming to the knowledge of Christ. It's also good for those who want to grow in Christ. You know we are all growing in the knowledge of God.'

'You mean they don't grow in Christ in your parents' Church?'

She laughed softly.

He loved the way she laughed. He smiled at her.

'I didn't say that,' she replied. 'I love to dig deep into the word of God.'

'That's the way you know so much about the Bible.'

'You're very correct though you have to make personal efforts to study the scriptures. If you don't, some people can use that to manipulate you. The devil, the archenemy of everybody can use ignorance of the word of God to oppress you or even destroy you. The Bible says in the book of Hosea chapter four verse six that the people of God perish for lack of knowledge. You see, ignorance is the main problem of the people, not even the devil or what they can perceive with their senses. Knowledge, especially knowledge of God is power. When you know the power backing you as a Christian, the devil will fear you but if you don't know, you will fear the devil and what he can do to you. So studying the scriptures and going to the Bible believing Church is very vital in the life of a true born-again Christian.'

He shrugged.

'You'll like to go?'

'Why not?' he asked. 'You can inform your father first.'

'I'll do that.'

Janet later went to Ben and informed him that she would like Nicholas to be going to Church with her every Sunday.

'Okay,' Ben said. 'The boy would need it anyway.'

'He's going to be a changed person, dad.'

'I hope so.'

'He's changing already.'

134

'I won't count on that yet until I see the change myself. If he changes, I'll give you an award.'

'Jesus will take the glory because he's the one that'll change him,' she said. 'I'll spend time praying for him. If I have to go on fasting to make him a changed person, I'll do that.'

'I'll like to see what will happen if you go that far for him.'

Through out the rest of the night and days after then, Nicholas could not help thinking of Janet. He could not quite understand how he felt about her but he knew he had a lot of respect for her. She seemed to possess the virtues that made him felt like a real evil person. He wished he could exhibit most of her virtues but it seemed so impossible, especially when the conflict between him and her mother seemed not to have an end. Because of what has happened, she saw him as enemy whom she must get rid of by all means. She was suspicious of him even when he did all he could to please her and to be at peace with her. She looked for every opportunity available to pick quarrel with him, including lying against him. If not for Janet who seemed to be having great influence on him, he would have probably beaten the woman one day. Since he did not want to disappoint Janet and Ben who remarked on the first day he was going to Church, 'you know you have committed so many sins, including beating up a boy for snoring in the middle of the night. So don't make the mistake of confessing your sins before everybody. If you do, people may be so provoked that they may stone you to death.'

The two teenagers had laughed whole-heartedly. It was the first time Ben would see him laughing like that. It pleased him to note that his daughter was positively making an impact in his life. When, a few months later, he observed some changes in his attitude at the workshop and at home, he had said, 'I brought a hoodlum into this house; I'm beginning to see a saint. That's great.' He looked at Janet. 'I give you a big kudos for that.'

'I give God the glory,' Janet said, looking at Nicholas with pleasure. 'I told you Jesus would change him.'

'Yeah,' Ben said. 'I can see the results of your prayers in his life.'

Nicholas looked at her as if to ask her if she really prayed for him to be changed.

Ben answered his unasked question, 'yes, she prayed and fasted for you. What else do you think could change a devil incarnate like you?'

The rest giggled. Ben seemed to love making them to laugh. Since then he always found time to chat with the two of them, cracking jokes and enjoying himself as they laughed.

Things seemed to be going on well until the day Sesan and Sunsomade and some other people traveled to another town to attend the funeral service of one of their friends. They went in an eighteen-seater bus in uniform attires. As they were coming, the bus had a fatal accident, making everyone except Sunsomade to loose his or her life. Even though Sunsomade survived in the accident, she had little or no hope to survive. In fact, the doctors could not explain how she managed to stay alive. Part of her internal organs like the lung and liver were seriously affected by the accident. When she was able to talk in the hospital, she requested to see her children and Nicholas. The news of the accident sent waves of shock to the people in the town. Gbenga, Seyi and Nicholas went to the hospital to see Sunsomade. They never knew she was in such critical condition until they saw her on her deathbed in the hospital.

'Gbenga,' she said in a very quiet voice.

'Yes, mother,' Gbenga replied, kneeling beside her bed, forcing back his tears. It was terrible enough to loose their father and traumatic enough to see her in such pain.

She called the names of the rest and said, 'I know I don't have much time.' Tears began to run down her eyes. 'You've all grown up now. I want you to be one even though…. Nicholas is not your brother.'

That did not register a surprise as no one had the impression that Nicholas was the real brother of the other two. Although Nicholas had wondered at one time or the other why his parents had abandoned him with the family, he never had any reason to think much of them. He was so well treated by his fostered parents that he never felt the need to think of looking for them.

'Nicholas,' Sunsomade said, 'I've hidden some truths from you. I have to tell you so that you'll not feel bad if you are not accepted by the people you think are your parents when they come to the town.'

Everybody was silent, expecting her to tell him the truth.

Tearfully, Sunsomade said, 'I don't know who your real parents are.'

The three young men looked stunned in spite their condition.

'I don't understand,' Nicholas said, wondering where he came from.

'I don't know your real family. I tried to look for them when you were a child but I couldn't.'

'Then how did I come to you?'

'You were lost when you were about two year old but I think your parents must be well to do. You were well dressed when I found you in the street. I think you were stolen from somewhere. At that time, some evil people steal children. I think you were stolen from somewhere. I wish I know where.'

Emotion engulfed Nicholas. For the first time, everybody would see tears running down his eyes. He had always heard it that the family of Kujor were nice people. It never meant anything to him until now. In spite of his misdemeanour, the family never made him feet he was not their child. They spent so much on him, caring for him everyday and in everything. They spoilt him with love. They would take the pains of putting things he had done wrong right. He was endured and tolerated despite his bad attitude. He could remember vividly how he was first taken to the school, how he had complained about the place and how they have explained to him why he had to go to school. He would never forget what his fostered uncle has said. 'We want you to become very rich. So you have to go school to know how to count your money.' They knew how to do something which would be beneficial to him and how to make him feel loved and happy. Now he was losing the people that have truly proved to be his real family. He wondered what was going to happen to him now that he just realized that he has no identity. Well, he consoled himself, if the people he thought were his family were not even related to him, he might as well leave the town to another place where he could hide under the identity of a stranger. Really, he was a stranger…

Nicholas knelt down, held Sunsomade's hand and began to cry like a baby. 'You're the greatest parents in the world, Mama,' he said within his tears.

Sunsomade began shedding more tears. 'I… would have gone home before now but I have to see you and say this.' She slowly laid her hand on his shoulder. 'God had always been with you and he will never leave you. There is a hand of God upon your life. You…know we did our best to take care of you.'

Nicholas was sobbing more hysterically now. 'I know… I gave you much problem…' he stammered with sobs. 'But you never give me up… What am I going to do without you…'

'God will be with you, child. I know he will…' she was growing weak now. 'I want you to do me a favour.'

'I will do anything for you… Mama…' he sobbed, feeling his heart vibrating with deep love for the woman he has come to realize meant everything to him.

'Nicholas… I want you… to… to change… and become a child of

God… that will grow… into a man of God.'

'I would change,' he said. 'I'm already going to the Church, Mama.'

She gave a weak smile. 'You will grow to become a man of God. You're going to be blessed.' She looked at her children. 'Gbenga, I want you and your brother to be of one accord. I want both of you to see Nicholas as your brother. If any of the three of you is blessed, I want you to help the rest. Would you do that for your poor mother?'

None of them could hide their tears as they nodded.

'I would have loved to stay with you longer than this but I can't. I want all of you to be godly people. That's the only way we can see in heaven and…' She could not finish before she became silent. She was dead.

The three young men burst into hysterical wails.

CHAPTER NINE

Nicholas became a very sorrowful person after the death of his fostered parents. He did not seem to have anything to rejoice about. He has no family, no friend and no identity. He was all alone in the whole wide world. He, however, took refuge in reading the Bible and singing the hymns every now and then through out his stay at home. He was to spend few weeks at home before the burial. After the burial, he would be on his own. His loneliness inspired him to write a song lyric.

I have been doing wrong all my life
Though I was too young to realize this
I was walking in the way of death
Yet I was very confident in myself

I was too happy about my life
Though it was in great danger
I was too carefree to know the Lord
Yet there was problem ahead of me

I was a terrible sinner with no hope
But I did not know sin leads to hell
I was getting nearer to the grave
Yet I did not know death was so near

I hurt people with what I was doing
But I never knew the implication
I never knew what true love is
Until I lost those who love me

Lord, I come to you with a filthy soul
And with a very heavy heart, I come
Take my life and make it yours
I cannot live this life again...

He became very reserved, preferring to be alone, thinking of the people that made life worth living before they died. He thought of what to do with what was left of the broken pieces of his life. As he once decided, he could go to a city like Lagos or Ibadan and look for a job. He would go to the university on part-time. Since he has no identity, he felt the best thing for him was to leave the town and get an identity for himself by becoming successful. If he became successful, he could propose to marry Janet and settle down with her if she loved him enough to spend her life with him. It would take long to achieve that but a hundred miles journey begins with a step and the will. Though he has the will that could see him through, he needed someone that would believe in him someone that would passionately push him to achieve what he wanted. Only one person could do that his master Ben or Janet. Both of them have proven it to him in so many ways that they loved and believed in him.

After a chain of thoughts of what he foresaw he would go through, he decided that he would tell Ben after the burial that he was going to leave the town.

Ben, Lade and Janet were present during the burial ceremony in the Kujor family house. Nicholas did not feature as prominently as Gbenga and Seyi, the children of the deceased. This was an indication that he was not even recognised by the family as one of the children of the deceased. It marked the beginning of loneliness. He felt isolated and alone in the world but he consoled himself by telling himself that he would soon be out of the town. He would not return unless Janet was willing to marry him afterwards.

When everything was over few days later, Nicholas went to Ben at home. Janet who was then sitting for the final year examination in secondary school was away. He had hoped to get Ben's permission and get out of the house before she returned from school. It seemed she was the only one that occupied the most sensitive part of his life. He was afraid she could stop him if he could not persuade her to let him go. So he felt if he could get Ben's approval, he would leave before she returned home.

'I want to have a word with you, sir,' Nicholas told Ben who was in the sitting room with Lade. They were discussing about how Janet could further her education. Ben was of the view that she should study medicine while Lade felt that teaching was good for women. He did not want her to become a teacher but they resolved that Janet should decide what she wanted to become. The couple sometimes have occasions to be together to discuss like that.

Lade smiled at him and stood up. 'I'll excuse the two of you.'

Ben gestured him to the chair beside him. 'Sit here,' he said gently.

'Thank you, sir,' Nicholas said in a quiet voice, sitting beside him.

'I really don't like the looks on your face,' Ben said, trying to cheer him up. 'I can do with some smiles.'

Nicholas forced himself to smile.

'That's better. Now tell me what the problem is.'

'First, I have to thank you for all God have used you to do. I must confess that it was your patience and tolerance of me that really influence the change in me. Like my fostered parents, you never gave me up despite my wrong behaviour.'

'Hay, Nicholas, how can I give you up? Have you seen a family giving up any of her members because he's a big problem? Besides, you're really not a problem. You were just going through a normal life as a teenager. Anyway, we thank God Janet was able to make you a Christian.'

'I'll never forget all you and my fostered parents have done,' he said quietly. He burst out in sobs almost immediately when he thought of what Sunsomade had said when she was dying.

Ben quickly put his arm across his shoulder and held him tightly as he shook with emotional sobs. 'I don't know what I would have become without your tolerance. It's impossible to find meaning to life without people like you… I never know how much my fostered parents… mean to me until I lost them.'

Though Ben was emotionally strong, he was so moved that he could not find anything to say to him. After a long time, he said, 'it's okay, Nicholas. Crying over the dead cannot bring them back. You've got to face life as it appears to you.'

'I don't understand my life,' he said, drying his tears with the edge of his shirt, 'so I have to…em… leave for the city to look for a job. It's the best I can do to take care of myself since all those who are taking care of me are dead.'

'Nicholas,' Ben whispered. His raising emotion made him realise that he really liked the boy. In fact, he was like his real son. 'You need a father and a mother, don't you?'

Nicholas looked at him with confusion.

'I know you don't have parents,' Ben said. 'Sesan told me the secret you just discovered.'

Nicholas looked more confused. 'He told you I was picked in the street when I was two years old?'

He nodded. 'He told me everything the day he brought you here.

141

He knew you were going to give me some problem. You really didn't give me any problem as he expected before you became a changed person. When I told him you've changed, he was very happy. He and his wife really loved you.'

'I know,' he whispered. 'That's what made it all the more painful.'

'You know we love you here too. That's why we have to tolerate everything you do.'

'I know that mummy doesn't love me that much. She tolerates me because of you.'

'Now that we are your only family, things would change; I promise.'

'That wont be necessary now, sir. I'm going to the city to look for a job. I would sponsor myself in the university.'

'You know I can't let you go.'

'Why not, sir?'

'I made a promise to Sesan that I'll make you an engineer, come what may. I'm obliged to do that. Besides, I can't let you go into the cruel world all by yourself without getting prepared. No, Nicholas, I can't let you go; no matter what you say.'

Nicholas was thoughtful for a moment. 'I...don't know what to say now except to thank you for the offer to continue to support me but I have to let you know that I've made up my mind to go to the city to get a job.'

'Except you run away, Nicholas, I can't let you go. If you run, you let me and Sesan down.' There was brief silence before he added, 'if you get a job in the city now, you'll be an unskilled labourer even with your school certificate. You know the condition in the country now, don't you? Getting a good job is as hard as coconut shell but if you have your own business you will have little or nothing to worry about.'

Just then, the door was knocked and Janet came into the sitting room. She stopped short when she saw Nicholas with her father.

'See, see, your girlfriend has come,' Ben said to him jocularly. He looked at Janet. 'How's your exam?'

'It's fine.'

'You'll pass it in flying colours.'

'By the grace of God, I would.'

He gestured at Nicholas. 'He wants to leave for the city.'

She frowned. 'Why?'

'You can ask and persuade him to change his mind.'

Janet slowly put down her bag and went to join them.

'Take him out and talk to him. He may listen to you.'

Giving him the usual captivating smiles and going to hold his hand, she asked, 'can we go out and talk about this?'

With what Ben had said and with Janet meeting him in the house, he knew there was no way he could carry out his decision.

Slowly he followed her, holding hands. She led him to the back of the house under a tree. There was a long bench where anyone in the house often sat or laid to relax.

They sat down. After a moment, Janet asked softly, 'why do you want to leave us?'

Her beautiful and innocent looks coupled with the tone of her voice made emotion to engulf him again. He wondered if he meant that much to anyone to make her said that. 'You know I can't stay here for life.'

'You need to complete your apprenticeship.' She was silent for a while. Then she asked, 'are you planning to leave because you lost your two relations that really matter to you?'

'Janet,' Nicholas said, in a shaky voice, 'I... have no relation.'

She frowned. 'What do you mean? What about your family members like your cousins?'

'They are not my family. It's... it's not an easy story for me to tell anyone.'

'It's okay if you don't feel like telling anyone.'

'I'll tell you,' he said slowly. 'I was picked in a street in Illisan when I was two year old.'

'What?' Janet was truly stunned.

'How do you know this?'

'Mum I mean Mrs Kujor told us before she died. Your father knows this all the while.'

'Who told him?'

'Mr Kujor told him.' There was uncomfortable silence. Janet was too surprised to say anything. He added in a very sorrowful tone, 'Janet, I have no identity. I have no family no relation because I don't know them.' His voice became very unsteady. 'I'm alone in the world.'

Janet held his hands in both of hers. He did not know she was so emotionally moved until tears ran down her eyes. After a while, she said, 'you are not alone. Remember the song the choir sang sometimes ago.'

He looked at her face. Her charming face was distorted with sorrow, concern and affection. He asked with tears, 'which one?'

'The one you told me to get the wordings from the choir mistress.'

'Yeah.'

143

'Can I sing it for you?'
He nodded.
Janet began to sing in a very appealing voice.

I'm not alone, I'm not alone
Jesus is with me everywhere I go
I am secured in his great love
No matter what comes my way,
I will trust in him all the time

I'm not alone, I'm not alone
Even if I'm forsaken by my people,
Jesus will never leave me alone
I may go through jungle of life
I know he is always with me

I'm not alone, I'm not alone
I may go through needless pain
I may be disappointed by people
And life may be very frustrating
Still, Jesus will not leave me alone

I'm not alone, I'm not alone
No matter what I'm going through
Jesus will never let me down
Everybody may decide to give me up
But Jesus will never give me up.

When she finished singing, she cleaned her eyes. She helped him to dry his tears. 'You may feel that you have no family but I can assure you that Jesus Christ is going to be your father and mother. He knows you more than anyone else.'

'I know,' Nicholas said in a whisper.

'He understands how you feel. I'm sure he'll do something about it.'

'Janet, you don't understand much, do you? Who can I call my mother or father? Who do I have as my sisters and brothers? When people ask, "where is your family," what would I say?' There was a brief silence.

'You did survive without your biological family till now. God can still use people for you.'

'People like who?'

'My father. You know he loves you very much. He will be your father as I'm your sister.'

'I can't call you my own family?'

'Why not? I'm your own, Nicholas,' she said, smiling.

He frowned. He wished she meant the relationship as something else but he knew she did not mean it that way.

She noticed the puzzled expression. She asked, 'don't you want me to be your own?'

'My own what?'

'Whatever you want as your own, I'll be. Cousin, sister whatever.'

He smiled faintly. 'I need both parents desperately. You want to be my mother.'

She forced herself to laugh. 'I would have loved to be your mother but you know I can't because you're older than me. But I'll be your sister because I love you like me real brother.'

Within the next few minutes, they were chatting and laughing like children. It was incredible how Janet managed to change his mood very quickly. Obviously, they were very fond of each other.

On Sunday, they went to the Church. The pastor preached a sermon that made a very serious impact on Nicholas. It was as if he understood everything about his life.

'There was a story in the first book of Chronicles chapter four verse nine and ten which I would like to paraphrase,' the pastor said. He was a very jovial man who loved to bring smiles on the faces of everyone with the word of God. 'There was once a woman who not only gave birth to a child in sorrow but also named him sorrow. Let's read verse nine of the chapter.' He looked at the Bible in front of him on the pulpit, opened and began to read the portion, '"And Jabez was more honourable than his brethren: and his mother called his name Jabez, saying because I bare him with sorrow."' He smiled at the people. 'Jabez's mother must have gone through a terrible experience to have named her son after sorrow. Imagine a woman calling her child sorrow instead of joy or blessing. If your name is sorrow or failure or frustration, God will change that named today as you hear his word this morning in Jesus' name.'

There was a shout of 'AMEN!"' among the congregation.

'So many things could have caused the sorrow of the woman,' the pastor continued after a brief pause. 'It could be that she has no money to take care of the child before he was born or after. We can also say that all the money the family has on earth was spent on the hospital bill. We can also say that the father of the child dodged his responsibility by staying away from the house or he eloped with another woman. It may be that Jabez's parents did not really prepare for his birth. So he was probably given away to someone else to parent. He could have been dumped somewhere he could be picked up like an item. He could have been sold or neglected because he was not welcomed. No one can really say what made the woman to call her child sorrow. So no one expect his parents to contribute meaningfully to his life. These are possible assumptions because the Bible never record any other thing Jabez's parents did except to call him sorrow. If the child's parents called him sorrow, they could as well do all they could to get rid of him. Why? It's because no one would like to keep sorrow. It was as if it was the child's fault to be born. The boy never picked them as his parents, did he? But let me tell you this: nobody has any right to write you off because you are Somebody's product. You are God's product. Only one person can write you off. It is only you, yourself. Even God who created you can never write you off. The reason is because God created you for a purpose. He cannot afford to let the purpose to be defeated for any reason or by anyone. Many people may say you're a mistake but you don't have to believe them. Instead, believe the word of God that says that you are fearfully and wonderfully made. Your parents may say you're not welcomed in this world but you can say you came for a purpose and nothing can hinder you from achieving that purpose.

'Because Jabez was born in sorrow, all his life was full of sorrow. The devil did one thing or the other that brought sorrow into the family and Jabez was the one that was blamed for it. When he started school, he was expelled from three different institutions because he always brought sorrow into the school. Anywhere Jabez went, sorrow always went with him. Jabez and sorrow were good pals. Anybody that made friends with Jabez made friends with sorrow. Everybody rejects Jabez because no one wanted to be identified with sorrow. Jabez could not understand his life because it was full of complications. He could have given himself up but he never gave up because somehow he knew all would be well. One Christian made friend with Jabez and advised him to give his life to Christ. Jabez became born-again. He became born-again! Hallelujah! He sought the Lord. He came across the word of God in second Chronicles chapter seven verse fourteen that says "if my people which are called by my name, shall humble themselves, and pray, and seek my face, and turn from their wicked ways; then will I hear from heaven, and I will

146

forgive their sins, and will heal their land."' He paused briefly before he continued, 'I have to quickly tell you four things that sin will do to you before we continue the story about Jabez. Turn with me to the first epistle of John chapter three verse eight. It reads like this, "he that committeth sin is of the devil; for the devil sinneth from the beginning. For this purpose the Son of God was manifested, that he might destroy the works of the devil."' He looked round at the people. 'From that passage, we can see that sin of whatever kind makes a person servant of the devil. By committing sin, you are serving the devil. I don't care who you are. You may claim to be a Christian or even a servant of God. Whoever you are, if you commit sin, the Bible says: you're a servant of the devil. So you need to repent of your sin if you don't want to serve the devil again with your sins.

'The second thing I want you to note in that passage is that sin makes you vulnerable to the attack of the devil. Thank God for sending Jesus Christ into the world to destroy the works of the devil in our lives. The devil can have a stronghold over your life through sin. So you need to allow Jesus to come into your life through the Holy Spirit.

'Let's read Ephesians chapter 5 verses 3 to 6 and see the other two things sin can do to sinners. The Bible says in that passage, "but fornication, and all uncleanness, or covetousness, let it not be named among you, as becoming saints; neither filthiness, nor foolish talking, nor jesting, which are not convenient: but rather giving thanks. For this ye know that no whoremonger, nor unclean person, nor covetous man, who is an idolater, hath any inheritance in the kingdom of God."'

He looked at the people again. 'From this passage, we can see that the third thing sin can do to you is to make God angry with you. And the fourth is that it can deny you from getting to the kingdom of God.'

He paused again to open the Bible to another place. 'Having explained the four things sin can do to you, we can now go back to the story about Jabez.' He looked round at the people to see if they were attentive. They were all very attentive. Some of them, including Nicholas and Janet were jotting some points. 'Sin is the real cause of Jabez's problem. Sin was what gave the devil room to plant sorrow into his life. His problem was not his parents who named him sorrow. It was not the devil and it was not what the people said about him. How many times have you been called failure because you could not achieve what was not in your power to achieve? Jabez's other problem is ignorance of God and his identity in him. If you believe that shout hallelujah!'

Most of the people shouted, 'hallelujah!'

'Some of you probably don't believe me. That's why you didn't shout but you don't have to worry about that. I'll convince you. Just turn your Bible with me to the book of Hosea chapter 4 verse 6. It reads: "My people are destroyed for lack of knowledge: because thou hast rejected knowledge, I will reject thee…" Etcetera. In that place, we see that Jabez went through sorrow or suffering because he lacked the knowledge of what to do. But somehow he got to understand that if he forsook his sins, humble himself before God and pray; God would heal his land. The Bible says in first Chronicles chapter 4 verse 10, "and Jabez called on the God of Israel, saying, Oh that thou wouldest bless me indeed, and enlarge my coast and that thine hand might be with me and that thou would keep me from evil, that it may not grieve me! And God granted him that which he requested." Did you see that? He asked God to keep him from evil, not just to enlarge his coast. God will grant you your request today in Jesus' name.'

There was uproar of 'AMEN' among the people.

'God granted Jabez that which he requested. Jabez later completed the school which sorrow had denied him and began to work. God bless him and he became a very rich and sophisticated man. He later married a very lovely lady who settled down with him. All the sorrows in his life came to an end the moment Jesus entered his life.

'One of the lessons in this story is that whatever conditions you are in this life; you're in sorrow if you don't have Christ. Without Jesus in your life, you'll not only be in sorrow but also in bondage. Everything about your life cannot be right. Remember what the Bible says in Deuteronomy chapter 28 verses 15 to 68 to the man that refuses to obey the word of God. The passage is full of frightening curses…'

When they were going back home, Nicholas was unusually silent for long time. He was thinking about the sermon which he considered the message from God. Was it true that he was dumped somewhere by his parents where the Kujor family could pick him up? If he was, why? Was he really not welcomed into the family of his biological family? By the way, where was his real family? They must be really wicked to have abandoned him at the time he really needed them. They must be very inconsiderate to have left him all alone in the world to fend for his life. But then, as he had been made to realize, he did not have to blame anyone for his problem. Now that he has Jesus in his life, it did not really matter whether his family neglected him for others

148

to look after or not. If he has no other identity, at least, he has come to realize his identity in Christ. He was a child of God and God has a plan for his life. That was why he was able to survive in spite of the fact that he did not have a family. It did not matter if the people that gave him life abandoned him or not. Jesus was always there to look after him. Just as his fostered mother had said before she died, God was always with him. He would not give him up. He would trust in him….

Tears blinded his eyes. He tried to dry it with the back of his hand before Janet who was walking with him silently saw it. She seemed to notice the impact of the message on him. She had also guessed that the sermon addressed his life. She held his hand silently. She did not seem to notice the tears but she sensed his feelings. She was sensitive and close to him to read his thoughts and feelings.

She smiled at him. 'You are silent, Nicholas. You are thinking about what the Pastor said, aren't you?'

Nicholas looked at her. 'Janet, I am Jabez.'

'I think so. Your life reflected in the story about him.'

'I don't know how I was born but I know my life had been full of sorrows. The only people that made me find sense in this life are both dead.'

'You don't have to think about the sorrowful part of the story. Instead, think about the amazing outcome of the life of Jabez. If you look at it in that angle, you will see that the sermon is a message of hope instead of sorrow. Going by the way the Pastor related the story, your life was changed and God blessed you so much that those who rejected you wanted to be your friend. Since you have given your life to Christ, so shall it be.'

A few months after the death of Nicholas' fostered parents, another incident happened that showed him the way out of the house. Jim, Ben's first child who was a student of the Polytechnics of Ibadan in Oyo state came home with his friend to get some pocket money from his parents one Saturday afternoon. By then, Ben had traveled to Abuja in search of contracts while Lade had gone out to a wedding ceremony of the daughter of one of her close friends in the town.

Nicholas and Janet were at the back of the house, engrossed in the study of the Bible.

'Obedience, unto the Lord,' Janet was saying Nicholas, 'simply means living your life for Christ. See what the first Epistle of Peter chapter 2 verses 5 to 10 that says, "ye also, as lively stones, are built up a spiritual house, a holy priesthood, to offer up spiritual sacrifices, acceptable to God by Jesus Christ.

149

"'Wherefore also it is contained in the Scripture, Behold, I lay in Sion a chief corner stone, elect, precious: and he that believeth on him shall not be confounded.'"

She paused, looking and smiling at Nicholas. She pointed the place to him before she continued to read, "'unto you therefore which believe he is precious: but unto them which be disobedient, the stone which the builders disallowed, the same is made the head of the corner,

"'And a stone of stumbling, and a rock of offence, even to them which stumble at the word, being disobedient: whereunto also they were appointed.

"'But ye are,'" She pointed at Nicholas who was very attentive, "'chosen generation, royal priesthood, a holy nation, a peculiar people: that you should show forth the praises of him who hath called you out of darkness into his marvelous light.

"'Which in time past were not people but are now people of God: which had not obtained mercy, but now have obtained mercy."

She smiled at him again. 'You see that place is telling us to offer ourselves as a sacrifice to God by living our lives for him. We do that by obeying his words. If we are obedient to God, according to the book of proverb chapter 3 verses 1 and 2 our life will be prolonged and we shall have peace. Apart from all these, we shall be blessed. If you look at Deuteronomy chapter 28 verses 1 to 14 you will see all the blessings that God attached to obedience. But a disobedient child of God will die prematurely. That reminds of me a pastor who boarded a bus from the north, coming to the south. The Spirit of God told him to get down from the bus. He obeyed without questions. You know what happened?'

Nicholas shook his head.

'The bus which God told him to leave had an accident. All the people inside died. You see if he had been disobedient, he would have been among the dead. Disobedience to God is a debt, which people would have to pay for even sometimes with their lives. Obedience on the other hand brings about great blessings, which often extend to other people. If you look at the same chapter of Deuteronomy verses 15 down to 68, you will see all the curses that are attached to disobedience to the word of God. The curses are so much that they can be transmitted from one generation to another. Disobedience is a very serious sin to God. God considered disobedience to his words as witchcraft. Let's look at the first book of Samuel chapter 15 verse 23. The bible says "for rebellion is as the sin of witchcraft, and stubbornness is as iniquity and…"'

Jim and his friend parked the car they have brought from Ibadan in front of the house. Jim told his friend to wait in the car while he went to get some money from his parents.

'You must make haste otherwise we may not be able to reach other places before we go back to the campus.'

'I'll be back in a minute.'

Jim went into the house. It appeared as if there was no one at home but most of the doors in the house, including his mother's room were opened. He called out, 'is anyone at house?' There was no reply. He went into the rooms. Some money was on the dressing table in his mother's room. Since that was what he came for, he took the money, counted it. It was enough for the rest of the semester. He took a biro in his breast pocket, took a small piece of paper on the floor and wrote on it. It read:

Mum, Dad, I was here to get some money from you. I could not find anyone at home. The doors including mum's room were opened. So I took the money on the table. I really need it in the school. We shall vacate in a couple of months time. I love you. I hope to call you soonest.

Cheers,
Jim.

He put the note on the table where he has taken the money but it was blown under the bed when he slammed the door in a hurry to go and meet his friend that was waiting in the car.

When Lade returned from the wedding ceremony in the evening, she began to look for the money. She searched everywhere, wondering where the money was. She was sure she put it on the table. She opened her wardrobe and searched everywhere. She went to Janet's room. She was reading a magazine. She asked her if she took it. She told her she did not know where it was. She went to search her room again. Then it occurred to her that Nicholas must have taken the money. Although she somehow noticed some changes in him, since he became acquainted with Janet who never hide it that she was fond of him, but she could not help thinking of his past. To her, he could still be a rogue in the house even though he claimed to be a Christian. Apparently, no one else could have taken the money except him. She was going to ask him to give her the money he took otherwise he would be dead before he knew it.

She rushed out of the room in fury and went to his small room where he was reading the Bible. He looked startled as she stared dangerously at him. 'You, crook,' she muttered. 'Where did you keep my money?'

'Which money?'

'My money!' she roared.

'Which money, ma?'

'You tell me where you keep it if you want to live.'

'I don't know what you're talking about.'

She looked furious. She snorted and looked round for something she could use to deal ruthlessly with him. She saw a very thick cable which he brought workshop on the floor. She grabbed it before going to face him. 'I'm going to beat sense into you now unless you give me my money right now!'

He stood up slowly, looking a little confused. 'Please, don't hurt me. I didn't take any money.'

'You lied!' She roared. 'Who else could have taken it except you?'

'You can ask Janet.'

'I've asked her.' There was silence as he wondered what else to say. 'I'm running out of patience!' she screamed at him. 'Where is my money?'

'God knows I didn't take any money. Please, I beg you in the name of the Lord; don't do this to me…' His innocence was written on his frightened looks but she could not read it. She was really blinded with the notion that he was a rogue.

'Don't try to play the innocent because you are not. Once a rogue, always a rogue.' There was a brief silence as she stared dangerously at him. She roared, 'I'm warning you, Nicholas!' she bellowed. 'Don't make me do what I have in mind to do. If I do it, by the time I'm through dealing with you, no doctor would be able to put you back to shape.'

'I …'

One lash of the cable on the head brought him on his kneels. His head vibrated, making him to give a sharp screen of pain. The second one threw him on the floor with a violent thud. Lade began to beat him so mercilessly that Nicholas who rarely cried began to cry for help.

Janet ran out of her room when she heard his voice. 'Mum!' she screamed. 'Please, stop it! Stop it!' But Lade had gone insane with fury. She rained more lashes at him until blood began to stain his cloth. Janet tried to pull her mother away. Only one stroke threw her backward. With that one stroke of the cable on her body, she knew it at once that she must have terribly wounded him. So she jumped

152

between them and shielded his body with hers. Lade beat the two of them together. Janet screamed, 'kill me too if you have to kill him!'

Lade tried to separate them but Janet clung to him. She struck her back twice. The pain weakened her. She pulled her away. But before she could hit him again, she had held the cable. While struggling it with her, Janet screamed, 'Nicholas, stand up and run!' But Nicholas was too weak to stand. Lade pushed her away. She stumbled backward and hit her head against one of the tables that were close to them. She exaggerated the pain by lying slumped on the floor. That seemed to work on Lade for she completely forgot about Nicholas. She rushed to examine her. To add more to her anxiety, the side of her neck where she had been beaten was bleeding slightly.

As soon as she rushed into the room to get first aid box, Nicholas crawled to where she was lying down. He touched her hand and whispered, 'Janet ....'

Janet opened her eyes and whispered. 'I'm all right. This is the only way I can stop her. So, please, go before she knows I'm alright.'

Nicholas stood up unsteadily and left the house. Few minutes later, Lade returned with first aid box. Even though she had no idea how to revive her, she began to treat her wounds.

It didn't take Nicholas much time before he began to regain his strength. He cleaned himself with the water coming from the public tap and went to lie down on some wood in an uncompleted building and began to pray. He prayed that God should forgive Janet's mother for what she did to him and her daughter. He thought of what to do when he finished prayer. He had not quite made up his mind until he slept. As if God wanted to direct his way through the dream, he dreamt that Sunsomade, his foster mother rushed into a Church asking God to keep and be with him wherever he went. She said, "make him your servant that will go around the world to preach the gospel of the Lord Jesus." The scene in the dream changed to the time he was walking down the street in a city where he met another woman that asked him if he would like to be her child. Because he was desperate to have a family he accepted the offer. The scene changed to another one where he was telling Janet that he was going to Ibadan to find his blessing.

He woke up with a start when he heard Janet crying and calling his name. 'Nicholas… Where are you?'

It was getting to mid night. Everywhere was dead silence. He stood up and went to see her, feeling much better. She was looking round the area, using torchlight to search the place. From the way she was moving around, it was obvious that she was still weak and probably tired.

'Nicholas …' Her voice was unsteady. She turned the beam of the light round.

'I'm here, Janet.'

She quickly turned the light to the direction. She hurried to hug him, crying over his shoulder. 'I'm … so sorry…'

Nicholas burst into emotional sobs. The proof of Janet's love for him was so mind bulging that he could not help crying.

'I've been looking for you,' she sobbed, still hugging him.

'Why?' he asked, trying to control his tears.

She released him slowly, looking at his wounds. She took his arms slowly and began to cry afresh. 'Why did mum do this to my Nicholas?'

'Your mum has to do it to me so that you may prove to me how much you care.'

She looked at him with strange expression. He was smiling. It made both of them feel better. 'You sound queer. You don't have to go through this before you know how much I care.'

'I know you care but I never know how much until now.'

'You mean you don't blame my mother for doing this to you?'

'No,' he whispered, holding her hand.

Suddenly she burst out in tears again. 'I think you're the most wonderful person in the world.'

'No, you're the most wonderful person.'

'It's hard to believe that you're not blaming my mother for this.'

'Janet, we've learnt a lot of things together in the scriptures,' he said gently. 'Besides, remember the story the Pastor told us in the Church about a man who wears black cloth, stealing and committing all sorts of crimes in the town. He removed the black cloth and put on white cloth, committing the same crime. He removed the cloth and put on another one until people see all the cloths he had used to operate. The people began to condemn the cloths. As you know the devil is the thief while human beings are the cloths he uses to operate. I don't blame your mother for what she did because she didn't know what she was doing. She believed I stole her money and she did what she felt was appropriate. So I don't blame anyone for my condition. If you ask me, I'll say that the only things I see in all these are positive things.'

'That's because Jesus had made you into a positive thinker.'

He smiled. 'There are two things I've come to realize now,' he said after a brief silence. He deliberately paused.

'What are they?' she asked.

154

'Are you sure you want to hear it?'

'Of course, I do.'

'You've proved it to your Nicholas that you love him. Tell me that's not true, then I'll call you a liar.'

She was silent.

'Janet, do you love me?'

'I'm your sister, remember.'

'I want something more than that.'

'What do you want?'

'Promise me you'll not turn me down.'

'You know I'll do anything to make you happy,' she replied softly. 'But don't tell me to do what you know I can't do.'

'Would you be my wife?'

'Your wife?' It really surprised her. 'You're not serious, are you?'

'I am, Janet. Only you can make me happy.'

'I still don't believe that you're serious.'

'I am,' he replied, looking more serious. 'If you are going to get married to someone one day, let it be me.'

She looked more puzzled. She said after a while, 'we are far away from marriage. We are still very young.'

'I know,' he said. 'A girl who is so loving and caring like you is rare. Think of what you've gone through with me. I … I can't help thinking of you as my wife in future. Even if I don't have a family, I must have you for life. You are the only one that can make up for what I don't have.'

Her eyes were filled with more tears as she recalled his pains, sorrow and the lost of virtually everything that was supposed to make life meaningful and joyful to him. 'Oh, my Nicholas, you know it's not proper to start a marriage courtship at this age. It can lead to sin. I'm sure you are not asking me to sin against God.'

'I need strength to hang on while struggling with life. You have to give me that strength by saying you'll put me into consideration when you're thinking of the man you'll marry.'

She looked more confused. She sighed and nodded. 'I'll do that but that's going to be years from now.'

'I'll wait,' he said.

'What's the second thing?'

'This is going to be very hard for me to tell you but I have to first tell you that this decision is based on what God revealed to me in a dream.'

'If you're sure is from God, I will bear it.'

He told her about the dream he had a while ago. Then he added, 'I

155

think God wants me to leave this town, going by the meaning of that dream. God has probably prepared another people to be my family. I will go to the city of Ibadan. That's the place I told you in the dream that I was going. I will look for a job and probably sponsor myself in the University. I really desire to be a University graduate. I'm ready to start by resitting for the General Certificate Examination.'

'Y- you really have to go away?' she asked sadly.

'Yes,' he replied in a whisper as if he regretted it.

She was silent, looking very thoughtful. 'Nicholas, you're going to the place you don't know anyone…' She began to cry again.

He held her hand and whispered, 'I know. I have no one to take care of me the way you've been doing.' Her hysterical sobs were moving him emotionally. 'Janet, you don't know how painful it is that I have to leave you. You're the only one I can call my own. You're always there for me all the time.' Tears began to flow from his eyes. 'But at this stage of my life, the only thing you can continue to do for me is to pray. I thank God than you so strong spiritually that I can lean my whole weight on you.'

There was yet another silence. She said quietly, 'you don't know anyone in Ibadan?'

'I know someone who knows everyone,' he said smiling.

'Who?' she asked eagerly.

'Jesus. You introduce me to me. He will see me through. I've come to realize that if he is for me, nobody can be against me.'

She smiled in the midst of her tears. 'You're no longer my son. You've outgrown that. You're now my father. I should have realized it that it was God that was directing you to leave the town the other time you told my father that you were leaving.'

'Actually, I didn't know then that the decision was in line with the will of God until now. You know that if not for that dream, I wouldn't think of leaving. You made me so comfortable here despite what I've had to go through.'

'When are you going?' she asked quietly.

'I'll leave in the morning.'

Her expressions indicated that she was about to weep again. He said, 'there is no need to feel so bad, you know.' He held her hand. 'I'm still coming back here because of you. You know I'll not let you down, don't you?'

She smiled and whispered, 'yes, I know.'

He sighed and said, 'thank God you didn't give me much problem. You're the only one who could stop me.'

'Are you coming to the house, at least to take the few things you need?'

'No. You have to help me do that.'

'Do you have some money with you.'

He shook his head silently. 'I don't have much except the little that was left from what I was given during the funeral of my fostered parents.'

'Where is it?'

'Everything I have is in the bag in my room.'

'My father gave me some amount before he left for Abuja. He wanted me to use it to take care of you and myself in case mummy… I mean it was like he knew this was going to happen. Apart from that, I was saving some money to give you a Christmas present. I'll give you everything. I think that would last you a while. With prayers, I know God would have come to your aid before you exhaust the whole amount.'

'Thank you so much,' he said in whisper.

'I'll bring everything as soon as cock crows…' She could not look at his face again. She turned quickly away from him and began to go when she felt like bursting into sobs again.

'Janet…' His voice shook with both love and emotion.

She stopped without looking at him.

'I love you.'

She nodded and went away, crying all the way home.

He prayed for sometime before went back to lie down. For about two hours, he tried to catch some sleep but he could not. His mind kept wandering from one thing to another. Although he was not very if the dream he had indicated that the future held him and Janet together but he was certain that the love they have for each other was strong enough to result into marriage. Going by what was now taking place in the country, the future seemed bright for hardworking Nigerians. Since the time the country has spent about years practising democratic government, sanity seemed to be returning though many did not care much about values. The havoc the military regime had wrecked on the values of the people was really affecting so many things but his joy was the Lord was always merciful to those who were his. From what he was hearing, corruption had eaten so deep into the entire system that even many people went as far as manipulating in the Church to get money from them. According to what his Pastor once said, there were three types of Churches now. One of them stood by the word and refused to compromise. The other one was a

157

commercial type while Satan or his agents established the third one so as to deceive the people. Often times, people who were looking for miracles instead of the word of God that can get them the miracles were deceived by the other commercial and Satanic Churches. But, according to the Pastor, through their fruits, people could easily identify these types of Churches.

The economic and social problems have prevented many Christians to compromise with their faith, preventing them from shining like stars in the grossly dark world. From all he had been receiving as messages from God, he was going to be a servant of God that would preach the gospel to everybody. He would not be many modern preachers that have powerful messages to preach but lacked the good works that could back them up. He would not like to be a borrowed vessel that would be used by God and then later cast into hell. This reminded him of the message of preacher that was invited from Lagos to his Church a few weeks ago. He had preached from the gospel according to Saint Matthew Chapter seven verses twenty-one to twenty-three which reads, "not every one that saith unto me, Lord, Lord, shall enter into the kingdom of heaven; but he that doeth the will of my Father which is in heaven. Many will say to me in that day, Lord, Lord, have we no prophesied in your name? And in your name have cast demons? And in your name done many wonderful works? And then will I profess unto them, I never knew you: depart from me, you that work iniquity."

'This passage gives me the impression,' the preacher had said, 'that there are certain vessels which do not belong to God but they are used to bless the people through wonderful works. Because the labourers the real ones are relatively few despite the number of so-called men of God we have around. There are so many borrowed vessels across the globe people whose righteousness are nothing to write home about, claiming to be doing the work of God. What they teach may be of benefit to the people who hunger or thirst after God. The people can follow what they teach them from the word of God but they must not follow what they do because, through their conduct, they are heading to destruction. Destruction will not be our portion in Jesus' name....'

Through the messages from God, Nicholas knew he was not only a genuine child of God but also going to be a preacher. It was also evident that Janet was a child of God. So God would take him and Janet to where they would find their blessings sooner or later. He has very strong feelings that his future was very bright. His story could be likened with Joseph in the Bible. Joseph was sold to the land he became a slave by his brothers. He ended up a prisoner who was later promoted to become the prime minister of Egypt. God later used him to save his family from starvation.

If he was right about his future, he wanted to share it with Janet who has done so much in his life. He has no idea how long it would take him to stay away from before he became successful but he would cherish the memory of the roles she had played in his life. She has done a lot that proved that she really loved him. She had stood by him right from the time he was made an outcast, praying and fasting because she to make him a Christian. She was always there to teach him the word of God that helped him grew in faith. She had ministered to his physical, emotional and spiritual needs. She was so confident in what the Lord had made his life to become that she trusted him with everything. Up till that moment, she never ask him if knew anything about the money her mother was looking for because she knew he was a child of God.

After series of thoughts, he knelt down and began to pray again. He prayed that God should forgive Janet's mother and make her realized that he was not the one that took her money. He asked for strength as he would embark on the journey that would take him to the unknown. Then he attempted to sleep again. This time, he slept.

CHAPTER TEN

Lade woke up at around 5 a.m when she heard the sound of the door closing from outside. She stood up and went to check the door. She saw Janet going out of the premises with a big bag, which either belonged to her or her brother. She did not need to investigate before she knew she was taking it to Nicholas. She attempted to run after her but something stopped her. She kept looking at her until she hurried out of sight.

Meanwhile, Nicholas was waiting for Janet after cleaning up. He had no idea what the time said. So he could not say if she was the one getting late or he was the one who was anxious to see her. After what seemed long hours, he saw her coming. The moonlight was bright enough to make everywhere clear.

He rushed to meet her. He embraced her. She broke the embrace after a while and went inside the building to lean against the wall, putting down the bag she was holding. She slipped down slowly, squatting on the floor. Her head was between her kneels.

He was not comfortable with the way she was feeling. He went to sit beside her and gently raised her head up. Her eyes were full of tears. He could see that she must have had sleepless night.

'You don't want me to go, do you?' he asked in a whisper. There was silence. 'I would stay if you want me to stay.'

'I've prayed about it,' she said quietly. 'I could not sleep well because I have to take time to pray. God confirmed to me that it is his will that you should go. You are going to be a Pastor. You truly have a great blessing ahead of you though I don't know how God will bless you. It would be wrong, therefore, to tell you to stay.'

He looked thoughtful for a while before he asked, 'did God tell you anything about our future together.'

She shook her head silently.

'But you do know I need you so much in my life?'

She was silent.

'Do you remember the sermon about Jabez?'

She nodded.

160

'It's about time the Lord does a new thing in the life of Jabez.' He paused before he said, 'Janet, apart from the way you have demonstrated how much you care, you never say you love me.'

'Love is better expressed in action than in words.'

He sighed and looked up thoughtfully. 'I don't know how to say this really but I have to express my fear that you may end up becoming another person's wife. That will devastate me if that happens.'

She looked at him.

He returned the gaze and looked up again. 'I wish you understand why I'm so desperate to keep you for life. When I needed someone to make me a new creature, you gave me Jesus. When I needed a mother, you were there to play that role and that of a sister. When I needed happiness to replace my endless sorrows, you were there for me with the word of God. When I went through so much pain yesterday, you went through it with me. When I needed an answer to my complicated life, you pray that God should explain it to me. You taught me the great value of prayer. What can I do without you? You mean... so much to mean, Janet...' Nicholas burst into hysterical sobs. Janet put her arm across his shoulder. She rested her head on the shoulder and began crying too.

'Life is so harsh on me,' he cried. 'I don't know why. I don't have any parents no family and no one to call my own except you, Janet. Just promise me that you'll be my wife. That's the strength I need to move otherwise I would not have anything to hang on. Please, give me that promise.'

'If ... if I promise you,' she said within her tears, 'and you fall in love with another person, what would happen?'

He looked straight into her eyes. 'If someone tells you I can love another girl the way I love you, would you believe it?'

'Time changes, so do people; Nicholas.'

'You don't seem to understand my feelings for you. One of the reasons I have to go out there and seek for the blessing God has for me is to have something to share together as a family and... you know, we have a ministry together. I'll become a pastor and you'll become Pastor's wife.'

She touched his cheek tenderly. 'I like your vision but we need specific instructions concerning that area of....' She stopped when she saw how disappointed he looked.

'Perhaps you're the one thinking of falling in love with someone else,' he said.

'You know that's not true.'

He looked at her. 'Am I asking for too much by asking you to give me that promise?'

'No,' she said quickly. 'The point is I may not be good enough for you. I don't even know if God means us for each other.'

'If God does not mean us for each other, why do we love each other so much?'

'You're my brother, remember.'

He sprang up on his feet. 'No,' He looked at her sternly. 'You are going to be my wife. Yes or no?'

She was silent, looking confused. 'Nicholas, let's ……'

'Yes or no?'

'If I say yes now and you find someone else, what happens?'

'I've made up my mind. It's either you or no one.'

She looked away. There was a long silence between them. Then she looked at him. 'You're asking me to make a vow that may keep the two of stick together for life or to be in bondage for the rest of our lives. That's the gravity of what you're asking for.'

'I know.'

'Are you sure you know what you're doing?'

'Yes, 'he replied quickly. 'In fact I need it as the strength I required to get the blessing God has for me for both of us. Once I have it at the back of my mind that there's someone else in my life, that feeling will help me to go through more odds to get the blessing God has for me so that at the end of it all, we'll be together.'

'Before I give you that promise,' she said, 'you will have to promise me that you will not let me down by forsaking Christ and by not coming back to see me.'

'You don't need to attach any of those conditions. You know nothing can take Jesus from me and nothing can stop me from coming to see you. If, however, you want me to state them in spoken words, I would. I vow not to forsake Christ and I promise to come and see you as soon as I have the chance.'

'In that case, I promise to be what you want me to be.'

He smiled and held her hands tightly he whispered, 'thank you. I'm ready to face anything now.'

She returned the smile. 'I'm glad it makes you happy.' She took the bag, opened it and showed it to him. 'I got you everything you need, including some of Jimmy's cloths, some canned food and soap for washing. Your bag is too small to contain everything. So I put them in this one.' She took out some money from the side of the bag. Feeling like crying again, she explained, 'the money in your bag was not much.

So, like I told you yesterday, I got you all the money in my possession. I wish I had more than this. The whole money would carry you for a few days. I have no idea how God is going to do it but I know he would not allow you to suffer.' She closed the bag answer gave it to him with the money.

He was moved to tears again but he managed to control his emotion and said quietly, 'thank you, my love. I know I can always lean on you. You can now understand why I cannot do without you.' He looked at the cloths he put on. It was dirty. He took out a native cloth with a cap out of the bag and went to change the dirty cloths. He came back and asked, smiling, 'how do I look?'

She stood up, smiling. She helped him adjusted the cap. 'It's lovely now. You are good looking.'

'Thank you.'

'I need your prayer, Janet,' he said gently. He knelt in front of her. 'I'm going on a journey that will lead to either blessing or suffering, depending how much you pray. Prophesy into my life and say all the things you want God to do for me.'

There was a long silence. She was trying to compose herself. Then she began to pray fervently, 'Lord, you have gone this far with your child. You know him more than he knows himself. You know all he's been through and what he is going to go through. From the way you've trained the people you have blessed both in our generation and in the Bible, you never train people you want to use in palaces of in luxuries. You called Abraham out from among his people and took him to where you blessed him. Jacob who became a great nation that is called Israel today has to leave his family and went to be trained under Laban. Similarly, Joseph had to be sold into slavery before he later became the second in command in the land where was a slave and prisoner. The list is endless until it gets down to our Lord Jesus who was born in a place where animals were born and who died a shameful death just before he could redeem mankind. Here is your child, Nicholas, going on a journey to the place he had never been to, let alone knowing whom he is going to meet. As he said, you know everybody there. Dear Lord, I pray that he will meet with your favour and favour of men wherever he goes in Jesus' name.'

'Amen,' he responded.

'Lord, make Nicholas a blessed child wherever he goes and open heaven so that your blessings would be poured out to him in Jesus' name.'

He responded to the prayer by saying, 'amen.'

It was a long prayer that lasted for about forty minutes. When she finished praying, he stood up. She said, 'I have back home before my mother wakes up.' They got out of the building. She asked, 'what do you want me to tell my father when he comes back? You know he will expect me to know your where about.'

'Please, don't tell him what your mother did to us. It can cause a problem between the two of them. What happened yesterday may not be a pleasant experience but God used it to bring us to another level in our relationship, apart from the fact that he used it to direct me to where our blessing is.'

She smiled at him. 'God has given the gift of wisdom but you are yet to tell me what I should tell my father when he asks of you.'

'You can tell him I believe God wants me to go to Ibadan. So I have to go. I'll be back as soon as I begin to earn a good salary.'

'Alright.'

They went to the commercial car park where he would take a taxi that would take him to Sagamu. From Sagamu, he would board a bus that would take him to the city of Ibadan.

When he entered the taxi, he covered his face with his palms and began to cry silently because he felt he was leaving someone that meant the whole world to him.

Janet hurried home, also crying on the way.

When she got to the house, she realized that her mother was already awake. In fact, she was waiting for her to come and explain where she went.

'I'm sure you went to see that rogue, didn't you?'

Janet was silent. She was too sorrowful to feel intimidated. 'Nicholas is not a rogue. He's a child of God, no matter what you think.'

'Child of God?' Lade snorted. 'I've always known him to be a rogue right from the time he came into this house.'

'He may be tough when he got here,' Janet said. She was feeling so emotional about it that Lade began to sense it that she was probably infatuated. 'He's born-again.'

'You want to claim to be righteous too?' Lade asked maliciously. 'Both of you are children of God children of God that steal. Nicholas stole my money and you stole a bag for him. I suppose he has gone to put up with a friend until he spends all the money he has stolen from me.'

Tears ran down Janet's eyes. She wondered how her mother could be so insensitive of her feelings. 'When dad comes,' she said, 'he's going to hear all about this. Yesterday, you wounded the two of us for

164

the money you misplaced. Today again you continue with the same accusation.'

'Are you threatening me?'

'I'm not,' she said firmly. 'But at least I have to offer dad an explanation why and how Nicholas who has no one to call his family left the house for Ibadan with wounds all over his body.' She ran inside the room, crying.

Lade shouted, 'come here, you bloody idiot!' She hurried after her as she entered her room. She stood by the door. 'You are aiding the rogue that took my money. Do you have any idea of what you are doing?' She paused, smiling maliciously. 'I think get the point now. He's you boyfriend!'

Janet was so dazed by what she said that for a long she did not know what to say.

'He's your boyfriend. Both of you are first class hypocrites, you know. The boy not only steals but also keeps you as his girlfriend. Don't forget to say that to your father when he comes.'

'Nicholas is born-again!' she screamed at her.

'See the way you're talking to me. Is that how you were taught to address your parents in the Church?'

Janet controlled her hurt feelings and said, 'Mum, Nicholas did not take your money.'

'How do you know this?'

'I know him. He's a born-again Christian. He didn't take your money. If he's not born-again, you can't beat him like that yesterday without him hitting you back.'

'Who took it then if he's not the one? You?'

'You could have misplaced it.'

'I'm not a dunderhead like you who trust everybody. I put it on the table or in the wardrobe or something.'

'See, see, mum,' Janet said, 'you're not even sure where you kept the money.'

'I kept it right inside my room! I'm sure of that. There are only three of us left in the room.'

'Perhaps dad took it before he traveled.'

'I saw the money after he's traveled. So give me another!'

Janet stood. 'I'll go and search the whole room if you don't mind.'

'Go ahead.'

She went to Lade's room and began to search everywhere. She searched the wardrobe, the table, the nooks and crannies of the room. After about an hour, she found the note Jim had written on the floor under the bed. She read it eagerly and ran to her mother who has gone to prepare the food in the kitchen. She gave her the note. The stern expression on her face changed when she finished reading it. She went slowly to sit down on one of the chairs in the kitchen. Suddenly, she began to reflect all that happened yesterday. She looked at her and asked in a very quiet voice. 'Where did you find this note?'

'I found it under your bed in your room. It must have fallen down there when Jimmy put it on the table.' There was silence. 'That confirms that Nicholas did not take the money. Do you believe me now?'

Lade was silent for a long time. She knew she was in trouble. If at all Ben spared her for what she had done to the poor boy, she would never be at peace with her conscience until she found Nicholas and asked for his forgiveness. 'Where is Nicholas now?' she asked. Her voice was full of anxiety and concern.

Janet sensed her anxiety. She thought she was probably afraid that if her father discovered what has happened, he would deal ruthlessly with her. 'He's on his way to Ibadan. In fact I expect him to be there by now.'

'Who does he know in Ibadan?' Lade was really troubled.

'He knows no one mummy except God.' Janet felt it was about time she let her mother know that she need a change of attitude. 'We are the only family Nicholas has. He could have left this house long before now but dad and I persuaded him to stay. He trusts us. So he stayed. Dad left for Abuja a few days ago. It was the first time he would leave the three of us at home. Instead of us to continue to make him feel part of this family, you beat so much…' She was crying now. 'Y-you beat him for the offence he had not committed. Supposing he's your child, would you beat him like that even if he's the one that took the money? He did what any normal person is expected to do. He left the place that was so full of hatred.'

For the first time in her life, Janet saw tears flowing from her mother's eyes. Even though she did not make a sound, Lade was crying within. 'Do you know which area he would be in Ibadan?' she asked after a while. Her voice was full of emotion.

'You want to go and look for him?'

'I have to… look for him…' Her weeping was becoming audible.

'He does not have any idea of the place he's going. So I don't know.'

'Y-you mean… we won't see… him again?' Lade stammered with

grief.

'He's not coming back until he's able to find a good job.'

Janet could sense it that she was broken down through the remorse that was written all over her face.

Lade held her daughter slowly and sighed. 'I'm sorry, Janet. I can't explain how terribly bad I feel.'

'It's okay, mum. There is only one person you need to say you're sorry to. It is Jesus.'

She nodded. 'How about Nicholas? I need to say that to him too. I don't think I'll be happy until I see him.'

'He knew you're going to find out the truth about the money. So he told me not to let dad know what happened. You know how much dad loves him. I have no doubt he has forgiven you.'

'Even if everyone forgives me, I don't know how I can possibly forgive myself until I do something anything to make him very happy.'

Janet thought of the promise she had made to Nicholas. 'I'm sure you're going to see him again. When you see him, he can tell you how you can make him very happy. For now, let's believe God used what has happened to direct his ways.'

Lade sighed and stood up to continue with the work she was doing even though she knew she would not be happy until she had seen Nicholas.

* * * *

Nicholas reflected what happened at Ikenne as he journeyed to Ibadan where he knew no one. He was never bordered about what he would come across in the place because he seemed so confident that God has something good for him. He had made up his mind never to give up or go back to Ikenne until he had gotten the breakthrough he needed. So all his thoughts were on Janet and his future with her. He knew that nothing could have made her vowed to marry him if not for what he had been through. With the promise she had made to him, he would give all he could to secure a bright future for the two of them. Then he would have a good story to tell their children.

His thoughts drifted to Janet's mother. He wondered where she kept the money that caused him and Janet so much pain. Actually, just as he had confessed to Janet, he was glad the incident occurred. It took his relationship with Janet to another level. What actually bordered him was the way her father who never cared to hide it from everyone that he loved him would react when he returned from Abuja. He recalled the first time he attempted to leave the house. He had persuaded him to stay and he was not even bordered to refer Janet as his girlfriend because he probably sensed it that they were in love. If not for his love and trust, he would probably be out of the house long before now. But then, it seemed God had to take him from that place to another by force for the purpose that was not quite clear to him.

The bus got to Ibadan at about 9 a.m. The journey between Sagamu and Ibadan was not as long as he expected. It was about an hour's journey.

He got down from the bus at a place called Challenge. Not knowing where to go and what to do, he began to walk round area; holding his bag.

He came across a big super market with a notice board that indicated that a sales girl was required. He decided to try getting the job, at least, for the purpose of getting something to start with.

The place was very big the biggest store he had ever seen in his life. A lady of about twenty-five years old was sitting behind one table. He went to her. 'Good morning, ma.'

The lady who was writing on a register looked at him. She smiled and said, 'good morning.'

He pointed towards the direction of the notice board and said, 'I …em … I saw a notice board ….. I need the job, ma.'

'Oh, I see,' the lady said. 'We need a salesgirl, not boy.'

'I can do the job if you can give a chance.'

The lady looked uncertain. 'I'm not sure if the manager will like to hire a boy.'

'You can persuade him,' he said quickly and hopefully. 'Please….'

'Where do you live.'

'I'm from Ikenne in Ogun State. I just come to the town.'

'Even if you're to be given the job, you'll need someone to be your referee.'

'I see,' he said. 'I didn't know that. I thought God would make everything so easy for me.'

For no apparent reason, the lady looked interested in him. 'What do you mean?'

'God actually told me to come to this city. I don't know anyone except Jesus. I expected to see someone who knows Jesus to help me.'

The lady looked thoughtful for a while before she gestured him to sit in front of her. 'I'm a Christian too,' she said.

168

'Really.' He looked excited.

She smiled, nodding. 'I'll see what I can do to get you the job,' she said. 'The problem is where you'll stay.'

'I can stay anywhere for the time being,' he said quickly. 'I can sleep at the filling station. I'm a village boy.'

'I can see that.' She laughed. 'But I'm not going to let you sleep in a place like that. But first, let me see what I can do to get you the job.' She stood up to go the manager's office.

'By the way, what's your name,' she asked before she left. Nicholas told her.

Nicholas waited for a long time before she came out.

'The manager would like to interview you now,' she told him. 'If he asks of our relationship, just tell him I'm your sister in Christ. Really, that's what I am.'

'All right, ma,' he replied. He dropped his bag before he followed her into the office. The office was not big but it was well furnished. Sitting behind an executive table that was clustered with papers and some items was a fat friendly looking man. He was dressed in a shirt that seemed a little too tight for him. His face brightened with smiles when he saw Nicholas.

Nicholas bowed, 'good morning, sir.'

'Good morning.' The manager has a deep voice. 'How are you?'

'I'm fine, thank you, sir.'

'Which school did you attend?'

'Ikenne community high school, sir.'

'Can I see your credentials?'

He pointed towards the door. 'They are in my bag, sir. Can … can I get them.'

'You'll give them to Lara later,' the manager said, nodding at the lady. 'You can write the letter of applications as a sales boy, attach the photocopies of your credentials and give it to her. You can start the job immediately.'

Nicholas prostrated on the floor. 'Thank you, sir.' He looked at the lady, 'thank you, Sister Lara.'

'You are such a lucky boy,' the manager said. 'If the girl that worked here had not been absent through out last week, you wouldn't be working here.'

'Thank you very much, sir,' Nicholas repeated.

When they got outside the office, Lara said, 'I'm sure this is the hand of God and that proves that you're truly a child of God. If not, like the manager said, you wouldn't be working here.'

'I really have to thank God more even for using you. You know, only God could move you to help a total stranger.'

She sat down. She gestured him to sit. 'Let me have your credentials.' As he brought them out, she got him a sheet of paper and a biro. He gave her the documents. She examined them. 'You have a fairly good G.C.E result.'

'That was the best I could get then.'

'I see.' She gave him the paper and the biro. 'You can write the application. When we sort things out here, we I can think of where you'll be staying.'

'Thank you, ma,' he said, writing the letter.

CHAPTER ELEVEN

Ben was in a very good mood as he parked the car in front of the house. He was just returning from Abuja after spend about two weeks in the place. He was really happy because he was just won a contract that would earn him a lot of money in one of the local governments in the area. It seemed that democracy was yielding its dividend at last after a long time of suffering under the military. Most of his colleagues in the place were urging him to come to the federal territory to continue his civil engineering job but he would rather stay in Ikenne, which was peaceful, and be getting contract in the place than to go to any place that was full of struggle. He did not see the use of making money at the expense of the peace he had been enjoying since he came to Ikenne.

He checked his time as he got out of the car. It was getting to 7 P.M. It has taken him almost ten hours driving home from the north. Now he could sleep for days if he liked.

Lade who had been feeling sorrowful since the day Nicholas had gone came to open the door. She welcomed him as heartily as her guilty feelings could permit her.

'Where's Janet?'

'She's gone to Church.'

'I suppose she went with Nicholas,' Ben said, getting his things out of the car.

Lade did not reply. She silently helped him took the bags and other things he had brought into the house.

'Please, get me something to eat. I'm starving,' he said, going into his room to clean up. When he came out some minutes later, he was a little refreshed. Lade had made the table. So he went straight to take his meal.

Lade waited for him to finish eating before she told him she had a confession to make.

'Confession?' Ben asked, a little surprised. He went to sit on the couch in the sitting room, wondering what she wanted to confess. 'I'm all ears,' he said after a brief silence.

Lade sat beside him and said, 'last week Jimmy came home when

171

no one was around. He found the doors open. I went for the wedding of Dotun's daughter. I left Janet and Nicholas at home. I don't know where they were when Jimmy came from school and entered the house. He went to take the money I forgot on the table and wrote a note that he had to take the money since he couldn't find anyone at home. I did not see the note when I returned. So I started looking for the money. When I couldn't find it, I thought Nicholas took it. I beat him so much that he left the house.' She became silent, trying to study his reaction.

He was expressionless. 'Where did he go?' he asked

'He left for Ibadan.'

'Ibadan?'

She nodded.

'How do you know?'

'He told Janet.'

'Who is he going to meet there?'

'I don't know.'

Ben looked sternly at her. 'You've always hated this boy. I don't know why. When he lost those whom he thought were his family, you didn't show much concern about him. You've always seen him as bad boy even when it was apparent that Janet has influenced him to become a Christian. Let's even say he stole your money, you should have considered the fact that we are his only family. You never consider his position.' He sprang up all of a sudden. 'You pushed him out there where he knows no one with nothing with him.'

The memory of the way she beat Nicholas with Janet flashed to Lade again and again. Suddenly, she burst out crying.

Ben was stunned. It was unbelievable. Lade whom he knew as an iron lady was crying for the boy she cared less about. Something must be happening to his wife, he thought.

She stood up, drying her eyes. 'I'll go and look for him at Ibadan tomorrow.'

'Do you know where he is in Ibadan?'

She shook her head. 'It's better than doing nothing.'

'There's no point trying to make things more serious,' Ben said. 'The boy will find his way here. If he doesn't come for you or me, he will come for Janet.'

'How are you so sure?'

'The kids are in love,' he declared. 'I'm sure they won't realize it until they are older.'

'Y-you mean… they…'

'Yes, they may end up getting married. I've seen it happening to people over the time.'

Lade was strangely comforted. However, she asked, 'don't you think they are too young… to…'

'I can assure you that they don't know this. Even if they do, they know better than doing anything funny. They are real Christians. They know how to pray to God for directions in everything they do.' He stood up to go to his room. 'Don't bother yourself about anything,' he said, yawning. 'Things will sort themselves out or should I say God will sort things out.'

By the time Janet returned from the Church, Ben has gone to bed. He was so tired that he had to sleep early. He did not bother himself much about Nicholas because he was certain that he would come back. He observed it shortly after he and Janet started going to the Church together that both of them were very fond of each other. They were always happy to be together. He knew they would make ideal couple. In fact he wished the love between them existed between him and his wife. Since he knew that the bedrock of every successful marriage was love with trust, he did not even discourage their relationship as it grew deeper.

Janet met her mother in the sitting room, looking moody. 'Mum,' she said, going to sit beside her. She put her Bible on the table. 'Is dad back? I saw his car outside.'

'Yes, he's back,' Lade said quietly.

'You told him what happened?'

'Yes.'

'Why? I told you Nicholas does not want him to know.'

'He did not react the way I expected him to react.'

'How did he react?'

'He took it calmly.'

'Then why do you look so sober?'

'Actually, I was thinking about you and Nicholas,' Lade said, turning to look at her. 'There is something between you and Nicholas, isn't it?'

'Why do you say that?'

'What happened the day he left the house proved it. Besides, your father observed it too.'

'What is it he observed?'

'Both of you are in love,' she looked at her eagerly. 'Is he right?'

Janet was silent for a long time. 'Mum, I like Nicholas.'

'You like or you love him?'

173

'What difference does it make?'

'One of the words is stronger than the other.'

'We are teenagers, you know.'

'It doesn't matter,' Lade said. 'You tell me how you feel about him.'

'I think he's someone I can marry.'

'Does he feel the same for you?'

'Yes.'

'Well then, you father is right to think he will come back for you.'

'I told you he would come back.'

'I just need assurance. Now that I got it, I can sleep with comfort.'

Janet put her arm round her shoulder. 'Can I assume that you approve of him as someone I can marry if I want to?'

'If you love him that much, why not.'

'Thank you, mum. I love you.'

'You're a very great child,' Lade said, smiling at her. 'And I love you too.'

* * * *

Linda drove her mother round the busy area of challenge in Ibadan, looking for where to shop.

Linda had come from America to visit her parents, Leke and Christie Temi who had been in the country running aviation, importing and exporting businesses for the past five years. Except on few occasions when Leke had to travel to Europe and America to hold meetings with the executives of his companies, the couple spent most of their time together; enjoying their early retirements and leaving all their children who have set up their families in America.

Leke had made so much money in America before coming home that he and every member of his family did not need to work again for the rest of their lives. Apart from the chain of businesses that brought millions of dollars into his account every month, the shares he had bought for his family in many companies were yielding so much that he did not know what else to else to do. He had been considered one pf the richest man in the country, making two strongest political parties to covet for his membership. He had even been given the chance to run for vice presidency but he told them point blank that he was not in the country to get involved in politics but to enjoy the result of his years of labour in America. To him, getting involved in politics was like sticking his neck into what could stain his reputation as a descent businessman and investor. Besides that, the political environment in Nigeria still has the reflection of the military rule. The people were not really practising true democracy. The elections of the present leaders which he had witnessed so far were not really elections but selections of people he considered rogues in the political class. Many of them were people were once military officers. It seemed the same set of people that rule during the military government were the ones in corridor of powers or dictating how the country should be administered. Consequently, so many promising Nigerians have fallen victims of assassination attributed to violent political rivals. Besides what he had experienced since he had come to the country, his brother, Tomi, who occupied the position of the leader of his family would not allow him to get involved in the politics in Nigeria. Although he had had cause to argue with him that if descent people shy away from politics, indecent people would be the ones that would rule but his brother believed that certain people must be eliminated before there could be sanity in the political system. As he always argued, Nigerians could not successfully elect their leaders. Few greedy people who have no vision for the country always selected their leaders. No one ever had argument with his brother about the country and win. He seemed to know so much about the country - much more than an average. Unlike Leke who had lived the most productive part of his life in America, Tomi had never stepped out of the country. He was well informed about the country, making Leke to trust his judgment on many things.

'Let's go to the shop over there,' Christie said, pointing at the big super market.

Linda drove the Toyota jeep which was one of the smallest of the cars she could find in her father's compound to the front of the super market. 'We should be able to get all need here,' she said as she put off the car engine.

'Don't count on it,' Christie replied. 'It's hard to find all we have in a single shop in Nigeria.'

'What?' Linda was a little surprise.

'Believe me.' They got down. Even though they were casually dressed, they still appeared very wealthy.

As soon as they entered the super market, Linda's attention was attracted to the teenager that was attending to the customers. He looked so much like Charles, her cousin's husband in America that she wondered if they were related. She looked at her mother who was already busy looking for the items they have come to buy. She went to tap her on the shoulder. 'Look at the boy over there.'

Christie turned round. 'Where?'

Linda nodded at his direction.

'Oh … what about him? … Wait a minute… Is he Charles' relation or something? They look so alike - carbon copy!'

'That's what I think.'

'We'll ask him a few question when finish shopping,' Christie said and continued getting the items. Linda stared at the boy, wondering how he came about the same features like Charles. It may be by mere coincidence that they came about the same features, she told herself. But deep inside her, she felt they must be related. Having the same big bright eyes, sharp lips, flat nose, and bushy eyebrow with coil hair was too much for coincidence. The features really made her wonder how they could be related.

As she waited for her mother to finish picking all the items she needed in the shop, she continued trying to link the boy to Charles. She didn't think Charles has any close relation that shared all these features with him in Nigeria. All his brothers and sisters were in America. He has no child that was as old as the boy except … wait a minute! She felt a bang in her heart. Mary had a child that got missing some years ago. The child was never fond. So it was assumed that he was dead. Could he be the child? That was the only way she could link Charles with the sales boy.

Unable to wait for her mother anymore, she went to the sales boy and said, 'hello, there.'

'You're welcome, ma,' the sales boy said. 'Can I help you, ma?'

'Yes,' Linda said, 'I just want to ask you a question. You look like the husband of my cousin in America. Do you have relation in America?'

'Oh, no, ma,' he replied. Her ascent sounded foreign. This was not strange as they often have foreign customers in the shop.

'What's your name?'

'Nicholas,' the sales boy replied. 'Nicholas Folusho.' Even then, Nicholas knew that might not be his real names, as he did not know his family.

'You don't know anyone called Olumbe?'

He shook his head.

'What about Temi?'

Again he shook his head.

Linda looked thoughtful. She was almost sure there must be a link between him and Charles. The resemblance was quite noticeable.

She was still thinking of how to link them when Christie came to join

176

them with the items she had selected.

'I can see that you've started interrogating him,' Christie said.

'Yeah, but I can find the link mum,' Linda said. 'I was even thinking he was probably he child that was stolen from uncle some years ago.'

Christie's eyes brightened up. 'You could be right!'

'I still can't link him.'

Nicholas who was silent all the while, thinking of what was going on raised an eyebrow when Linda expressed his thoughts.

'Young man,' Linda said, seeing the surprises on his face, 'do you know your parents?'

'Actually, I ... em ...... I don't have parents,' he said slowly.

'The couple that adopted me are dead. They died in a car accident.'

'You must be... em... seventeen or sixteen years, am I right?' Linda asked.

Nicholas nodded thoughtfully.

'Do you have any idea how old you were when you were adopted?'

'From what I was told, I was two years old,' Nicholas replied, looking confused.

'Yes!' Linda shouted. 'You must be Mary's child! You were stolen from you grand parents at the age of two.'

'Yes can't be so sure,' Christie said.

'I'm sure!' Linda was excited. 'I can still recall how Mary reacted when the news about missing child was broken to her.'

'Let's do it this way,' Christie said, putting the items on the table for the cashier to see before she gave her the bill. 'We'll take him to Mary's parents to identify him.'

'Okay,' Linda said quickly. 'With the information we got from him and the features of Charles written all over his face, I'm very sure he's the missing child.'

Christie looked at Nicholas and asked, 'Can we take you to the people we think may be your grand parents. If what we think is right, your real parents are in America.' She paused, looking at Nicholas who was both puzzled and uncertain.

'Listen, child,' Linda said. 'We are your real family. Your mother is my cousin. We just want your mother's parents who look after you when you were a child to confine that you're their grand child. We'll bring you back if they you are not.'

'Let me get permission from my boss,' Nicholas said and hurried to Lara who was at her desk as usual, keeping records of items that were bought.

Lara had been playing the role of his sister for the past six months, ensuring that he was comfortable in the city. Even though she didn't know much about him except the place and the people he had lived with, she could not help putting so much trust in him. He had proved to be not just trustworthy but also a very fervent Christian.

'Sister Lara,' Nicholas went to tell her. She looked at him. 'I have to go somewhere now.'

'Where one you going?'

'I'll explain later.'

'How long would it take you to be back?'

'I don't know.'

'Nicholas ...'

'Please, Sister Lara.'

'Okay,' she said. 'But don't take so long.'

'I won't,' he said quickly. 'Thank you.' He hurried to Linda and Christie who were waiting for him at the entrance. 'I've been granted the permission.'

'Let's go right away,' Christie said. They went to the car. When Nicholas saw the car, he began to wonder if the blessing God has promised him in the dream would come through the people. Even though it seemed as if he was acting on impulse, he could not help feeling that the people may turn out to be the family he had been craving for since he discovered that he was not related to Kujor family at Ikenne in anyway.

Linda got behind the wheel while Christie sat beside her. Nicholas sat behind them. 'We'll go to my uncle now,' Linda said, kicking the car and driving away. 'Nicholas.' She looked at him through the rear mirror.

He was very passive. 'Yes, ma.'

'If I'm right in what I'm thinking, nobody will allow you to go back to that place.'

'Why, ma?'

'You're asking why. It's because you're simply a lost child that is now found.'

'The people would be offended.'

'What I mean is that you'll come back to tell them you're not coming back.'

'I see.'

'Tell us about your past. The one you're been told or the one you can remember - everything - anything,' Linda said. 'Do you think you may be our child I mean family?'

'I .... think it is possible, ma,' he said. 'That's the reason I'm not reluctant to follow you.'

'We can see that,' Christie said. 'What is it you were told about yourself?'

'Mrs Kujor who actually found me in the street in a town called Ilishan was the one that adopted me as her nephew. She and her husband told the people in the town that I'm her brother's son in Ghana. I didn't know that I was not related to her until she was about to die in the hospital after a car accident. It was as if she knew I'm going to need the information. If not for that, I won't believe that she is not my real family. If I believe she is my real family, I won't consider the possibility that we may be truly related.'

Christie looked back at her. 'How old were you when you were found in the street?'

'I think she said I was two or three years old. I'm not sure.'

'Can you remember the year?'

'There's no way I can know that. I was so frantic at the thought that Mrs Kujor was going to die that I could not ask her all the questions I needed to ask.'

'It's okay, sweetheart,' Linda said softly, trying to comfort him from the pain of the past. 'Everything is going to be fine. I'm sure of that. We just need your grand father to confirm that you're the child we were looking for about fifteen years ago although, going by what we have right now, I have no doubt that you're the child.' There was a brief silence as she recalled all the things Mary had gone through in Nigeria when her parents were told of the pregnancy. She told her all the mental tortures her father had subjected her into until she was rescued by her mother. She became so fond of the child that she was constantly calling her parents to find out how he was doing. She remembered how she felt when she told the child fell on a pressing iron that caused a permanent scar on his body… Wait a minute, the scars must still on the boy's body if it was that indelible.

She looked at him again through the rear mirror. 'The year before you got lost, your mother told me you fell on a hot pressing iron which burnt one side of your one of your legs and ankles.'

'Yes!' Christie said. 'I remember the incident. I even saw the pictures in America them.'

Nicholas stiffened with awe. Of course, he had always seen the scars on his ankle and leg. He did not know how it came about.

Seeing the expression on his face, Christie quickly said, 'can see your ankles.

He showed her. The scar was still there quite alright.

179

'Oh, my God!' Christie screamed.

Linda quickly pulled the car by the side of the road and stopped the engine. 'It's there?'

'Let's see your legs,' Linda said, getting down from the car. She opened the door of the side Nicholas was sitting and pulled his leg. The scar was on the left leg. 'I knew it! I knew it! I knew he's Mary's son!'

Christie was a bit sceptical at the initial stage became stunned.

Linda jumped back into the car. 'I'm taking you straight to your grand parents.' She kicked the car and drove away.

'They are not going to believe this,' Christie said as if she was talking to herself.

There was silence through out till they entered a very big compound. Everybody was trying to recover from what appeared like a surprise.

Tomi and Ayanfe who moved from their old house in one of the busy arrears in Ibadan to the big house which Mary bought for them in a quieter environment now lived in luxuries. They could afford to live like first class citizens in the country because their only daughter and her husband were in every standard multi millionaires. The engineering company which they jointly owned in America had grown big enough to make them very rich. Apart from constructing houses for people, they owned, bought and sold houses in America. Leke really influenced and helped the couple to increase immensely their asset base through his counsel and supports. Since the couple were already blessed with three beautiful girls, everybody except Ayanfe seemed to have forgotten that they ever had a child called Tokunbo. Ayanfe who had become a devoted Christian since the child got lost constantly told her husband that she had the nagging feelings that Tokunbo was not dead. She believed that she would still come across him. Even after well over fifteen years, the feelings persisted. She once told her husband about the feelings but he had told her to forget about the past. 'I know you won't understand the feelings. I know this is from God. I even dreamt it that he was walking down the street one day.'

'You should have picked him up in the dream,' Tomi had said in irritation. 'Look, woman, forget about this child. If he's going to be found, we would have found him since. You keep dreaming of the child because you'll not let him go in your mind…'

When Linda drove the jeep into Tomi's compound, she jumped out of the car and asked Nicholas to get down. Christie followed them from back, still dazed with the stunning discovery. Linda was so excited that she held Nicholas, pulling him as she strode inside the house. She pressed the door bell. The housemaid opened the door. 'Is my uncle inside?'

'Yes ma,' the lady replied.'

'And aunty?'

'They are both in the sitting room.'

Linda burst into sitting room and startled the couple. Tomi was reading a magazine while Ayanfe was reading the Bible. She smiled at them and asked, pointing at Nicholas who was walking behind her, 'guess who this boy is.'

Tomi removed his glasses and studied Nicholas. 'Is he related to Charles. They look so alike.'

'That's your grand son, uncle!'

Ayanfe jumped on her feet, 'Tokunbo?'

'That's right?'

Tomi stood up. Just then, Christie came in. 'Are you sure there's no mixed up here somewhere?' he asked.

'I thought that until I saw the proof myself,' Christie said.

'What's the proof?' Tomi asked.

'You remember the time he fell over a pressing iron and burnt himself on the leg and ankle?'

'Yes, yes!' the couple said at the same time.

Linda looked at Nicholas and said, 'show them the ankle and the leg.'

Nicholas showed them the scar on his ankle before he rolled up the left side of his trousers and showed them the other scar.

Ayanfe gawped at him and screamed, 'thank you Jesus! I knew you will not let me down!'

Tomi was too surprised to say anything. He shook his head in awe and sat down heavily on the chair as if he was in stupor.

Linda went to hold him, 'uncle, don't you think I deserve an award for this.'

'It's unbelievable,' Tomi muttered, trying to recover quickly. 'Where did you find him?'

'He was working as a sales boy in one super market.'

'Sales boy?'

'Yes,' she said. 'I told him he's not going back there.'

'Please, sir,' Nicholas said quietly, 'I'll like to go and ....'

'You're going nowhere!' Ayanfe cried, going to grip him on the wrist. 'You don't know what we've been through for years. I was the only one who believed that you'll be found because Jesus never failed me since I've been serving him.'

'I'm a born-again Christian too, ma,' Nicholas said quietly. 'Jesus told me to come to Ibadan…'

'Where were you all these years?'

'I was in Ikenne.'

'What?' Tomi looked more surprised. 'You lived in Ikenne?'

'Yes, sir.'

'Your grand father is from Shagamu, the town close to Ikenne,' Ayanfe said. 'We'll talk about this later but if you have to go anywhere, I'll follow you.'

'Please …' Nicholas pleaded.

'I'll take him there,' Linda said, 'and I'll bring him back.'

'Wait,' Ayanfe said, going to the room. 'I'll go with you.'

* * * *

Janet was sitting at the back of the house where she and Nicholas were fond of sitting, reading the Bible. She was full of thoughts as she glanced at the Bible without actually seeing the words. All her thoughts had been on Nicholas for the past few months, wondering what was happening to him. By now, he was supposed to have come to visit her at Ikenne. It was now getting to a year since he left home and she hoped he was not facing hardship. He has been through enough at Ikenne without having to go through any rigour again. Even if he could not get the blessings he expected from God on time, he was supposed to come home; at least to let everyone knew he was alright. Her mother had worried so much about him. She had to relieve her of her worries by assuring her that he was doing fine. Now that everybody, including Jimmy who was told of what happened, seemed to be getting over their feelings; she was recalling what happened over and over again. At times, she would laugh but in most cases she cried. She knew Nicholas has formed part of her life. His absence has caused a great vacuum in her life. She wondered if he felt so much about her. Well, she thought, she could not say if he was worried now but at least she knew he loved him once very much. How such great love could result into neglect was a great concern to her. She knew Nicholas could not just neglect her just like that without a good reason. Besides, both of them were not only bound by the vows they have exchanged but also by their feelings for each other.

As if God was trying to give her a hint of what to expect, an elderly

182

couple came into the town on Sunday; looking for her family and that of Kujor. After meeting with the surviving children of the Nicholas' fostered parents, they came looking for her family.

Lade was busy in the kitchen with Janet that day while Ben was in the sitting room, watching the television. He was not actually interested in the program but waiting for food to be ready.

The door bell rang and Ben went to open the door. The couple stood by the door, smiling at him as they greeted. 'Good afternoon.

Ben looked at then. He said, 'good afternoon, sir ma.'

'My name Tomi Temi,' the elderly man said. He gestured to Ayanfe. 'This is my wife. I believe you're Mr Ben Janosi.'

'That's right, sir.'

'You have a daughter called Janet?' Ayanfe asked.

'Yes, ma.'

'You know the young man called Nicholas?'

'Nicholas!' Ben looked so excited that he quickly held Tomi. 'Y-you know where he is?'

'Yes, of course.'

'Please, come in.' As couple entered the sitting room, he said, 'we're been worried sick to know where is he?'

'He's in United States,' Tomi said.

'What?' Ben looked. 'Is that a joke, sir?' He gestured them to sit on a couch.

'It's not a joke at all,' Tomi said, laughing with his wife. 'It's a long story,' Tomi said, 'but we are here to tell you the story.'

Ben went to called Janet and Lade in the kitchen. 'There's a message from Nicholas.'

The two rushed out of the kitchen to the sitting room. They looked so anxious to here the message that the couple knew at was that they love their grand son in the family.

Tomi and Ayanfe smiled at them. 'You're Janet, I believe,' Tomi asked, looking at her.

'Yes, sir,' she replied quickly and politely.

He took an envelop from his pocket. 'This is a letter for you from him. You don't need us to keep in touch with him. All you need to contact him is there.'

She wanted to hurry into her room and open it.

'You're supposed to hear our story before you read that letter,' Ayanfe said. She could sense her eagerness in her.

The three members of the family sat down to hear the couple.

Tomi gestured at Ayanfe to tell them the story.

Ayanfe began, 'about twenty years ago, our only daughter called Mary went to study in America. She wouldn't spend up to two years there before she become pregnant. She has to come to Nigeria to deliver the baby. He was the boy you called Nicholas.'

The listeners exchanged glances. They all looked stunned.

'Mary went back to America to continue her studies while we my husband and I took care of the child. The child was very playful. So there was a time he fell over a pressing iron and got permanent scar on his leg and ankle. The scars were to form part of what proved that he is our grand son.

'He was at day care centre when he was stolen with other children. I remember the day that I ran into the church and prayed that God should protect the child and bring him back to us. Anyway, we never saw him again. God made sure that he was in the save hands of Mrs Kujor and your family. He told us so much about the families, particularly you, Janet. He told us how he gave you problems until he became born-again.'

'How did you come across him again?' Ben asked eagerly.

'Well,' Tomi said, 'I must say here that God still performs miracles. My wife used to tell me that she dreamt that we found the boy. I never believe we could until my niece who came for a visit from America went to shop with her mother at a super market. She saw a sales boy at the supermarket. The moment she saw him, she knew he must be related to my son-in-law who happens to be his father. They are so alike that you don't need anyone to tell you that they must be related. She questioned him. You know, one thing lead to another until they brought him to us. We later confirmed that he is our grand child. The moment her parents got to know that he's been found, they told my niece to bring him to America immediately. That's why he could not come to see everyone. He made me promised that I would see you and tell you the story. You know irony of it is that I'm from Shagamu even though the child was stolen from Ibadan. This God we serve is great.'

It took the listeners a long time to recover from the loads of surprises which the couple had brought.

After a long silence, Janet asked, 'when is he coming back to Nigeria?'

'I knew you will ask that,' Tomi said. 'He's started school now at Arizona State University. He's going to be an engineer like his father and also a pastor.'

'Great!' Janet said. 'I know he'll be a pastor.'

184

'He may come to see you after the end of the first semester.'

'I don't know if he said that in the letter,' Ayanfe said. 'But he wants me to remind you at your promise. He said you'll understand if we tell you that.'

'Yeah,' she said, nodding.

Lade stood up suddenly. 'I forgot what I'm cooking in the kitchen. Please, give me a second to check it.' She went to the kitchen. Janet followed her.

'From what Tokunbo I mean Nicholas told us about Janet,' Tomi told Ben, 'you have a very wonderful daughter.'

'Thank, you, sir,' he replied. 'Tokunbo is Nicholas' real name?'

'Yes,' Tomi said. 'We forget to tell you that. He's Tokunbo Olumbe.'

Ayanfe leaned across her husband and whispered something into his ears. He nodded before he looked at Ben, cleared his throat before he said, 'we've seen the children of the Kujor family to reciprocate the things their parents have done to our grand child. We are thinking of doing the same thing to you.'

'Oh,' Ben said quickly, 'that won't be necessary. What is important to us is that the young man is fine.'

Janet later came with a tray of drinks and placed it in front of them.

'We hope you'll take that with love,' Ben said.

'Alright thanks.'

Janet went back to the kitchen.

'I don't know how to say this,' Tomi said. 'But I cannot help telling you that your daughter meant a lot to our grand son.'

'I know,' Ben said. 'We knew he would come for her one day. That was what prevented us from declaring wanted.'

The couple laughed. Tomi said, 'If you refuse what we want to do, he will come here and do it.'

'Let him come and do it himself,' Ben said. 'That'll afford me the opportunity to see his stubborn face once again.'

The couple laughed and began to take their drinks, chatting endlessly about all the things Nicholas has done to prove that he was a tough boy.

CHAPTER TWELVE

Janet's eyes were full of tears as she lay on the bed in her room, reading Nicholas' letter the third time. There was a hundred dollar note enclosed with the letter in the envelop. The more she read the letter the more her heart was tied with his. The letter read:

Dear Janet,

I am sure this letter will come to you as a pleasant surprise. Up till now I'm yet comprehend the mysterious ways of God. God had worked things out in my life. Remember I said my life was full of complications. I can now understand my life because I have found my true identity. I did not look for it. God found it for for me. I now know who I am. My real name is Tokunbo Olumbe. My father is from Ondo State but he is based in United States. Where my mother came from is quite a surprise to me. She is from Shagamu, the neighbouring town of Ikenne where I lived most of my life! My grand father is from Temi family in Shagamu. He is a very wonderful man full of wisdom but he marveled at the wisdom of God which I got through you. I told him so much about you and everyone God have used to help me. He promised to see everyone of you. If you are reading this letter, that means he had seen you. I do hope all is well.

I would have come down to you but no one wants me out of the house. It was as if they were afraid I would get missing again. Even if I have to go to the town, my grand mother and her driver would take me there.

I am down here with my parents in United States. I am now in Arizona State University. I really can't list all the blessings I have been receiving from God through my family. But there's nothing I can compare our love with. When I remember all we've been through together, I could not help crying. When I was faced with a lot of things, you were there for me. Your life did more of the preaching of the word of God. Nobody could have influenced me to be a born- again Christian except someone like you who is truly a child of God. When I was all alone in this world, you stood by me. You shared my pains and sorrow. Remember when I have to sleep in that uncompleted building,

186

you came; looking for me. Janet, I'm crying now but I want to assure you that there is no more tears to shed. Jesus has removed all our sorrow. It is now time to rejoice because we have hope. Our future is bright. I can see it from here. We've got joy in the Lord which is our strength. You gave me strength to hang on until I got what God planned for me and you. We are going to share our lives together. I'm going to be a Pastor and engineer and you are going to be the Pastor's wife. We need each other to become what God ordained us to become in life. So whatever I've become, I own it to you, my love and my joy. One of the things that gives greatest joy in my new life is the thought that someone like you is going to be my wife. I'm not sure if anyone else know about our intention but I know your father seems to notice our love for each other. Please, let him know that I really need you in my life. If he doesn't give you to me, he should consider me a dead man. You're my heart. Without you, I can't breath. You're that one that gave me the definition of life when life has no meaning. You gave me reason to live when I felt like dying. You gave me hope when I lost all hope. You gave me joy when I needed it desperately. You accepted me the way I was when I was an outcast because I was so unruly. You made it happened with your prayer. You're the one that prayed for me to be changed. It was your prayer that brought me this far. We are going to tell the story to the world how we overcome together. I really need you to set a godly family and to build a ministry. I'm sure you're not going to walk out of me now and go to another man. I told God that if that happens, the ministry is history already. He assured me that He is going to give you to me.

I told my grand mother who seemed to understand so many things, including how I feel about you. She asked me if I wanted to marry you. I told her I want to if the family does not oppose it. I prefer to marry someone who went through so much with me even when I was nothing and when it looked as if I have no future. I told her how I made you promised me you'll marry me. She promised to remind you of the promise when she sees you but, you know, that was a secret between us. She gave me the freedom to tell her anything I have in mind. So she knows virtually everything about my thoughts. The only thing I did not tell her was what your mother did to us. I hope you did not tell anyone about it as you promised me. You know, she is going to me my mother-in-law. So we cannot afford to let anyone have a wrong impression about her. I know that by know, if the money had been found, she would have realized her mistake. Besides, to me, God just used the incident to get me to the place I would find my family. It was like the story of Joseph who was sold to Egypt where he was to be used to preserve his family years later. Please, tell your mum not to regret anything. There's nothing to regret. You must let her feel the need to forgive herself and put the past behind her. Tell her how much I miss her. I'm really eager to see and tell her how much I love her.

I told my parents down here so much about you. It's like I could not hide how much I feel about you from them. Guess what they said. They wanted to give you a scholarship to any school you want to go within or outside Nigeria. I'm sure my grand father would discuss this with your parents. Please, write to inform me of their decision. If you want to know what I feel about it, I want you down here in Arizona state university. It's a wonderful school. Having you here would fill the only vacuum that needs to be filled in my life. What do you think?

Cheers,
Tokunbo Olumbe

Janet folded the letter and put it back into the envelop with the money. She thought briefly of what to do. She really wanted to be with Nicholas wherever he was but she knew that would not be possible without her parents' consents. With the new image of her mother, she could count on her consent but she was not sure if she could persuade her father to let her go. She decided to try using her mother to get her fathers consent which she knew would be difficult to get. She was in at the back of the house, reading a Christian journal. She smiled at her as she walked to her.

'Mum,' Janet said, sitting beside her on the bench, 'I have something to share with you.'

'What's it?' Lade asked softly though she suspected that it has something to do with Nicholas. She has been having the funny feelings that what the letter he had written to her must very crucial her. She wished she was given the privilege to know what was written inside the letter but she has come to respect so many things about her daughter, including her privacy. So she had avoided asking her anything.

'It's about what Nicholas told me in his letter.'

'What did it tell you?' Lade asked, keeping her eagerness under check.

She brought out the letter and gave it to her. 'You can read it.'

Lade took it reluctantly. She looked at her, expecting her to change her mind.'

'Read it, mum.'

188

She removed the letter from the envelope with the money. She looked at her for explanations.

'He just gave me the money.'

'I see.' She gave her the money and began to read it. She was not even half through the letter before she began to cry silently. She managed to finish reading it before she gave it back to her.

Janet misunderstood why she was crying. She said, 'you read what he wrote. It's over. You've got to let go the past. God have achieved what he wanted. It's left for us to make best use of what he has for us through what has happened.'

Lade put her arm across her shoulder. 'Janet, I'm just having mix feelings. I'm feeling both joy and sorrow. Ever since God have assured me that he has forgiven me all my sins, I've been feeling differently. I know I'm not the one that did what I did. It was my old creature. I'm a new creature. I'm feeling joy because you and Nicholas have proven it beyond any doubt that the love you have for each other is divine. Nobody can stop it from resulting what God ordained it to be. I know your marriage with him is going to be blessed by God. I'm happy for that. The sorrow I feel was bore out of the fact that I never had the chance to contribute meaningfully into Nicholas' life. Instead, the devil used me to make life terrible for him.'

'Mum, it's still part of the game. If you don't play that role, there's no way Nicholas would know and appreciate my love for him. I would never forget what he said the day of the incident. He said that he loved what happened. It proved it to him that I loved him. You may not like the role you played but it was necessary for other things to come up.'

Lade smiled at her. 'Even though you're a girl, you talk like an old woman.'

'An old man is living inside me,' she laughed.

'Yes. The old man turned you into an old lady.' Lade added with laughter. 'Old lady, I need to learn from you.'

'Mum, on a serious note. I need you to persuade dad to let me go and meet Nicholas in America.'

'I can't do that.'

'Why?'

'It's because I don't want you to go not now. I need you here. In fact, the first person you have to tackle before you tackle your father is me.'

'Do you really think you're that difficult for me to handle?'

'Try me.'

'You've become my daughter in the Lord since you gave your life to

Christ.'

'I'm still your mum, no matter what.'

'Think of it,' Janet said persuasively, 'I've not been able to get admission to the University since I completed my secondary school despite how much we pray. It may be that God planned that I should study in America.'

'Here comes the old lady talking,' her mother said, laughing. 'You can go and tell your father about your intention first. Let me know what he says. I'll know where to come in.'

Janet looked so happy that she hugged him. Lade was again moved to tears. She was happy that at least, she was about to do something that would make up for all the wrongs she has done to her and Nicholas.

Janet stood up and went to her father in his room. He was going through some papers on the table when she knocked.

'It's opened,' Ben said without looking away from the papers.

Janet went to sit down close to him. It was when she said, 'dad,' that he realized that it was not his wife that came into the room.

He looked at her. He was observant enough to see that she looked a little pale. 'What's wrong?'

'It's Nicholas, 'she said quietly. She was going to use what he observed to appeal to him.

'What about him?' he asked, looking puzzled. 'You are supposed to be happy about the news his grand parents brought to us today.'

'It's the letter he wrote to me that … em …'

'Can I see the letter if it's not too personal?'

'It's very personal but you can read it because I need your help.' She handed it to him. He took it opened. He was a little so surprised to see the hundred dollar note. He gave her the money and began to read the letter. After he finished reading, he learned back on his chair thoughtfully.

'So there's something between you and Nicholas all the while,' he said unexpectedly as if he was not aware of it.

'Before the last time we saw, there's nothing,' she told him. 'Actually I have to agree that I'll marry him because he felt that was the strength he needed to start the struggle in Ibadan. He didn't know he was going to find himself in U.S.'

'Okay, okay,' he said, smiling at her. 'Actually, I knew he needed you. That's why I didn't frown at the closeness between the two of you.'

She returned the smiles. 'He said something about a scholarship in the letter. Did his grand parents make any offer?'

Ben shook his head. 'No,' he said. 'Actually, they said something about reciprocating which I didn't encourage. I didn't know they wanted to talk about scholarship. Even if they are, I wouldn't encourage it.'

'Why, dad?'

'You know I can afford to send you to school, don't you?'

'But I want to go United States and study there.'

'I know that's what you to say. You want to go and meet him, don' you? Well, I won't encourage it.'

'Why, dad?'

'Something else can happen.'

'What?'

'I'm sure you remember the story about how Nicholas was born.'

'We are Christians, dad.'

'Christians do make mistakes, don't they?' He knew his excuses was not really tenable but he had to say something to discourage the idea of studying overseas.

She was silent for a long time. Tears ran down her eyes. 'You don't trust me and Nicholas. You think we are doing things which we are not supposed to do.'

'It's okay, Janet,' Ben said. 'I trust both of you. I know both of you are Christians but the truth is: I don't want Nicholas to take you away from us yet. Your mother wont like it and I wont like it.'

'If I'm not in the place Nicholas is, I'll not be happy and he'll not be happy too.'

'But he's still coming back.'

'Yes, I know,' she said. 'I want to inform him to start the process of getting me an admission into the University there since I could not get any here.'

'I'll discuss it with your mother.'

'Okay, dad.' She stood up to go.

'I'll try to be on your side,' he said before she got to the door.

She looked at him, smiling. 'I don't need to be told that you are on my side. Because I know you are going to support my going to America.'

'Don't count on it, child,' he said jocularly.

* * * *

Tokunbo was teaching his parents and sisters the words of God at the family alter which he organized when he came to America. It has become a regular practice to share the word of God and lead them in prayers everyday whenever he was at home with his family.

When Charles and Mary were first informed that their child who was lost many years ago, at first they found it hard to believe it. Linda gave them the details of how he was found, including the evidence that confirmed he was their son. Within a short time, arrangement was made to have him brought to America. As soon as the couple and their children set their eyes on him, they did not need any other evidence that he was actually part of the family. His facial look was enough to prove that he was Charles's son. He spent only few weeks before he began to sit sat for all necessary examinations which he readily passed. A few months after then, was enrolled as a student at Arizona State University which was located in another state in U.S. To the family great delight, Tokunbo was not just a strong Christian but a charismatic and influential person who knew how to lead people to Christ. The way he taught the word of God and prayed distinguished him as a very experience minister. Before long, his family and even fellow students in the school began to see him as a minister. He normally related the story about himself and when he did, he always moved most of his audience to tears. Before anyone knew it, he was endeared to the heart of everybody. Even then, deep inside him, he was not a very happy person as people thought. He longed to see Janet because there was no way he could separate her from his life. His parents observed this and told him to influence Janet to come to America so that his and their joy could be full. He, therefore, wrote the letter which he sent through his grand father. He talked to him on the phone and asked him and his grandmother to visit all those who had helped him in Ikenne.

Tokunbo read from the Bible he was holding, 'The Bible says in the book Colosians chapter 3 verse 17, and whatsoever you do in word or deed, do all in the name of the Lord Jesus, giving thanks to God and the father by him." He looked at everybody. They were all very attentive. He knew they always enjoyed the way he ministered to them in the word. 'Obedience to the according to the passage means doing things and saying things in the name of the Lord. So many people preach the word of God only in words and not in deeds. It is not enough to preach it, we must live it. The world is full of hypocrites but, as I used to tell everyone, we are all going to account for our lives. God is going to judge us according to our deeds, not the deeds of others. So if anyone preaches the truth, I'll follow it and not what he does.

'When we obey God who is our Father, our days are prolonged according to Proverb chapter 3 verses 1 and 2. That passage says, "My son, forget not my law; nut let thine heart keep my commandments. For lengths of days, answer long life ...." The Bible does not stop at long life but goes on to say ..... "Peace shall be added to you." It is not everybody that live long that live a peaceful life.

'Obedience to God brings blessing and wisdom according to Proverb chapter 8 versed 33 and 34. That passage reminds me of how God instructed me to leave Ikenne when I was in Nigeria and go to Ibadan. If I had not yielded to that instruction, you wouldn't have found me. Sometimes, it may be difficult to do what God tells us to do but if we obey, there will be joy, peace and blessing for us.

'What happens to someone who does not obey God? We need to ask ourselves that question. In the book of Psalm chapter 66 verse 18, the Bible says, "if I regard iniquity in my heart, the Lord will not hear me." That place tells us that the prayer of anyone who is disobedient to God will not be heard. If he prays for any things, it is the devil that will hear him, not God. You know what happens if he devil hears the prayer of a person. If he prays for peace, he will get trouble. If he asks for blessing, he will get curses and if he asks for joy, he will get sorrow. Everything he would get would be the opposite of what he asks for.

'There is an interesting story in the book of Acts of Apostles chapter 19 verses 13 to 16. It reads, "Then certain of the vagabond Jew, exorcists, took upon themselves to call over them who had evil spirits the name of the Lord Jesus, saying, we adjure you by Jesus who Paul preaches.

'"And there were seven sons of one Sceva, a Jew, and chief of the priests, who did so.

'"And the evil spirit answered and said, Jesus I know, and Paul I know; but who are you?

'"And the man whom the evil spirit was leaped on them, and overcame them, and prevailed against them, so that they fled out of that house naked and wounded."' He smiled at them as they all looked amused. 'You can see that if a sinner calls upon the name of the Lord Jesus, it is the devil that will answer him.

'The last thing I want us to see is the end of anyone that disobeys God in he book of Revelation chapter 21 verse 8. The word of God says in that passage, '"But the fearful, and unbelieving, and the abominable, and murderers, and fornications, and sorcerers, and idolaters, and all liars, shall have their part in the lake which burns with fire and brimstone: which is the second death."'

193

He paused for a moment before he said, 'so many people deceiving themselves and other people by saying there is no hell. According to that passage, there is hell. I expect that portion to be in every version of the Bible except if the people who claim that there is no hell remove the passage from theirs. It is in the original copy of the scriptures that was written in Greek. People often frowned when others take risks of their physical lives which are temporary but very few are moved when they put their eternal lives into jeopardy. We cannot afford to risk our eternal lives by saying hell does not exist. If we think like that and live our lives anyhow only to discover when we die that there is hell and heaven as the Bible says, what shall we do? It's my prayer that the word of God will not stand against us on the day of judgement. Shall we pray?'

Everybody knelt down and began to pray. After that, they all stood up to go and do other things.

'Son,' Charles said. He has grown more masculine. Apart from figure, he did not look much different from the time he was in school. Although Mary looked rather too young to be Nicholas' mother yet she had grown a little plump and more matured than the first time she first came to America. 'I forgot to tell you had a mail from Nigeria.'

'Where's it, dad?' Tokunbo asked anxiously, thinking it must Janet. He had been expecting her letter for so long.

'It's in my case in the room,' he said, going into his room.

He followed him. Within some minutes, Tokunbo was in his bedroom, reading Janet's letter.

Hello, Tokunbo!

Your grand parents delivered your message and the good news about what the Lord had done. I was so happy when I heard it that I lost my appetite for days! I burst into tears when I read your letter even though, according to you, there is no more tear to shed. Thanks for the letter and the money. May God continue to bless you.

I would have written you long before now but my father and my mother were taking time to think over the idea of studying in America. My mother gave me her consent almost immediately I shared the idea with her. My father appeared as if he would support the idea at the initial stage but after a second thought, he decided against it. My mother tried all she could to get his consent too by saying that he should not hinder our love. He said that if he must release me to you, I would have to complete all my education in Nigeria. You know how much my parents love me and my brother, being the only children they have. Since he made that decision, I was never happy. My mother told me to tell you that you need to come to Nigeria during you vacation and persuade him. She said when he sees you, he would not be able to resist you. He loves you that much. He suspected all along that we may end up getting married. That was why he did not discourage our deep friendship. Besides, he knew how much you needed me during you trying period; the time you lost your fostered parents. I think my mother is right to think you could persuade him to let me come to America. I really want to be where you are because, as you know, I love you very much and I missed you a lot. I've waited for you to come home for so long but you never showed up on time. I was heart-broken, thinking you have let me down by not coming to at least tell me how you are feeding down in Ibadan; knowing fully well that I would be waiting to hear from you.

It would be of interest to you if I tell you that I found a note which Jimmy wrote to my mother about the money the same day you left for Ibadan. He was the one that came home to take the money on the day my mother was looking for it, but, like you said that day, it was God's way of directing you to go. The chances are that you wouldn't go if my mother didn't do what he did to us. Besides that, the incident made mother to hand over her life to Christ. She is now a born-again Christian. That was possible because she could see that she was a miserable sinner through what she did to us. I know you have long forgiven her but she longed to see you and make you feel happy. If you come to Nigeria and explain to my father how much we need to be with each other before we can be so happy, perhaps things will to go the way we want.

I guess I have to stop here until we see. When we see you, my parents will call for celebration. Nicholas, you complained that I never say I love you because I expect you to read it in all my actions. I will say to you now and again that I love you. If you love me as you make me believe, come to Nigeria and persuade my father to let me come to you. I can't wait to see you. Please, don't keep me waiting again. You've kept me waiting long enough.

Your love,
Janet.

Tokunbo finished reading the letter and read it again the second time. He knew he has to talk to his father about this. He went to him in his bedroom. Mary was with him. 'I want to talk to you, dad.'

'Is there any problem?' Charles asked.

'It's about the letter from Nigeria.'

'The letter is from Janet, right?' Mary asked quickly.

He nodded.

'What about it?' Charles asked.

'She wants to come down here to school but her father doesn't want her to come. She said her father does not want to release her to me until she had completed all her education in Nigeria.'

Charles looked at Mary who also returned the stare. He looked at Tokunbo and said, 'at least, her parents are not against your relationship with her.'

'No,' Tokunbo replied. 'They all like me in the family.'

'So what do you want us to do now?' Mary asked. 'It seems you have to wait before you can bring her down.'

'She wants me to visit Nigeria and persuade her father to let her come down here. He may consent to her coming here to school if I persuade him.'

Charles went to pat him on the shoulder. 'I know how you feel about this girl and I can understand why but if her father has made that decision, why must you try to reverse it?'

'We've stayed away for too long already, dad. I want her to school here or I go to Nigeria to school there.'

'You're kidding us, right?' Mary said.

'You're already in the University here,' Charles said as if he did no know.

'Honey,' Mary said, looking at Charles, 'you remember how we both felt when I have to be in Nigeria when I was pregnant of him while you're here.'

'But that's different.'

'It's not. It's the same feeling.'

'We can't allow him to go back to Nigeria,' Charles said firmly.

'I'm not saying we should. Let's give him a chance to go and talk to the girl's parents and see what comes out of it.' She looked at Tokunbo. 'Is that not what you're saying?' He nodded, smiling. 'We can think of what else to do if he cannot persuade them,' she told Charles.

Charles was thoughtful for a while. 'Listen, son, you'll go to Nigeria during your vacation and talk to her parents. I respect people's decisions. So better do all you can to persuade them. If you can't get their consents, you'll have to wait for her to complete all her education in Nigeria as her father said before you can see her as you want. Do you understand?'

Tokunbo nodded.

When he left, Mary said, 'the boy had become your pet.'

'He's my guarantee for early retirement.' He kissed her. 'So I can't afford to let him out of my sight,' he added in a whisper.

'You better continue to thank God that you found him,' she said in the same whisper.

'Yeah....' He went to look the door so that the children would not come to disturb them as they were about to play the game of love.

* * * *

The jeep was parked in front of Ben's house. Tokunbo jumped out of the car and went to press the door bell. As it was Sunday afternoon, he expected the family to be around.

Jimmy was the one that came to open the door. 'Nicholas!' He screamed and hugged him tightly. The rest of the family except Lade who looked uncertain rushed out of the rooms when they heard his name.

Ben tore the two young men apart and pulled Tokunbo inside, looking very excited. 'You run away bad boy!' He pushed him on the chair. 'Where the hell do you spring from? Come on, talk to me Yankee boy!'

Tokunbo laughed so loudly that his voice rang in the house. He stood up and prostrated. 'Good afternoon, sir!'

'Happy new decade!' Ben said.

'Same to you, sir!' Tokunbo said happily. He looked at Janet who was smiling at him with joy. He winked at her. She returned the wink. He looked at Lade and went to hold her two hands. 'If you are not ready to give your runaway son a hug, he would like to give you a big one if you don't mind.'

Lade suddenly burst out laughing. He grabbed her and decorated her face with kisses. 'Come on, mother, what do you have in your kitchen? Your boy is starving!'

'We don't have hamburger here,' she said.

'Hamburger is not the only food in the world,' he said. 'Give me Eba - anything.'

'Alright, be a good boy and stay here while I prepare it for you,' she said, going to the kitchen.

Tokunbo eased himself on the couch, removed his shoe and began to chat with the rest.

Janet went to help her mother in the kitchen while Jimmy and Ben chatted with him.

'I'm glad to see you again,' Ben said. 'Everything about you,

197

including your name has changed.'

'Yes, sir!' Tokunbo said jocularly. 'There's no way anyone would change environment without adapting to the environment. I tried as much as I could not to behave or talk like Americans but there's no way I could.'

'How's your Christian faith?' Jimmy asked.

'Oh,' he said quickly. 'You won't believe this. I pastor my family at home in U.S and I preach in the school chapel. It's like I'm needed to preach everywhere. Most people I shared the word of God with are always interested.'

'That's very good, boy,' Ben said. 'I'm very proud of you.'

'You don't have to be proud of me,' Tokunbo said, pointing to the kitchen. 'You should be proud of Janet. You remember all the problems I gave you a few years back.'

'Oh, that!' Ben laughed.

'With that kind of attitude, I would have been out for long. You remember the day I punched one of the boys in the face for snoring at night.'

Ben laughed the more. 'Yeah. How can I forget?'

'You couldn't hide it from everyone that you love me by bringing me to the house.'

'Actually, the most powerful consideration I have to give you is that you had no family then. There is nowhere I could take you to even if you're worse than that. I decided that I'm taking you as my own. You know a proverb that says that the parents of a child cannot throw him away. Boy, was I happy when you changed?'

'You're!' Tokunbo said, laughing. 'I remember you saying that I should not make the mistake of confessing my sins. If I did, according you, I'll be stoned because it's so much!'

Ben and Jimmy roared with laughter. The chat was endless until everybody was called to the table. At the table, Tokunbo continued to chat with them, making everyone to laugh. Obviously, Tokunbo was very happy to see them and they were very happy to see him too.

'You have no table manners,' Janet remarked, laughing at him.

'What I have got to do with table manner when I'm with my family. Keep your table manner to yourself and keep your mouth shut!'

Everybody laughed.

'Now I have to beg you, Nicholas,' Lade said. 'Give us a break if you don't want the food to come out through our noses.'

Laughing, Tokunbo said; 'Okay, okay, mother.' He paused suddenly and said, 'Janet; better get the driver something to eat.'

198

'Y-you mean there's a driver in the car outside?' Lade asked.

'Yeah,' Tokunbo replied. 'Actually, he told me he would love to remain in the car.'

'You can get him something to eat,' Ben told Janet.

'There is still some rice in the kitchen,' Lade told Janet who stood up to get it. She came back to join them after a while.

When they finished eating. Tokunbo began; on a more serious note as Janet and Jimmy cleared the table, 'I came down to Nigeria purposely because of this family. My grandfather told me he had narrated the story you need to know.'

'Yes,' Ben said. 'It's full of pleasant surprises.'

Janet and Jimmy came back from the kitchen to join them.

'When you see my father,' Tokunbo continued, 'you won't doubt it that he is my father. It took me time to get used to the fact that I still have parents and sisters. I'm the only male child and the first child. So I'm being treated like a gem. My father had the vision to hand over his engineering company and numerous investments to me.' He looked at Ben and said. 'It was as if God was preparing me for that company by making me your apprentice. You know, like we have it in Nigeria, every child of a big gem is expected to go to college. So a lot of money was invested on me before I could get admission to Arizona State University.' He paused. Everybody was very attentive. 'I don't want you to have the impression that I'm very happy there. You make my joy full. If you ask me where I prefer, I would love to school in Nigeria but, of course, my parents would have none of it. It was like they were afraid I would get missing again. My grand father strictly told his driver to take me to anywhere I want and he must not loose sight of me. Imagine them treating me like that. I don't blame them. I was told when I got lost, the whole family including my father's in America was shaken. My grandmother, according to them, would have died of sorrow if not for my grandfather that helped her recover from the pain. Considering the fact that I'm already in the school in the states and the reaction of any family, it is almost impossible to stay in Nigeria without causing panic…' He looked at Ben and Lade before he looked at his hands. 'I have a feeling that you know what's on my mind.' He smiled at Ben, 'am I right, sir?'

'You're right about what?' Ben asked.

'About what's on my mind.'

'How am I supposed to know what's in your mind? Am I God?' There was a brief silence. 'What's on your mind, boy?'

'My parents are giving Janet and possibly Jimmy scholarships in

199

U.S. They'll be solely responsible for everybody about them. They would get them employed when they graduate.'

Ben and Lade were silent. They looked at him for a while.

'I'm not comfortable with the way you're looking at me,' he said, shifting from one side of his chair to another. 'Please, be merciful and say something.'

Ben roared with laughter. Lade smiled, looking more jovial.

'I feel better with that laughter, sir.'

'Nicholas,' Ben said, 'Janet told me about it. I've thought about it. It won't work. I've decided that we'll see her through her education down here. Jimmy is completely out of the issue. Just as your father is grooming you to take over his company, I'm doing the same for Jimmy. Besides, you know he's doing his Higher Nation Diploma in civil engineering. So he is out of question.'

He looked at Lade. She had not said much since. She looked as if she has something to say.

'Nicholas,' Lade said, 'first of all, I'll like to say I'm sorry for all I did to you.'

'Oh, mother, what are you talking about?'

'Let me relieve myself of the burden by saying it to you, please.'

Nicholas sighed and said, 'okay.'

'I tried to look for you but there's no way I can trace you. So we kept praying that God should keep you.'

'Actually, mother,' Tokunbo said, 'I don't expect you to refer to the past. No matter what you think, you are still my mother. No matter what happened, I'll still love you as my mother. Really, whatever happened, it was ordained by God and there is no way you could have stopped it. As the Bible says, whatever happened to any child of God is for his good. The joy in all that has happened is that it drew you closer to God and it made me come across my family. That's all what God wanted to achieve in everything that happened.'

'You are a very intelligent boy,' Ben said. 'I can see why you are seen as a pastor.'

'Thank you, sir.'

'You know,' Lade went on, 'going by African custom, it is inappropriate to take anything from you. Going by what Janet told us, you hope to get married - right?'

'Yes, ma,' Tokunbo said silently, looking gentle. It was strange how he had suddenly turned into a gentle young man who has come to ask for a lady's hand in marriage.

Lade's voice became very shaky as she said, 'I can see that you loved each other very much … When I recall the incident about the money, I could not help saying to myself that only death can separate these youths. You are in American where you have access to everything you want including any lady, yet you came for her.' She smiled at Ben, 'You know my position in this matter. It may not be proper as we think but I think you to reconsider your position. I believe God wants Janet to school in America. That's why, as she told me the day she shared idea with me, she could not get an admission in Nigeria. If God wants her to school in Nigeria, by now, she ought to have been in school because we prayed. So…' She knelt down in front of Ben. 'Please, let's give them a chance.'

Ben looked a little puzzled. The rest, including their children and Tokunbo went on their kneels; all were appealing to him.

Ben looked very thoughtful for a long time. 'Nicholas, you're a good fighter. You know how to get what you want; including using my family to get it.'

There were soft chuckles among them.

'Are you sure I can trust you with Janet?'

'Don't trust me, sir. I want you to trust Jesus who had brought this far.'

Ben took and let out a deep breath. He said, 'I'll give you my conditions. First, you must not get so close as to give room for temptation. You kids are Christians and I expect you to know better than playing any game of love. The other condition is that both of you must always come to visit us one or twice in a years.

Nicholas nodded, smiling. 'I accept the conditions with joy.' He looked at Jimmy. 'You'll also be visiting us once in a year.'

Jimmy smiled. 'I'll be delighted if I'm given the opportunity.'

'Don't worry about the opportunity,' Tokunbo said. 'By the grace of God, It'll come.'

And so, the following year, Janet went to join Tokunbo in United States to study computer science. Both of them worked with Charles when they graduated. They later came to Nigeria with Tokunbo's parents and got married. Few weeks after their wedding, they went back to United States to set up their own family.

CHECK OUT OTHER BOOKS BY DIPO TOBY ALAKIJA
Each Serves Either As Edifying Or Evangelical Or Missionary Or Academic Tool At Home, School, Bible Clubs, Sunday Schools, Church, Office And Other Fellowships

BLOODSHED IN CAMPUS
ISBN: 978-07350-3-8 ISBN: 978-978-07350-3-6

A poor widow tearfully warned her son, Richard, against joining the bad wagon when he got an admission into one of the Nigerian Universities. He resisted the membership of groups of students, including the Christian Fellowship until he had an encounter with a member of The Black Skulls - a deadly and ruthless secret cult on the campus.

Before Richard knew what he was up against, the head of The Black Skulls had arranged items for his initiation into the cult. While resisting being initiated, he ran to the Christian Fellowship for help. The leader of the Christian Fellowship dragged The President of Students' Union Government (S.U.G) into the conflict. With the involvement of the S.U.G President, another formidable cult called The Red Eyes felt obliged to team up against The Black Skulls. Then the campus turned into a battlefield and BLOODSHED became the order of the black day.

THE UNROMANTIC LOVE BIRDS
ISBN: 978-49847-5-7 ISBN: 978-978-4974-5-5

And other short stories about love and marriages

They were very much in love right from their school days but when they got married and had children, romance became the game Charles' wife refused to play. No matter how much he tried to make her understand the unbearable condition her unromantic attitude has subjected him into, she would not change. Consequently, after enduring for so long, he was forced to look for the women that would make up for her weakness. He unofficially married a beautiful lady of insane jealousy. Though she was ready to give him what was missing in his marriage, it soon dawn on him that he has solved one big problem only to create a bigger one.

FOOTSTEPS IN THE MUD
ISBN: 978-36348-9-5 ISBN: 978-978-36348-9-3
The Drama Package Of Results Of Research Works That trace Global And Societal Vices To The Corrupt Or Lost Of Family Values

The 13-Episode drama book involves Bosede who learnt many wrong things from her parents' conduct and foul language. She was forced to marry Kola when she became pregnant. Using her mother's method to handle her father, she tried to subject Kola to her control. In the course of that, she made life terrible for him. Although her mother tried to warn her of the implications of maltreating her husband but Bosede has grown out of control. Consequently, while looking for peace, Kola was pushed out of the house. He made friends with some guys who taught him the unholy ways of life and influenced him to become a menace in the house.

Junior who was born at time the couple never proved to be responsible parents also learnt wrong things from them. He decided to follow his father's footsteps by taking alcohol when he was in primary school. As if that was not bad enough, he tried to teach other children in the school the madness in his home. A school teacher, however, was able to influence him and his mother by teaching them Christian morals. Even then, Junior was soon caught in the crossfire at home as his father tried to enlist him as a future member of a secret cult that posed as a social club.

SUCCESSFUL CHRISTIANITY AND BASIC MINISTRIES
ISBN: 978-49874-6-0
A Collection Of Resource Materials That Precedes Christian Ministries And Basic Leadership Course Book

The first question is how Christianity is practiced even in a hostile environment. Next to that is the question about the potentials of Christians in spite of their apparent limitations. The other issues are connected to the successes, deliverance, callings, basic ministries of all Christians and evangelism. Various schools of thoughts have attempted these questions but many answers only portray Christianity as a form of religion instead of a way of life as specified by God. Some answers give room for compromise, hypocrisies, dogmas and denominational doctrines. The misconceptions about these areas of Christianity have brought

about worldliness instead of righteousness and false achievements instead of fulfillment.

This book which contains six different subjects had been used to hold seminars at various levels, train ministers and Christian workers in Bible Schools and to equip the Church. It explains in simple terms the seemingly complex issues on practice of Christianity, Potentials, Deliverance, God's Kind Of Success, Evangelism and Basic Ministries of a Christian with Biblical principles, life transforming stories and illustrations.

INSANITY OF HUMANITY
ISBN: 978-36348-6-0 ISBN: 978-978-36348-6-2
The Results Of Research Works Into Various Methods Of Brainwashing

Man is made to exercise his freewill. The mind of his own and the power to choose between right and wrong, good and evil, light and darkness is about to be washed away through brainwashing. The agents of control dubbed as Secret Government by John Todd (the top Illuninati defector) have put necessary machinery in place to ensure that all human beings are in conformity in their thinking and ways of life, trying to wipe away diversity, which makes each person unique.

This book attempts to shed light on how the techniques of mind control are applied through the use of propaganda, education, entertainments, drugs, religions, media and other means of communications. It is the result of research works, some of which are based on findings of various researchers and writers like Bugger Lugz, Edward Hunter, Hadley Cantril, Herbert Krugman, David L. Robb, Vaughan Bell, Juliana Gomez, Ryan Duffy Vice, Henry Makow, David Nicholls, Fritz Springmeire, Steven Hassan, Renate Thienel, Debra Pursell, Mary Pride and a host of others who are acknowledged in this book.

THE BATTLE OF THE CONQUERORS
ISBN: 978-49874-7-3 ISBN: ISBN: 978-978-49874-0-7-9

Wickedness takes over the land of Bondage from First Couple and subjects everybody into slavery without giving anybody the chance to be free. Love brings The Redeemer from Eternity and offers the slaves the chance to escape. Wickedness soon declares war and engages everyone in the battle. The Redeemer makes the redeemed people Conquerors by giving them the armour of war and Comforter but Wickedness cannot be undone. He has several thousands of years of experience in the war. So he is quick to recognize the weakness of the redeemed people who are ignorant of their strengths and advantages. Although the Conquerors fight like immutable giants, rescuing victims of war, many people suffer heavy casualties.

Since King Wickedness knows that a redeemed person is strong enough to chase one thousand of his warriors at a time, and two would put ten thousand into flight, he enlists as one of his warriors the people's deadliest enemy called Disunity.

Wickedness is able to strike the people by making them to fight with

204

one another, turning what is supposed to be their best moments in the battle into tales of woes.

CHRISTIAN MINISTRIES AND BASIC LEADERSHIP
ISBN: 978-36348-7-9 ISBN: 978-978-36348-7-9

A Collection Of Resource Materials That Follows Up Successful Christianity And Basic Ministries Course Book

As it is common to say that the hood does not make a monk, the dignified positions and bogus titles of many Christian leaders in modern days do not really make them Gospel Ministers.

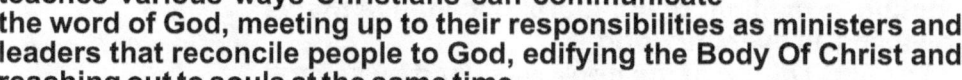

This course book - a compilation of five resource materials on Missions And Outreach Ministries, Christian Communication Arts, Christian Leadership, Christian Education Methodology and Ministries Of Improvisations - aims at making every matured Christian an effective minister and leader at their respective homes, communities and nations. It teaches various ways Christians can communicate the word of God, meeting up to their responsibilities as ministers and leaders that reconcile people to God, edifying the Body Of Christ and reaching out to souls at the same time.

All of the resource materials are in use in Bible Schools like College Of Christian Education And Missions, in Churches and other ministries to raise Christian workers, Evangelists, Missionaries and other Ministers that serve at various levels and leadership capacities.

NETWORK BIBLE CLUB
YOUTH AND ADULT BOOK ONE
ISBN: 978 - 978- 49874-9-X ISBN: 978-978-49874-9-3

A collection of 26 life transforming stories, 26 poems, 26 hymn tuned songs and weekly Bible lessons

The issue of moral instructions in schools and at homes is threatened with extinction. Consequently, so many youths are involved in prostitution, drug addictions, cultism, fraudulent practices, armed robberies and other crimes. Those who are supposed to be trained as leaders in various walks of life are the ones posing serious threats to many lives. Many parents who fail to add moral values to the upbringing of their children often times breed potential criminals under their roofs without knowing it. Apart from these, many other people negatively influence young ones through the media, music, publications, films, conduct and foul language; making them to lose their moral and family values.

This book one just like the rest of other volumes is an attempt to bring back moral instructions into schools and campuses through the use of stories, hymn tuned songs, poems, Bible lessons and class activities. It is designed to assist teachers and ministers in Secondary Schools, Bible Clubs, Churches and Campus Fellowships to teach people, especially youths the Word of God and serves as a school text book in subjects relating to literature, music and other creative works.

FOUNDATION BIBLE CLUB A-Z STORY BOOK
ISBN: 978-49874-2-2 ISBN: 978-978-49874-2-4
Volume 1 With 26 Stories, 26 Bible
Lessons, 26 Rhymes And 26 Songs For Book For Young Minds

An adage says, "a man who builds a house without building his child builds what the child will later sell." Proverbs 22:6 says, "train up a child in the way he should go: and when he is old, he will not depart from it." This book is an attempt to assist parents and teachers to meet up to the challenges that befall them in carrying out this important function in the light of the moral decadence that is prevailing all over the world.

The first edition of the book was used by several thousands of teachers, ministers and parents in schools, Churches and homes to build the moral values of young ones. Apart from the stories, songs and Bible passages for the young ones to study, there is a seminar material that is based on the lecture which the author delivered to school proprietors, children ministers and Christian professionals in this volume.

RANSOM FOR LOVE
ISBN: 978-49874-8-1 ISBN: 978-978-4987-4-8-6
She accepted his marriage proposal without knowing the kind of person he was. She soon discovered that he was a mean and ruthless guy who was always ready to get whatever he wanted by all means even if he has to pay for it with the lives of others. She was in his bondage, especially when her parents who believed he was a generous and gentleman were on his side.

Because she considered the proposal to marry him as a marriage engagement with the devil incarnate, she decided that she would rather die than to share her life with him. Then out of the blues, this passionate gentleman sneaked into her life despite all she did to discourage him. She could not resist his love for her when he offered to set her free from the devil incarnate. Then the battle began – sooner than they anticipated.

THE WEIGHT OF DEATH
ISBN: 9978-36348-0-1 ISBN: 978-978-36348-0-0
(Story Of The Spirit Eyes Series)

PLAY ONE: HORROR IN THE FAMILY: Talimi probably did not envisage his death when he was trying to compel his son, Damola to succeed him in the occult Brotherhood. Other members of the secret cult were aware of the battle between them. So when Talimi died; his family, especially Damola who was a diehard Christian began to fall prey to the cult. Using all their powers and the spirit that posed as Talimi's ghost, the cult waged war against the family, tormenting and making them to be at loggerheads.

PLAY TWO: RITUAL KIDS' KIDNAPPERS: Victor and the rest of the members of the School Bible Club were taught that there are lots of evil people in this world but he did not understand why God allowed him to be among the children that were taken away from their parents. He soon understood that he was to be used by God to rescue other children who did not know that everyone that truly believes in Jesus has the power to overcome evil.

PLAY THREE: THE WEIGHT OF DEATH: Awoseun would not have known the real source of problems of mankind if his father had not given him the power to see demons tormenting the people in different ways. What he was yet to know, however, was the power of light over darkness. When he was caught in crossfire between these powers, he desperately sought for deliverance.

CALVARY ROCK RESOURCE BOOKLETS
ISSN: 1595 93X
The Quarterly Missionary Booklets That Are Designed To Teach Children, Youths And Adults In Schools, Fellowships, Churches, At Homes, Office And Other Places.

Although all the various volumes of this booklet can be used independently of other books but it is recommended that it should be used as part of supplementary materials to make up for Foundation and Network Bible Club Story Books for both children and adults in

School, Church, Campus, Office and other Fellowships.

Each of the volume is rich with quarterly Bible lessons, stories, drama, songs, seminar, tract materials and a host of other things that can be used to edify, educate, entertains and evangelize every category of people, ranging from children to elderly persons.

Every volume is designed to equip school teachers, ministers in Churches or campus or office fellowships and other people who wish to work with the Lord.

All These And Other Books Are Distributed Worldwide And Published By The Publishing House Of Calvary Rock Resources

*Ikenne-Remo, Nigeria
*Manchester, United Kingdom
*New York, United States

www.calvaryrock.org

www.ingramcontent.com/pod-product-compliance
Lightning Source LLC
Chambersburg PA
CBHW020841260626
47169CB00003B/1089